SKERRETT

Liam O'Flaherty titles published by Wolfhound Press:

The Pedlar's Revenge and Other Stories (1976)
All Things Come of Age: A Rabbit Story (1977) – for children
The Test of Courage (1977) – for children
The Ecstacy of Angus (1978) – a novella
Famine (1979) – a novel
The Black Soul (1981) – a novel
Shame the Devil (1981) – autobiography
Short Stories by Liam O'Flaherty (1982)
The Wilderness (1978, 1986) – a novel
The Assassin (1983, 1988) – a novel
Insurrection (1988) – a novel

Limited first editions, handbound, signed and numbered
The Pedlar's Revenge and Other Stories (1976)
The Wilderness (1978)

SKERRETT

Liam O'Flaherty

WOLFHOUND PRESS

This edition 1988
WOLFHOUND PRESS
68 Mountjoy Square,
Dublin 1.

© 1988, 1982, 1977, 1932 Liam O'Flaherty

British Library Cataloguing in Publication Data

O'Flaherty, Liam
  Skerrett.
  I. Title
  823'.912   [F]   PR6029.F5

  ISBN 0-905473-11-6

Cover design: Jan de Fouw
Typesetting: Redsetter Ltd., Dublin.
Printed by the Guernsey Press Co. Ltd., Guernsey.

CHAPTER I

On a wild day in February 1887, the hooker
Carra Lass brought David Skerrett and his wife from
Galway to the island of Nara. They left the town at
dawn and then tacked down the bay, through ice-
cold rain and hail and lurching seas that rode white-
maned across the hooker's bow. It was already noon
when they came abreast of the Black Head, lying
close inshore for shelter.

Then as the boat lay upon the heaving water like
a brown-winged fly, beneath the towering, black
mountain, along whose rain-bright upper slopes
great shreds of cloud were driven by the wind, the
sky grew sudden clear and the sun came forth. Up
rose the island to the view, ten miles to the south-
west, a black speck upon the horizon, a dismal sea-
lashed rock, lying across the harbour mouth from
land to land, except where two foaming channels
east and west made roadways to the ocean. Through
the eastern channel the ocean's fury swept into the
bay, so that when the hooker tacked west into the
wind, she bounded like a ball. The wind-filled bellies
of her sails near touched the waves and she seemed
like to founder with each careening plunge.

Amidships in the shallow hold, her passengers lay
crouched among their cargoes, all island men and
women. The women, with their red petticoats and
many-coloured cashmere shawls lashed about their

bodies, moaned in a great agony of fear and sickness. The men, though neither sick nor afraid through use of seafaring, had until now lain sombre and silent. When the sun came out and the ocean became dazzling in its light, they sat up, stretched themselves and began to chatter in loud voices.

Attracted by the sudden speech, Skerrett crawled up the hatchway of the fo'c'stle, where he had been waiting on his sea-sick wife since leaving port. The islanders in the hold examined him with interest, he being a stranger. They saw a man in the prime of life, tall, of heavy build, with a brown beard that masked the almost brutal coarseness of his countenance. His thick, moist lips curved outwards and his nose was like that of a prize-fighter, being short, thick and flattened at the end. His brown eyes were bold and sullen. A loose oilskin coat covered him from head to foot.

" When do we reach the island ? " he called out to the people in the hold.

They looked at one another and whispered in Irish. As he had spoken in English they did not understand him. Then a man with a crooked leg came forward and spoke in English, though with a foreign accent.

" By night-fall, sir," said this man, " or a little sooner. There is Nara out there."

Skerrett looked, blinking, at the distant rock, that seemed to rise suddenly from the ocean and then disappear once more, as the hooker plunged from crest to trough of the waves. His forehead became furrowed as he looked. Then he shaded his eyes with

6

his arm and glanced all round, at the white-ridged sea, at the black mountain falling fast astern, at the low dun line of mainland going west upon the north. All looked dismal, cold and savage to him, though there was beauty in the sunlit, foam-capped sea and vigour in the strong perfume of its brine, carried on the wind.

" It looks a lonely and a wild place," he said gloomily.

" It is faith," said the man with the crooked leg. " Though it's old and honoured in the history of man. The island of saints and scholars it's called in the story books. It's how in the early Christian times it was inhabited by saints that near covered it with churches and monasteries. But the marauding Danes and then the robber English came and destroyed everything. They burned the saints in boiling oil and now there's only poor people on the island, except a few protestants that are put there by the government to tyrannise."

The man spoke with great energy.

" Do you live on the island ? " said Skerrett.

" I do faith," said the man. " I'm Pat Coonan, the rate collector. I live at Ardglas, where we are going to land. It's the most important place on the island. It will soon be a town. You are Mr. Skerrett, the new schoolmaster at Ballincarrig. I heard you were coming. You were pointed out to me yesterday in the main street of Galway."

Skerrett nodded his head without looking at Coonan. His eyes were still fixed on the rock and his face was gloomy.

7

" Have you no word of Irish at all ? " continued Coonan.

Skerrett turned to him angrily. Coonan was a tall, lean man, with a brown skinny face and peering eyes like a small bird. Though only about forty years of age, five years older than Skerrett, his body had already shrivelled, through scanty nourishment, hardship and exposure to the wildness of the island climate. Skerrett seemed to be of quite another race, heavy, well-fleshed, placid, slow of movement, dominant.

" I know no Irish," he said. " I'm from the county Limerick. They have no Irish there."

" It's a pity, then," said Coonan, " for without Irish you'll have a hard job of it in Ballincarrig. Around Ardglas, where I live, the people speak English. God knows, it's a poor sort of English we have, but we get along with it. It's how we get in the habit of speaking it to the coastguards and the police and the government people that do be coming and going. In the west of the island, the people speak no English at all. Only an odd person understands it."

He looked behind him towards the islanders in the hold and then said in a fawning fashion :

" The place you're going to, they're half savages. They have no word of English at all."

Skerrett looked at him arrogantly, stroked his beard, threw back his powerful shoulders with a jerk and then said in a booming voice :

" I'll soon make them learn it."

" God bless you, sir," said Coonan. " I hope you will. The school there is not long open, only five years. But you know that yourself, I suppose. There was only one regular teacher there before you. Up to that, the young people used to come into Ardglas to school and it was only an odd person that came. But Mr. Scanlon was there in Ballincarrig for five years and faith it was little good he did."

" Huh ! " said Skerrett contemptuously. " Why was that ? What sort of man was he ? "

" It's like this," said Coonan. " He was a quiet sort of Christian man at first and he lay a great compliment on what he did and said. But sure they made a show of him and then he took a conceit to the place altogether, as he was able to teach them nothing and only an odd person came near his school at all. So he began to drink, until in the end he had to be sent to the madhouse."

" Huh ! " said Skerrett again.

" Yes, sir," said Coonan. " Sure enough it's a wild place, but faith we are making great changes in it. We have a great priest there now, Father Harry Moclair. He's like a king over us. Before he's done with the island, we'll be as rich there as in the fine fat county you came from. God bless you, sir."

Skerrett looked gloomily at the distant rock that now began to lengthen in the sea. Then he shrugged his shoulders and crawled down the hatchway into the fo'c'stle, where a woman's moaning could be heard. Coonan walked, bow-legged, back to the shallow hold. There the islanders gathered around him, asking questions about the new master.

Coonan treated them as he himself had been treated by Skerrett as a social inferior. They all wore

9

the native costume of the island, rawhide shoes, blue frieze drawers held with a belt, hand-knitted, of coloured threads, a sleeveless frieze waistcoat, blue in front and white at the back, dark blue frieze shirt with white bone buttons from throat to breast, wide-brimmed black felt hat. Coonan wore shop clothes, a swallow-tailed coat, trousers, boots and a cravat. Although, at birth, his condition had been identical with theirs, he had begun the slow ascent towards the bourgeoisie by virtue of his position as rate-collector ; a type of Irish middle class man in the infancy of that class, when it began to detach itself from the peasant stem. He affected difficulty in pronouncing the Irish words when he spoke to them and in almost every sentence he inserted an English word or phrase ; just like a slightly educated African negro posing before his fellow tribesmen on his return to the bush from a Christian settlement. Indeed he filled his pipe and began to smoke before he condescended to answer their questions. Then he said :

" He seems to be a tough man, this new schoolmaster. A proud and uncivil sort of man."

" What did he say ? " said an islander with buck teeth, squatting on his heels and pulling at the stump of a clay pipe.

" He said he was going to make the Ballincarrig people learn English within a month or dance on the guts of their dead bodies," answered Coonan.

" Huh ! " said a handsome young man, who lay on his back with his cap over his eyes. " He'll soon find himself stretched flat with a broken skull if he isn't careful."

"We don't want any English," said another. "The language our ancestors spoke since God made the world is good enough for us."

"Hold your whist and don't talk nonsense," said Coonan indignantly.

"Sure without English ye'll remain in misery and poverty and ignorance, same as ye always were. How can ye go to America without English? How can any of ye get a job like I have without English? It's English gave me bacon of a Sunday morning for my breakfast and gives me tea twice a day, while ye all are living on Indian meal porridge and potatoes and salt fish."

There was general agreement with this statement.

"Faith," said one, "you're becoming a sort of little half-sized buck, Pat Coonan. It's true for you."

"Of course, it's true for me," said Coonan. "This man 'll be the makings of ye over there in the west of the island, for he's a tough man to handle."

He looked furtively towards the fo'c'stle and lowered his voice.

"I heard the whole story of how he was driven out of his last school from a man in Galway," he said. "He beat a scholar and the lad's father came to complain. Begob, Skerrett laid out the father with a blow of a fist and the poor man's jaw was broke. There was a rumpus in the place so the parish priest had to ask him to resign. So then Father Moclair took pity on him and gave him this school in Ballincarrig."

"So that's the class of a man he is," said the islander with buck teeth.

" That's the class of man he is," said Coonan. " He's a proud and saucy man, but maybe he'll get tamed and go away with his tail beneath his belly from this place that he despises. So I say and I know a thing or two."

Later the wind changed and blew upon the hooker's stern and she raced south-west at a great pace. The island grew distinct, until the people could see the boats riding at anchor in the roadstead of Ardglas. The rocky land rose high to a great ridge of cliffs that stretched from end to end of the island facing the southern ocean.

As the boat entered the harbour, Skerrett came out of the fo'c'stle, supporting his wife. She was a little round woman, big with child, wearing a black cloak and a feathered bonnet. Her face was yellow with sickness. He pointed to the island and said fiercely :

" That's where you brought me to live. Look at it."

She looked in wonder at the rocky place that was like a chess-board with an immense multitude of stone walls encasing stony fields. She shuddered and clung to her husband's arm.

" It's like a wild desert, David," she said.

" And to think," he growled, " that only for you, I'd be on my way to America now, instead of coming to live on this bloody rock."

He frowned upon the island and in his sensual face anger blazed against the fate that had driven him hither. In the light of the setting sun the island rock was radiant with a gaunt and fearsome loveliness, but the cloudy eye of this unhappy man saw only its stark and lonely nakedness.

CHAPTER II

THE HOOKER sailed slowly up the little harbour, through the anchored boats, past a new pier that was being built. She was moored to a rough stone jetty at the foot of the steep hill, on which the houses of Ardglas were huddled in a disorderly mass. As soon as the boat was made fast, Skerrett took his wife in his arms and went ashore. Father Harry Moclair, the parish priest, came forward from among the crowd on the jetty and saluted them. He led them away at once to the hotel that adjoined the landing place, a long, slate-roofed house with white walls. At that time it was the only hotel on the island.

" You must be perished," he said. " I ordered a meal for you."

He was a tall man, over six feet in height, a year older than Skerrett, strongly built, handsome in appearance, of striking personality. His shaven face looked subtle and refined, especially his hawk-like blue eyes, which seemed to smile continually. He wore top boots over his priest's black trousers and flicked his thighs as he walked with a riding crop, which he carried between his clasped hands behind his back.

Walking a little to the rear, Skerrett examined the priest with suspicious hostility. Wet, cold and hungry, his anger against the savagery of the place fixed on the priest, who had brought him thither.

Mrs. Skerrett, on the other hand, was fulsome in her thanks, as she trotted beside the long-striding priest, who looked down at her now and again, smiling his queer smile and belittling the favour he had conferred on the couple. Skerrett bit his lip in shame at his wife's servility. His dripping oilskin coat made a rustling noise as he shrugged his body in anger. He looked coarse, aggressive and brusque beside the subtle priest.

They entered the hotel, where in a small room with a fire, a meal of boiled eggs, tea, bread and butter was already laid for them. Skerrett immediately sat down and began to devour the food greedily without troubling to take off his dripping coat. Mrs. Skerrett was too sick and excited to eat. She sipped her tea and continued to shower thanks on Father Moclair, who stood with his back to the fire, flicking his thighs.

" We'd have to go to America," she said, " only for you giving us this school."

" I wish I had gone to America," muttered Skerrett to himself.

" There is nothing to thank me for, Mrs. Skerrett," said the priest. " I think your husband is exactly the man I want at Ballincarrig. They are rough people over there and a determined man is exactly what is necessary for them. If he does his duty, he needn't be afraid that I won't back him up."

Skerrett looked at the priest, threw out his chest and said almost insolently :

" No man yet could prove that I ever failed to do my duty. What I undertake I fulfil."

For a moment the priest's eyes grew cruel as they

looked into Skerrett's insolent face. Then he smiled gently and said :

" I think we'll get on well together, Mr. Skerrett."

" Oh ! I trust in God you will, father," said Mrs. Skerrett fervently.

The priest excused himself, after explaining the arrangements he had made about their lodgings and a conveyance thither.

" You'll find it rough here at first," he said, " but everything is going to change for the better. Great things are happening and greater things are going to happen."

He smiled and left the room, flicking his thigh with the crop.

" Huh ! " said Skerrett to his wife. " You have too much to say."

" Sure I only thanked him as was fitting," she said. " We'd have been left to starve only for him, after you were driven out of the school. Nobody else would give us a school."

" Why should I thank him for bringing me to this place ? " cried Skerrett. " Only for you I'd be in America now."

Mrs. Skerrett began to sob.

" Stop crying," he shouted. " I curse the day I was fool enough to marry you. You are a weight around my neck."

He lit his pipe and strode up and down the room, smoking moodily, until the hotel-keeper's wife came to announce that the cart was waiting outside. In the road, a stocky man with a whip saluted them. A red-painted cart, harnessed to a grey mare, stood nearby. Two drunken islanders stood at the mare's head, keeping her quiet. She was very excited, whinnying for her foal and stamping her hind legs, to ease the pain in her taut udder. In the cart there were two barrels of porter, sacks of flour, a bag full of groceries and Skerrett's two trunks. They all climbed into the cart, the two drunken islanders sitting at the rear with their legs hanging. Mrs. Skerrett sat on a barrel. Skerrett sat in front opposite the driver. The cart moved off. The two drunken men clasped hands and began to sing.

" I'm John Corless," said the driver. " I own the public house at Ballincarrig. That's me. I'm a rich man. This is my cart. This is the first cart that ever came to Nara. I brought it here. No other man on the island has a cart but me. So I'm a rich man."

Skerrett could hardly understand the man's broken English and he shrank from the fellow, as from an uncouth and dangerous savage. The man looked ridiculous in a swallow-tailed coat over a white frieze shirt that was tucked into his belt. His face was puffed with constant drinking and all round his mouth there was a wet rime of the tobacco he was chewing. Although the mare strained, groaning under her heavy load, up a steep hill, he lashed her brutally.

It was now dusk and the stars had come out. Sand and wisps of seaweed were flying in the fast cold wind as they skirted the shore. Curlews cried. The sea roared against the cliffs to the south. On either side of the road groups of people stared at the cart and jeered at the singing of the drunken men. They

passed a straggling line of miserable thatched huts
and then mounted another hill beyond the village,
going westwards along the island's back. Here all
was silent and empty, naked and savage in the darkness. There were no trees, no shrubs, no soft shapes
of grassy mounds on the horizon to soften the
desolation of never-ending rock and sea.

As Skerrett looked about him, he thought of his
own rich, soft countryside and again he cursed the
fate that had brought him to this dreary place. Then
it became so dark that he could see nothing beyond
the dim outline of the ragged stone walls that bound
the road.

Now and again they passed a little hamlet and by
the light of a lamp shining through the open door of
a cabin, he saw a dark kitchen, with pigs sleeping on
straw and barelegged children gaping.

" Oh ! God ! " he kept muttering to himself.
" What brought me here ? "

Four miles west of Ardglas they reached Corless's
public house at Ballincarrig. In a large, stone-flagged
kitchen, a crowd of men were waiting for the arrival
of the porter. Skerrett and his wife went to bed at
once ; but it was nearly dawn before they slept,
disturbed by the wild singing of the men drinking
in the kitchen.

CHAPTER III

Next morning, Father Moclair came early on horseback from Ardglas and brought Skerrett to his school. Mrs. Skerrett went also, although she was already six months with child. She was her husband's assistant. The school was a fairly new building, like the tavern in which they lodged, of one story, with a slate roof. But although it had only been built four years, all the windows were already broken. Slates had been torn from the roof, by stones which the mischievous scholars had thrown. The floor was also torn. The desks and forms were mangled by penknives. In fact, everything was in a state of fearful disorder. Nettles grew up to the doorstep and the yard was full of every conceivable kind of dung and rubbish.

Most astonishing of all were the scholars themselves, who had gathered in great numbers, out of curiosity to see the new master. Some of them were already grown men and women. Their wild appearance terrified Mrs. Skerrett. Hardly any of them wore shoes, even though it was still wintry weather and there had been a heavy frost on the previous night. They looked famished. The big girls carried their little sisters within their shawls for warmth. Nearly all of them appeared to be lousy, by the way they kept scratching their heads and bodies.

"Well! Here you are," said Father Moclair,

pointing to the scholars who sat on the forms or stood around the walls, their wild eyes peeping sheepishly from above protecting arms. " See what you can do with them. I'll stand for anything short of manslaughter."

Then he laughed, went out, mounted his horse and rode away. Skerrett set to work at once. Picking up a stout birch rod he had brought from his lodgings, he went to the rear bench where a group of the largest pupils were sitting. They were whispering in Irish, but ceased on the master's approach. Without warning he cut the nearest fellow across the shoulders with his birch.

" I won't allow any talking in this school," he cried.

The youth's eyes looked startled and then clouded in anger. He was about nineteen years of age and nearly as tall as Skerrett, with a lithe, supple body. He stared at Skerrett for a little while, his nostrils twitching like a frightened animal. Then he growled and jumped at Skerrett's throat. The two rolled backwards to the floor. The young children screamed and Mrs. Skerrett flopped into a chair, groaning and beating her breast. All the other youths on the back bench jumped on Skerrett to assist their comrade. They kicked him, tried to gouge out his eyes and gnawed at his hands. Yet they could not hold him down or knock him unconscious. Soon he struggled to his knees, punching them one after the other with great force and growling with each punch. In a few minutes he had scattered them. Some took to their heels from the school. Others, unable to run, lay on the floor moaning. These he kicked to their feet and flogged with his birch rod. Afterwards he drew a chalk line on the wall, against which he stood them, with their hands stretched above their heads as far as the chalk line.

" Let this be a lesson to everybody here," he said, shaking his birch.

Then he called the roll and organised the pupils into classes, giving the smaller children of both sexes into his wife's charge. He set them to work cleaning the school, lighting a fire with the sods of turf they had brought, setting the yard in order. At noon, he had water fetched, a basin, a towel and some soap. Then he made them wash their faces, their hands and their hair.

" If anyone comes here to-morrow morning," he said, " with dirty hands or face, or with lice in his hair, I'll flog him to within an inch of his life. The first thing you have to learn here is to keep clean and to be obedient. Yes, and I'll flog your parents too. I'll go into your homes and flog everyone in them if you come here dirty."

In the afternoon, when he began to teach, he found that he had to start practically at the beginning with the majority of them, as they did not even know the alphabet. Only a few understood more than twenty words in English. But he was not disturbed or discouraged by this, having effected his chief purpose, to establish order in his dominion. When he closed the school at three o'clock, the scholars ran to their villages with a wild story of the new master, who struck terror into everybody.

Skerrett went to his lodgings and after a miserable supper of potatoes and salt fish, he wandered alone over the rocks until nightfall, cursing his fate. Then, oppressed by loneliness and anger, he returned to the tavern, where he drank himself stupid with porter, until he had to be helped into bed beside his wife.

Such was his beginning in Nara.

CHAPTER IV

FOR THREE months Skerrett lived at Ballincarrig
as an enemy of the people. He regarded the life
about him with aversion, taking no interest in anything but his school and the mastery of his scholars.
Even these latter he regarded merely as enemies
to be conquered. After the experiences of the first
day, they began to stay away in large numbers, but
he went into their villages, as he had threatened,
and attacked them in their homes ; even assaulting
their parents, if any attempted to protect the defaulting scholars. He received many a bruise and was,
indeed, one evening caught by a gang on the dark
road at night and beaten unconscious. Yet his
strength, courage and the support of the parish
priest, enabled him to have his way. Soon only the
largest and most tough of the scholars dared to play
truant. In the school there was perfect discipline.
The boys came with clean faces. The girls had tidy
pinafores and well-combed hair. As yet there was
little progress made with scholarship, but otherwise
the change was startling. In any case, Skerrett paid
little attention to scholarship at the beginning.
In those days, he himself was informed in a very
paltry fashion, but he set out to be a master rather
than a teacher.

As he said over his porter at Corless's public
house :

" Never you fear. They're not going to send me to a madhouse. I'll see them all in hell first."

In the four hamlets of Ballincarrig, Kilchreest, Cappatagle and Tobar Milis, from which children came to his school, people touched their hats to him within a month as to a landlord. Indeed, no fine gentleman had ever been seen on the island as pompous and arrogant as he, who hardly nodded to their salutations, who rushed to blows at the least insult to his dignity, who eschewed all social inter- course with the people and only conversed with the coastguards and police, when these chanced to come westwards to Ballincarrig on their duties. With these servants of the government, whom the people hated, he felt at home and eagerly agreed with their sneering references to the " natives."

No fine feeling or intelligent ambition seemed able to penetrate his soul. Outside school hours, when he was not making punitive expeditions into the ham- lets, to satisfy his vanity and his lust for blows, he was drinking with his cronies at Ardglas, or flirting with whatever women he could find ; and this, even though his wife was nearing confinement.

There she was, left alone practically every evening in the gloomy tavern, listening to the drunken brawls in which her husband joined on occasion ; yet he never once unbent to say a kind word to her or to cheer her loneliness with a show of affection. The child that was now kicking in her womb he regarded with horror, as a bond that would make his escape impossible. For he still cherished hopes of America. Often, walking alone by the southern cliffs, he listened to the thunder of the sea and thought how good it would be should she die in childbirth and let him free, to wander off in search of golden riches and the lusty life of an adventurer. He forced her to attend school to within a week of her confinement. Her deformity of motherhood, which softens the most cruel men into pity and tenderness, seemed to have the opposite effect, of arousing a hatred that was quite inhuman.

Yet when they came to him in school and told him that his wife had been delivered of a son he was strangely moved. At first he seemed unable to believe that he was a father. Then, when he realised that it was true, he was overcome with pride and joy. Nature had struck a mighty blow on the cold anvil of his heart, which hitherto had never moved to love. He rushed from the school to his lodgings. He could hardly be restrained from shouting and laughing in the bedroom, where his wife lay pale and silent and the midwife was dressing the new-born infant. He was like a drunken man and when he was alone with his wife that evening, he whispered endearments into her astonished ears.

Indeed they were the first she had ever heard from him during the two years of their married life. She was a year older than himself and their marriage had been forced by her becoming pregnant through a previous intimacy. He had taken her without love, finding her handy to his passion, as she was school assistant to him at the time and he was not particular about the object of his lust. When she miscarried and he found himself tied needlessly to a dull and unattractive woman, indifference became hatred in him.

Now he behaved as if she had ever been the idol of his life ; so that the poor woman believed she had at last aroused his tenderness. But it was not so. He merely had found something before which he could humble himself ; not his wife, but his infant son. He had hitherto felt alone and without purpose, in rebellion against a fate that denied him all love, predominance, wealth to satisfy his ambitious lusts. Now there was this infant that would call him father and grow up in his image. The fierce conflict of the past three months was over, as he must put aside all thought of flight and work to maintain a home for this infant. Nara would have to be the battleground on which he had to struggle for existence.

The instinct of dominant natures is to deck their brows in defeat with the wreath of victory. And so did Skerrett set about to turn the hell from which he realised there was henceforth no escape into his chosen paradise ; even lashing himself into a belated love for the dull wife, whose dry lips and flaccid bosom froze his lust. Even so, he was now a father and lust unsated in his bed could spend itself in hunting for his young. So from that day he began to change his mode of life. He no longer looked upon the people as his enemies, nor on the land as alien. He began to learn Irish and saw the island with new eyes that had lost their sullen anger. The rocks lost their nakedness and he saw how they were holy with the imprint of man's feet through the centuries and how this barren wilderness could speak of beauty to those with ears to listen, of ghostly things long dead but still remaining on the wind and in the earth's substance. The sea, in thunder or in sunlit peace, became the blue dreamland of his awakening mind and not a ditch impassable beyond his prison walls. The island became his home and began to draw him towards its savage bosom.

He left Corless's public house and took lodgings in the house of a peasant called John Kearney about half a mile to the east on the outskirts of Ballincarrig.

" A public house is no fit place for us," he told his wife. " From now on I'm finished with drink."

" Thank God for that," said the poor woman, who hardly ever ceased praising God since the change in her husband's nature.

Indeed he became a fanatical teetotaller and now went to the same extreme in his opposition to drink, that he had formerly gone in his addiction to it. Furthermore, although he had never taken an interest in religion, beyond the superstitious awe of the next world in general use among our people, he now became devout. He ceased to swear and to use coarse language. He went to confession and to Holy Communion once a month. He made pilgrimages to the various holy wells and ruined churches scattered over the island. He put his head in the air and passed by without salutation when he met a coastguard or a policeman on the road, while he eagerly tried to identify himself completely with the islanders. He had to be restrained by the parish priest from adopting the island costume, but he insisted on wearing rawhide shoes in the evenings, after his work in the school was over. These vagaries almost brought him into ridicule with the more skittish of the people, until they found that his old brutality still lived strongly under the thin paint of his conversion, for he set upon and thrashed a man who dared to make an impertinent remark.

" He may be a bit touched in the head," the people said after that, " but he's a dangerous customer and it's best to leave him alone."

So they still raised their hats to him, even though he had begun to call them " brother " and " sister " in his broken Irish. He remained a master in their eyes.

To Moclair he behaved as to a woman with whom he had fallen in love. He doted on every word and action of the priest ; thought and spoke of him continually and went into a frenzy when anyone dared suspect the integrity or wisdom of the priest's least judgment. When Moclair came on horseback to the school, Skerrett rushed out bareheaded, smiling like a lover. He offered his hand, his knee, and even his shoulder to aid the descent. It is still told among the older people on the island, how one day in the church at Tobar Milis, when Father Moclair was walking down the aisle to the confessional before Mass, Skerrett rushed out of his pew, knelt on both knees and wiped a speck of dirt from the hem of the priest's soutane with a handkerchief.

And as a man in love adores the ground on which the beloved walks and the people among whom she has her being, if they be serving to her from afar, he exalted the virtues of the people whom he had formerly despised as savage and barbarous. In particular, the couple with whom he lodged, John and Barbara Kearney, excited his enthusiasm. They were in the first joy of their mating, a young and handsome pair of outstanding virtues. The wife especially was very beautiful, tall, slender, with extremely refined features and a grace of movement that resembled that of a young thoroughbred filly. Her voice had a delicious thrill like the singing of a blackbird. Her eyes were deep blue and her complexion, beyond the brilliant glow of her cheeks, was white and pure. She wore her hair parted in the middle and coiled at the back, so that she looked like a most beautiful Madonna. Nor was her husband's male beauty less splendid, even though he lacked delicacy, being crude and solemn except when his body was in action with his daily work. Yet when he leaped upon a horse, or waded, waist-deep in the sea, collecting the golden weeds in his strong arms, or again worked in the fields at his crops with sweat upon his lean forehead, there was a fine quality in his supple energy.

A silent and meek couple they were, who hardly ever spoke to one another above a whisper, industrious as honey bees and in all ways desirable.

Skerrett's admiration of them was mixed with jealousy. At first he was astonished that they, having so little, could be content with their lot, sharing all their joys and sorrows in common and continually raising their voices to God, as the lark soars towards the white face of the sun, in wondering gratitude. They had no leisure or security, being always giddy with their work, like beasts of chase in a forest. Their holding of rocky land, scattered here and there over the village territory, was just sufficient to feed a cow, a horse, a few sheep and to raise a crop of potatoes, while around the house they had pigs and fowl. Yet they rarely showed sign by word or action that they wanted more. Their fields and beasts were things personal and friendly to them and even the savage sea sometimes gave them joy by delivering its riches ; or a consciousness of sublime woe when it swallowed a life into its maw.

And then he saw with jealousy the holy key to their happiness in spite of hardship, the pure ecstasy of their young love ; how it made them holy in pure contact with the harsh earth and sea ; noble in their simplicity. And he was sad, seeing himself cut off from such happiness.. He ached at the thought of their beautiful young bodies locked in an embrace at night, loin to loin and chest to paps that already swelled with the milk of pregnancy, while he himself lay supine and silent beside one who was repulsive to him.

One evening indeed his lust so gained the mastery of him as he watched young Barbara stoop before the fire that he wished to lie on her. He had to rush out from the house and wander over the crags. On and on he went, climbing the steep height that led to the southern cliffs, groaning aloud in an access of despair. For his lust died down only to make room for a bitter darkness, wherein he heard voices singing the beauty of his fading youth. All gone and nothing left but a dull wife, who again became so hateful to him in this agony that he cried out several times in the dusk asking God to deliver him of her.

A heavy fog came down with the fall of night and in a bleak, rocky field near the cliff tops he came upon two sheep. They stood on a smooth rock in the middle of the field, moaning in fear of the heavy fog. They shivered and tried to hide their heads under one another's bellies. The mist shone on their bedraggled wool and round their white bodies the naked rocks were black with rain. There was no sound but their drear moaning and the gloomy thunder of the sea.

Then, as he stood looking at them, he felt over-come with a terrible pity, not only for the sheep but for himself and for all living things that suffered and were afraid. Of what ? This emotion that was strange to his harsh nature so overcame him that he quite forgot himself and stretched out his hands towards the sheep, calling to them like one foolish. Then he ran towards them, babbling, as if to give them comfort ; but they only became still more afraid. Snorting, they ran away and leaped a wall in such haste and terror, that the stones fell beneath the impress of their clumsy bellies. They left a trail of sodden wool where they had passed and they were swallowed in the fog, while their mournful bleating became more distant until it died out and there was nothing left but the dark fog and the sea.

Tears poured down Skerrett's cheeks as he stood helplessly on the crag and he began to shout, rebel-ling against all this unreasonable phenomenon of pain and lovelessness that disfigured God's kingdom ;

until suddenly he had a vision of Moclair's hawk-like blue eyes, smiling subtly and then he saw the priest lordly on horseback, serene in the execution of his duties. He grew terribly ashamed of his emotion and hurried home over the rocks, begging God's forgiveness for his sins of lust and rebellion. He knelt by the cradle of his infant son and prayed. Then he stripped to his shirt and lay beside his wife, whom he took in his arms and possessed, as if doing penance before God. Yet when she sought his lips with hers and fondled his hair with greedy fingers during his embrace, he groaned within himself and saw the sheep fly bleating through the fog. Through a dark, loveless world, a gelding chained to unrewarded toil.

CHAPTER V

AND SEEING how Moclair was happy without love of woman, Skerrett tried to shut out from his mind all thought of ever again feeling the joy of amorous tenderness. So, although he was no fanatic, he was driven towards fanaticism in order to escape from the growing horror of his lovelessness. And for the moment all went well with him, as the life of his new community was aflame with the enthusiasm of revolution.

It must be remembered that this was the period when the whole of Ireland began to emerge from feudalism, as the result of the guerilla war waged by the peasants against the landowners. Even in Nara, that remote and poor island, which had experienced no change for hundreds of years and where people still used the tools and dwellings of prehistoric times, the will towards civilisation had been stirred into life. And the island had been fortunate in the possession of Father Moclair to direct that will.

He had come at the very height of the Land League agitation and he had at once taken command of the people as a soldier and statesman as well as a priest. Roads, piers, lighthouses, fishing boats came in his trail rapidly and in Ardglas a native trading class came into being, together with a little group of petty officials, a rate-collector, a sanitary officer, a harbour master, all tending to give the people an idea of their new importance and dignity.

Skerrett saw the priest reigning like a bountiful father over a people that worshipped him, more as a god than as a father. In his eagerness to forget his unhappiness, by submerging himself completely in the personality of another (just as a miserable slum dweller deifies a revolutionary leader who is merely a paltry charlatan) he saw nothing but altruistic social enthusiasm in the priest's labours. Yet the devil of avarice had found a place in the priest's soul from the very beginning.

Nowadays when priests are half gentlemen, the social equals of rich merchants and officials, it is somewhat difficult to realise the position of a parish priest in those days on an island like Nara. He was merely a distinguished serf, a spiritual bailiff to keep the people in order. He had to rely for his liveli-hood on the charity of the peasants, who had practic-ally no money ; so that he got paid mostly in kind. His poverty can be imagined from the fact that the parish priest accepted presents of potatoes and salt fish in payment for special Masses, for which it is practically necessary to cross the hand with silver or gold, as in dealing with a sorceress or fortune teller. It is even on record that a public subscription was made in the year 1872 to buy a suit of clothes for Father McNally, Moclair's predecessor.

When Moclair came to Nara, his parochial house, on the brow of the hill overlooking the harbour of Ardglas, beside the white wall of the coastguard station, was but a three-roomed, thatched and white-washed cottage like that of any other peasant. But almost at once he started to put himself on a different social footing to that of former parish priests. He did not have a penny in his pocket or a proper coat to his back, but he quickly used the force of his personality and the grace of his manner to procure money.

" It is about time," he said from the altar, instead of preaching about the salvation of souls, " for the people of this island to see that the priests of the church are treated with a fitting dignity. If your priests are beggars then you'll remain beggars. But if you help your priests your priests will help you. I am your representative in the struggle against your enemies, the landowners and the government. Let me treat with them on your behalf, confident in the belief that you are solid behind me. Then I'll do good work for you. But an army marches on its stomach. The least you can do is feed and clothe your shepherd. I am the shepherd of my people. Give then, out of your generosity, a little to your pastor. No sum can be small enough for a poor man like me."

Although he spoke from the altar with the humility of the lowliest beggar, that humility sat well on his lordly countenance and became the condescension of a king ; so that the people gave and bowed down after giving. In faith, Moclair instituted such a cunning system of blandishment and persuasion and promises that he soon levied his dues Christmas and Easter, on birth, marriages and deaths, on tomb-stones, prayers, incantations, earth money, and thanksgiving for harvest on sea and land, with a greater sureness than the landlord levied his rents.

Amazed at the prosperity that kept pouring in on them, the people were as generous as he was insistent. A goodly proportion of their wages from the road-making, the pier-making and the fishing found its way into the priest's pockets.

He added a fourth room to his cottage with the first money he earned. This room had a slate roof, a separate chimney and a fireplace. He furnished it like a proper parlour of the gentry, with gay curtains on the windows, a case for books and a carpet. He made this room his study and in it he held conferences with the chief men among his parishioners. Realising the importance attached by our people to political associations of a semi-terrorist nature, he founded a society called the People's League, over which he reigned as dictator, without committee or rules. After Mass on Sundays at the parish church in Tobar Milis, he held public meetings, where he issued his orders for the week. All the islanders gathered round the chapel gate and listened to the advice of their pastor. It was a kind of parish council, dealing with the tilling of the soil, fishing, the sale of cattle, sheep and pigs, sanitation, social conduct and co-operation. His sound advice and the magnetic influence of his personality made these meetings extremely beneficial ; and if any man, through jealousy or meanness, tried to go against the priest's decision, he was set upon by the mass without mercy.

As a true statesman, he set a more distant goal to his own and the people's ambition, by hinting vaguely that the time would come when the island and indeed the whole country would be the property of the people, when " the tyrants would be over-thrown " and when " freedom would be won." Without committing himself to anything rash, he hinted that the police and the coastguards and the government officials and Mr. Athy, the local squire, were enemies of God and of the people and that they were to be avoided, treated with hostility ; until the time was ripe to smite them hip and thigh. Yet he himself, being as he pointed out the people's ambassador, was friendly with all these gentry.

Skerrett believed all this implicitly and set about giving what help he could to furthering the priest's efforts. The new God to which Moclair had introduced him was practical, being served by good works rather than by prayer ; and in work something could be achieved which the unthinking Kearney could not achieve between the warm, young thighs of his sweet Barbara. Now he read everything on which he could lay his hands in order to widen the scope of his information and from the old people he stole the treasure of the island's history, handed down from mouth to mouth through the centuries. Not satisfied with the amount of work he did in the school during the day, he organised night classes, to teach the grown people how to read and write and to transact business. His energy and enthusiasm appeared fantastic ; for he was at work among the people practically every moment of his waking hours, sowing the seeds of civilisation. It was he who put into execution the practical suggestions thrown out by Father Moclair at the church gate.

Nor was he loath to use his hands ; as when the

children of a Cappatagle peasant took fever through living in the same kitchen with three pigs. Skerrett went to this peasant and said :

" Make a sty for your pigs."

" Mind your own business, schoolmaster," said the peasant.

" It's my business to see that your children go to my school," said the fierce Skerrett, " and that they are not compelled to stay at home through sickness. I'm going to get those pigs out of your house or break every bone in your body."

Then he gathered together some men of that hamlet and under his direction they built a pig-house in a few days, in spite of the peasant's protestations. Then Skerrett drove the pigs out of the man's kitchen and put them in the sty. The peasant tried to drive them back again, but Skerrett thrashed him.

" They'll perish in that cold sty," said the peasant, after he had been beaten, " without fire or warmth."

" You scoundrel," said Skerrett, " your children may die of fever, but you only worry about your pigs. I'll teach you how to behave."

And he gave the peasant another whack. So that the man left the pigs in the sty. And lo ! The other men of the village, seeing that the sty was good and that the pigs prospered therein, made similar little houses for their own pigs.

In such ways did he work, so that life became a hymn to labour and to love of his fellows for this strange man, who had come to the island as a surly bear, enchained and snapping at his fetters. He became rooted in the rocks and a man of consequence, especially when he occupied his new school-house and his new residence in the year 1891. The new school was much finer than the old one, built on a level space between Kearney's house and Corless's tavern. It was a long single-storyed building, very broad and squat, divided into two sections, as there was henceforth a separate school for girls. A high stone fence surrounded it. The walls were grey like the surrounding rocks, so that it looked rather desolate. But it was a palace to the simple Skerrett, who began to swell with pride as he watched it nearing completion.

The residence was a little farther to the west, on the brow of a hill, which soon became known as Skerrett's hill. It was a paltry cottage, one story and a half in height, with a slate roof, which had a wedge-shaped protuberance in front to make room upstairs. There was a stone wall about it and in front there was a little garden, with a gravelled path up the middle. To Skerrett it looked even more magnificent than the school ; especially as, at that time, there was no other house on the island west of Ardglas of more than one story, with the exception of Kilchreest House, the residence of Mr. Athy, the local squire.

" There you are," said the people. " Our schoolmaster is getting on in the world. He is now a slate-roofed gentleman like the best. And high up too."

In faith, perched up there on the top of a hill, within everybody's view, it added greatly to his importance. It was like a large advertisement in a newspaper. Little by little, the couple set to work

39

making a garden on the naked rock in front and furnishing the five little rooms of the house. Such was their poverty at the time, for Skerrett's salary was very small and in spite of his harsh exterior he could refuse no poor person alms, that it took them more than two years to furnish the house with an appearance of comfort. Skerrett himself made most of the fittings in the kitchen ; being busy with a saw and hammer in the evenings. He became quite proficient at carpentry and even made a fair book-case for the sitting room. But what he loved most to work at was the garden. He gathered earth scrapings from the road and sand mixed with rotten seaweeds from the shore and covered the rock and made things grow. It was a day of great glory for him, when he saw the first bud break through the dark earth that he had made upon the naked rock.

Yea ! They were great years for Skerrett, with his school, where children learned from his mouth, and his four hamlets, whose people treated him as a wise chief, and his garden and his house and his little son. It was the son, above all else, that made life beautiful and full of munificent purpose. And through the agency of the little boy, his wife also became dear to him. In their common love for the child they forgot their unsuitedness and the lack of passion in their marriage bed. There he was, trotting about the house, a precious miracle growing up before their eyes. Already he had his little toy saw and his hammer and his spade, assisting his father to make some gadget in the kitchen or to sow in the garden.

In weaving the web of this young life they spent themselves without regret and they forbore to eat the honey of desire. And at night time, when the lad was sleeping upstairs, the couple knelt and recited tht rosary and gave thanks to God for all the blessings that had been conferred on them. They asked protection for the little one who was the apple of their eye.

It seemed that the fierce soul of Skerrett had found permanent peace. From his high hill, he looked out with pride on the sphere of his influence, which kept continually widening, like the spreading branches of a tree ; so that even the island, which had at first appeared cruel and barren to him now assumed a darling beauty. Often in the evenings he looked out over his wall and thought how beautiful it was ; even the naked crag that stretched for a mile south of his house to the hamlet of Cappatagle, a squat cluster of grey cabins pitched like insects on the rocks, with the ocean rolling beyond without limit. And on the north, the land dropped steeply to the narrow sea that cut the island from the mainland, where the blue mountains rose, peak upon peak, to the far west, until they were drowned in the mists of the western sea's horizon. On the west, down in the hollow, was the harbour of Kilchreest, between two long promontories that lay in the evening light like fallen spears upon the water. He could hear the rumble of oars as the curraghs passed in and out the harbour. He heard the men sing as they rowed and he saw them stand like spars to set their nets. He saw them leap onto the land, as they grounded on the sandy shore that looked white in the distance. He heard the lowing of cows, the neighing of horses, women calling to their children, the shouting of men coming from work, the singing of birds, the sighing of the evening wind.

Or maybe it was the rain upon the crags he heard, or the thunder of the southern sea, or the whirring of a wild swan's wings, passing unseen upon the upper air.

All was woven into a cloak of peace and happiness that fell upon his soul ; the gentle happiness of a good man who is doing good work and is at peace with his fellows ; who watches old age coming in the distance with honour and security upon its back ; who sees a young tree rising from his seed ; who believes firmly in immortality.

Indeed, he began to pray aloud often to the bountiful God after the manner of the people.

CHAPTER VI

THEN suddenly in the Spring of 1894, when the child was seven years old, disaster came with the fury of a thunderbolt.

One afternoon, as Skerrett was preparing to close his school, a scholar who had just been dismissed came running back and said :

" Oh ! Sir, the mistress wants you. She said to hurry."

" What's the matter ? " said Skerrett.

" I think, sir," said the boy excitedly, " that it's how something happened to Michael. The mistress was crying. She ran out into the road and then she ran back again."

Skerrett muttered something and put his hand to his beard as if to stroke it. But instead of stroking it, he clutched it fiercely. Then he trembled from head to foot and said in a calm voice :

" Run back and tell her I'm coming."

He stood for a little while without movement and then he said :

" God have mercy on me if anything terrible has happened to my son."

He locked the school and marched back the road to his house with dignity. He kept his eyes on the ground and he tried not to listen to the excited voices that he heard before him. At the gate he saw a group of his pupils, who drew back in timid silence at his approach. A man was coming down the path as he entered by the gate. The man mumbled something which Skerrett did not understand. Mrs. Skerrett came rushing out of the house, waving her short arms in a foolish way.

" Oh ! David ! " she cried. " Something terrible has happened to our Michael."

Skerrett halted as if he had been paralysed. Then he walked slowly towards his wife in a strange manner, quite on tip-toe, stealthily. His wife became transfixed, her eyes on his face. Even in his moments of most violent rage in the old days, she had never seen his face like this, grey and drawn, with his thick lips fallen back from his teeth, like the mouth of a gasping fish. She clutched her breasts and shivered.

" Don't strike me, David," she said, as he came up to her. " It wasn't my fault. Oh ! God ! He was there one minute and then I heard the shout."

" What has happened ? " he said.

Her lips moved without voice and then she uttered a strange sound like the moan of an animal in pain.

" Get out of my way," he said.

He brushed past her and strode into the house. He paused in the little hallway and put his head to one side, listening. There were voices upstairs. Then he moved furtively into the kitchen on the left. The servant, a great lump of a girl, with heavy breasts and a blood-red face, stood before the fireplace toying with the tongs, obviously overcome by excitement. He looked at her for a moment, as if about to question her. Then he moved across the

44

floor to the stairs. He looked up. Then he came over to the servant.

" What is it ? " he whispered.

His voice was hoarse and scarcely audible. She dropped the tongs to the floor with a clatter and then began to fumble with her apron. She could say nothing. Suddenly he bounded up the stairs, grasping the banisters with such force that he seemed like to tear the bars of wood from their sockets and bring them after him in a heap. In the large bedroom to the left on the landing he saw two men and a woman. The woman came towards him and said in a mournful voice :

" God pity you, Mr. Skerrett."

" What is it ? What is it ? " he kept saying, as he moved slowly towards the bed.

His son was lying in the bed, the face all white and still, like the face of a dead thing, the eyelids closed upon the eyes, the lips without movement, the golden hair fallen over the forehead in long uneven curls, one little hand lying crosswise on the breast. He looked at this silent figure for a long time and then he threw himself on his knees by the bed.

" Have courage, sir," the woman said. " There's life in him yet. Maybe the doctor can do something."

Skerrett looked at the woman and said :

" What happened to him ? Is he dead ? What is the meaning of this ? "

" I'm afraid, sir, he's badly hurt," said one of the men. " We sent for the doctor. It was how he fell over the hill out there into my field and a stone fell over him."

" It fell right on his back," said the woman. " Oh ! Virgin Mary pity him. I was spreading seeds in the garden and I heard the shout."

" It would strike terror into ye, the way he shouted," said the other man.

" Have courage, sir," said the woman. " There's life in him yet. We sent Patcheen Derrane on the horse for the doctor. He's gone now. Maybe the doctor can do something."

Skerrett got to his feet. His shoulders drooped and his whole body seemed to disintegrate, so that he looked like a dead person, hanging by a neck-rope from a gibbet, all limp and useless. Several times he tried to pull himself up and stiffen ; but each time he shuddered and went limp.

" Have courage, sir," the woman kept saying. " Put your trust in God. He gave up His own blessed Son for all sinners. May the holy and immaculate Virgin Mother of our Divine Saviour look down in pity on your sorrow."

" Is there no hope, then ? " muttered Skerrett. " Where is he hurt ? "

There was silence for a few moments, as they looked at one another, timid of answering him. Then one of the men said :

" It's his back and his neck."

Skerrett understood and clenched his fists.

" Hadn't you better go down and take a sup of something warm ? " said the woman.

" Can I do nothing here ? " he said.

" Put your trust in God, brother. There is no use in crying out against the hand of God. Bow down your head and pray."

He sighed and left the room, followed by the woman. It was terrible the way such a strong and fearless man had completely crumpled up and become helpless. The servant rushed out of the kitchen when he came in sight, stumbling on his unsteady legs. Mrs. Skerrett was still outside the door, moaning.

" Can't anyone come and save my little child ? " she kept saying. " Oh ! Doctor, why don't you hurry ? "

Skerrett went out and took her by the arm.

" Come indoors, Kate," he said quietly. " You are only giving scandal to the neighbours."

He brought her into the sitting-room. Then he flopped into a chair.

" Neighbour," he said to the woman, " do whatever is necessary. I must rest for a minute."

He lay back and closed his eyes. His mind was completely blank, except for a white cloud that kept whirling round and round before his closed eyes. The neighbouring woman went into the kitchen to make tea.

" You won't kill me on account of this, David," said Mrs. Skerrett, coming over and putting her hand timidly on her husband's shoulder.

He said nothing.

" Oh ! God ! " she continued. " He just ate a slice of bread and butter and then he went out. ' Where are you going, Micky ? ' I said. ' I'm only going out into the garden,' he said. They were the last words I heard from his lips. Please God, maybe I'll hear him again. Oh ! David, I couldn't help it. Don't blame me. When I heard the shout, I ran out. I saw them around him in the field. Have pity on me, David, and say something kind to me. My head is going round. I feel like a bird in a cage."

" It was birds' nests he was after," said the neighbouring woman, coming back into the room. " That old wall there on top of that hill is rotten. Ye see, it's a dangerous place, not fit for a goat. He slipped over the wall and then he fell down into the deep field, with the big stone on top of him. I was spreading seeds when I heard the shout. Then I looked and saw something in the field. Not another sound did I hear. When I came over he was lying there like a dead thing, beside the stone."

" Oh ! God ! " moaned Mrs. Skerrett. " Don't take the only thing I have in the world."

Then Skerrett lost control of himself.

" Silence woman," he shouted at his wife. " What have I got ? Does he mean as much to you as to me ? "

He gave her a look of bitter hatred. The neighbouring woman said afterwards to her friends :

" The cut of her woe'd soften the heart of a stone, but 'faith it was how she made him rampant with fury."

Indeed nothing could be more pathetic than Mrs. Skerrett's behaviour and appearance. She moved about, fidgeting with things and mumbling to herself. She had grown fatter with the years. Her face had lost all comeliness ; little red cheeks like the tops of buns, a pinched mouth, upturned nose, pale blue eyes that had lost their lustre. Her grey hair was disorderly. Her stubby hands were swollen. Her ugliness, which in the ordinary way would repel an onlooker, now increased the feeling of pity inspired by her helplessness in sorrow ; for beautiful or talented people can afford to lose a great deal and yet be sufficient to themselves, while the loss of a single groat is untold tragedy to those ungifted.

How she whispered to herself, enumerating all the beauties of her little one ! The stories he used to tell when she put him to bed at night ! How pretty his infant hands were ! What a clever remark he had made a few days before ! And last winter, when he had a heavy cold and a high temperature, he was so brave. He sat up in his little bed and said : " Will I die, mummy ? "

Yet Skerrett seemed unaware of her sorrow, or rather indifferent to it. Indeed, he appeared to be indifferent to his own sorrow, outwardly, after he had drunk some tea and had become used to the realisation of what had happened. After a while he went upstairs and stayed there watching the boy. Only once, when there was a little flicker of life on the child's lips, did the father lose control of himself.

He stooped over the bed and whispered excitedly :

" What is it, Michael ? What did you say ? Are you very hurt ? "

Again the mouth was still and the father straightened himself very slowly. His lips dropped back from his teeth, like the mouth of a gasping fish.

At last, the doctor and Father Moclair came on a jaunting car. Skerrett went out to receive them. For the first time since his conversion he did not fawn on meeting the priest. Now he fawned on the doctor, looking into his face with foolish eagerness, taking his bag and saying :

" I want to know at once if there is no hope, Doctor Melia. Do your best, but don't keep me in agony."

The doctor, a tall, dark man of forty, who had just come to the island and to whom Skerrett had not spoken before this, looked at the schoolmaster with interest and said :

" I'll do all I can do."

" Thanks doctor," said Skerrett. " But for God's sake let me know at once."

Mrs. Skerrett clutched at the doctor in the hallway and said :

" Oh ! Save him, doctor. Save my little son."

Father Moclair put his arm around Mrs. Skerrett's shoulder and began to soothe her. Skerrett went out into the garden to wait for the news.

The sun was now setting and there was a wild chorus of bird music. The earth smelt rich and pure with the sap of spring. The seeds in the dark earth of the garden had already put forth shoots. A nesting robin with a tiny bit of moss in its beak hopped along the wall. The air seemed to sing of life and joy and the exuberance of growth. A man on horseback passed along a winding lane among the crags to the south. The steel hoofs of the horse rang merrily on the loose stones of the lane and the man was singing. Afar off to the north-west, a white-sailed boat lay slanting on the smooth sea that gleamed in the light of the setting sun.

Neighbours passed him on the gravelled walk, offering words of sympathy. He could not speak.

Then, at last he heard a cry of anguish from the house. He took off his hat, made the sign of the cross and bowed his head. A mist came before his eyes and he muttered :

" God have mercy on me."

The doctor came out and took him by the arm. He pressed the arm and said something which Skerrett did not understand. They went upstairs. Women had begun to chant the death wail. Men stood about in silence with their heads uncovered. Mrs. Skerrett was kneeling by the bed. She had grown calm. The floodgates of her sorrow had burst and tears flowed down her cheeks. She was telling her beads. Father Moclair was reading some prayer. Skerrett went on his knees and tried to pray ; but he could think of nothing. His mouth was still like the maw of a gasping fish. A white cloud whirled before his eyes. Even the little dead body that had been his son a few hours ago awoke no understanding in him when he looked at it.

Afterwards Father Moclair talked to him for a while in the sitting-room, about fortitude in accepting the will of God. Skerrett did not understand anything of what the priest said. But when Doctor Melia came and shook him by the hand in silence he felt comforted and tears nearly broke from his eyes. Then the priest and the doctor went away and the wake began.

CHAPTER VII

People came in great numbers from all parts of the island to the funeral. Skerrett felt exalted by their sympathy. He saw how fine was their humanity and how much they loved him. Even the most crude of them, rough fellows from whose mouths words came with halting difficulty, found some gentle phrase to ease his sorrow.

Again and again he heard them utter the plaintive peasant cry over the death of an innocent child and he was comforted.

" He went straight to Heaven to sing among the angels on God's right hand."

" He has become a bright star in the sky at night."

" At every dawn he will dance among the sunrays."

Their voices, rising towards Heaven from the place of death, made his soul rise in union with their simple fortitude, which turned ugly death into a holy sacrifice. Yet, when the death wail rose again as they were putting the child in the coffin and he came for a last look at the body, faith died under the weight of his sorrow. His face went gray and his lips fell back from his teeth, like the mouth of a gasping fish. He rebelled and the wild strength of his being sought some violent outlet. His wife now suffered far less, since she had begun to weep. Even when she kissed the dead forehead and took the lock of hair they had

53

cut, she looked composed. She seemed unable to comprehend her loss any longer. She followed the coffin out of the room like a little dog after its master.

Offerings for the dead were taken in the sitting-room. A table covered with a white cloth was placed near the door. Father Moclair and Skerrett stood beside the table. The people came in, bareheaded, with their offerings. Coming in, they bowed to the corpse in the kitchen. Then they placed their coins on the table, bowed to the priest and went out again, crossing themselves as they passed the kitchen door.

Skerrett stood a little to the rear, with his arms crossed on his chest, watching the priest. Moclair now seemed to be quite a stranger to his former worshipper. Skerrett noted with displeasure how greedy the priest's eyes looked and how stout the man had grown. Beneath his long priestly frock coat his belly had begun to swell. His neck had got red at the back. A large pimple had come out on his right cheek near his nose. His nose was heavy, with a sharp point. It was rosy, like the nose of a good liver. His mouth looked cruel.

Skerrett especially noted the priest's eyes darting hither and thither. They fixed on each person that entered and then followed the coin from the hand to the table. They sparkled at the sight of each new coin.

Then the demon of jealousy found voice in Skerrett's mind. Suddenly it appeared evil to him that the priest, whom he had thought good and pure in all ways, should stand greedily watching coins in the house where his beloved son was dead.

" That's all he really cares for," thought Skerrett. " For money. He has no thought for my sorrow. See how he watches the money like a hawk. He doesn't suffer."

And again he thought :

" Look at his red nose. He drinks with Athy and the government officials. He feeds himself well on the money he gets from the people. He only thinks of the money that's thrown on the table to him."

When the people had ceased to come, the priest went to the door and looked out.

" Is there anybody else there that wants to make an offering ? " Skerrett heard him say in a loud voice.

Skerrett shuddered with anger. This remark appeared very shameful to him. Then Moclair came back eagerly, with a slight smile on his face and without looking at Skerrett. He again took up his position by the table, watching the door. An old man named Cooney entered slowly. He was a toothless old fisherman, very ragged, with a yellow muffler around his neck. He was noted in his village as a miserly fellow. Very slowly, he took out a red handkerchief, which he unwound deliberately, glancing as he did so from Skerrett to the priest. At last he took a shilling from the handkerchief. He toyed with the coin as he put it on the table. He did not drop it, but laid it down gently on the heap of coins and he withdrew his fingers with obvious regret from contact with it.

" It's all I have," he said in a mournful voice to Skerrett, " but God bless you, sir. It's the least I could do for your kindness, to honour your dead."

A lump came into Skerrett's throat as he remembered how he had now and again given a little to this old man, who was very poor and lived in a miserable hut with a childless wife. He wanted to pick up the shilling and return it to the old fellow, but Moclair came forward eagerly even before the ragged man had left the room.

" We better count it now," he said.

When the money was counted, he put it in his large pocket.

" This life is a vale of tears," he said to Skerrett. " But be of good heart. You now have a soul praying for you by the throne of God."

Skerrett found his words barren and without comfort. Instead of giving him comfort, they made him feel savage. His faith in the priest received at that moment a blow from which it never recovered. When Moclair took his hand and pressed it, something sour came up his throat.

The coffin was put on the cart and the funeral set off towards the graveyard above the beach at Kilchreest. Three women sat on the cart with the coffin. Skerrett and the priest walked behind, followed by a long line of whispering people. A woman came up to Skerrett and said :

" We had to put the mistress to bed. She broke down."

Skerrett started. He had forgotten all about his wife since the previous evening. Then he thought :

" From now on, I must treat her kindly. Michael was all she had. It's little comfort I've been to her. I've only thought of myself."

Anger then swelled within him against Moclair to whom he had given most of his thoughts during recent years ; to that man whose greedy eyes devoured silver coins in the house where a dearly beloved son was dead. Even when they lowered the coffin into the new grave and the priest was reading the prayers, Skerrett felt anger instead of sorrow. Then the people scattered and he went home to his wife.

He went quietly into the room where she lay on her bed. He intended to lie down beside her and tell her what was in his mind, about his lack of sympathy with her in the past and how the two of them must cling together in the future, in order to bear this sorrow that had come to them and find peace in one another's love, now that they were both getting old and cured of youth's follies. But somehow, as he stood within the doorway and looked at her, he found it impossible to say anything of the sort. She lay like a bundle under the clothes. The expression on her face, as she turned towards him, was vacant and remote.

" Don't you feel well, Kate ? " was all he could say to her.

She shook her head in answer. It seemed to him that she was no longer interested in him ; so he could not say any of the things that he had intended. He walked over to the window instead of approaching her. With his hands behind his back, he looked out

over the crags. A drizzling rain had begun to fall
and the rocks were quite black. Looking at these
black rocks he remembered how he had hated her
on hearing about the accident. Overcome with
remorse, he went to the bed and again tried to say
that in future they must go hand in hand through
life, seeking together the peace and companionship
of old age.

But he only said :

" Is there anything I could do ? Could I get you
something ? "

" No, David," she said in a tired voice, without
any feeling. " My heart is bad. I've had pains in it
this long while."

" Why didn't you tell me about it, Kate ? "

" I didn't like to worry you."

" I see."

She moved and put her hands out over the clothes
to change her position. He saw that she had the lock
of golden hair wound around the fingers of her left
hand. Then indeed, at sight of this golden lock of
hair, his loss became terribly personal to him, instead of the dull ache it had been until then. His
memory suddenly grew crowded with impressions
of the dead child. He sighed heavily and dropped
his head to his wife's side. He took her hand and
pressed it. Yet neither of them said a word. Neither
did they weep nor come any closer to one another.

And the thought came into Skerrett's mind that
it was now too late to establish any closer intimacy
with his wife. She had become a stranger ; the only
bond between them having been broken by death.

So he stood up and arranged the clothes about her clumsily.

" I'll tell Lizzie to bring you a cup of tea," he said.

She did not answer and he turned to leave the room. Then she said : " I think a drop of brandy would do me good."

" Brandy ? "

" Yes. They say it's good to ease a pain in the heart."

" Brandy ? " he repeated. " But you always said you couldn't take it."

She turned her head to one side and said pettishly :

" All right. Don't bother."

" Of course I'll get it for you if you want it," he said.

" Anything at all," she said. " Whiskey or brandy."

" All right. I'll send Lizzie for it."

He moved to the door again and was going out, when he halted and looked back at her. It appeared very strange to him that she should want to drink spirits at this moment.

" It's very funny," he thought. " She always had a horror of drink."

Noticing that he was watching her in silence, she raised her head. Her face looked awful. Her eyes were bloodshot. Her cheeks were covered with queer blotches of colour. She seemed to have grown into an old woman suddenly. He could not endure the sight of her face and he rushed over to the bed. He threw himself down beside her and began to mutter her name.

" Oh ! Kate," he said, " why can't I do something for you ? "

She began to tremble in his arms, but she did not weep and he felt her body struggling weakly away from him.

" Forgive me, Kate," he whispered, " for every bad thing I ever said or did to you."

But she only pushed against him weakly with her hands and she said :

" I'm so tired. I want to be quiet. Could you get me a little brandy ? "

Then he let go her body, stood up and looked at her in stupid wonder. He could not understand why she had suddenly become a stranger.

" God ! " he muttered. " All this is so sudden. At one moment everything is all right and then everything turns upside down. What is the meaning of it all ? "

He left the room slowly. Going downstairs he halted several times, asking himself the meaning of this astounding change. Having sent the servant to the tavern, he tried to read, but found that impossible. Then he began to wander around the house. Everywhere he saw signs of the child's existence, an old toy, or a shoe, or a little coat.

Suddenly he cried out :

" Oh ! God ! I can't endure this. I know why she wants brandy. She wants to forget."

He took his hat and dashed out of the house, not knowing exactly where he was going ; and then he met Doctor Melia at the gate.

" Good evening," said the doctor. " I brought

some medicine for your wife. She told me she had trouble with her heart."

" God bless you, doctor," said Skerrett, seizing Melia's hand eagerly. " You are a good man. I don't know where I was going, or what I'd do only for you came at this minute."

The doctor looked intently at Skerrett and said softly :

" I can imagine very well what you are suffering. If you can bear it, it will be good for you. But it's no use running away from suffering."

" You are a kind man," said Skerrett. " I won't forget it of you."

" It's of no consequence at all," said the doctor. He looked embarrassed.

" Ah ! But it's of great consequence," said Skerrett eagerly, " at a time like this, to find a person that you feel sure is good and kind. I said to myself this morning——"

Suddenly he stopped, having become ashamed of this show of emotion. He drew himself very erect, threw out his chest and said gruffly :

" Maybe you'd go up and speak to my wife."

" I'll do that," said the doctor.

Skerrett waited in the sitting-room rather nervously for the doctor's return from upstairs. Doctor Melia had made a deep impression on him.

" There is a really fine man," he thought. " His eyes look you straight in the face. How kind he is ! I wish I could make a friend of him."

Being essentially a rather stupid man, of very slow understanding, it was vitally necessary for Skerrett to rely on somebody of greater intelligence for a plan of life. Now that his confidence was shaken in Father Moclair he was already seeking elsewhere.

" What sort of man is this doctor ? " he thought.

Beyond the man's outward appearance and the manifestations of a kindly nature shown during their slight intercourse, Skerrett knew practically nothing. The doctor had now been a month on the island, but the islanders, in spite of their love of gossip and their positive genius for probing one another's inmost secrets, had learned nothing of his history. Skerrett had heard vague rumours about some tragedy in the doctor's life and that he came of a good family. But everybody said that the doctor was " as silent as the tomb."

This mystery added to his charm at this moment in Skerrett's imagination. The doctor definitely appeared to be a rock to which a drowning man could cling. He was like Father Moclair, living alone, secretive, belonging to a large world of the mind ; and yet he was different.

" In what way is he different ? " asked Skerrett.

He was very excited when the doctor came down to the sitting-room.

" How did you find her ? " he said.

The doctor sat down without speaking. Skerrett sat opposite him. Stroking his beard, he stared arrogantly at the doctor and yet he felt timid, just as he used to feel in Moclair's presence before he lost faith.

" You'll need to take great care of her," said the doctor quietly.

" I see," said Skerrett.

" There's nothing really the matter with her," continued the doctor. " I think her heart is slightly affected, but that's only natural for her age and constitution. However . . ." he paused, looked closely at Skerrett and cleared his throat, " she's hovering on the brink."

The doctor's face became so intense as he said the words " hovering on the brink " that Skerrett felt afraid. Suddenly his wife became the most important thing in the world for him ; and that also astonished him, since she had been for years an unnecessary and almost useless encumbrance.

" How do you mean ? " he said.

Doctor Melia rubbed his hands together and said : " It's hard to explain."

He was very dark. His short, thick hair was of a brown colour and yet he gave the impression of being all dark. It was his sombre countenance that caused this. And yet he exuded gentleness and peace. His face was very strong ; clear-cut in every feature ; quite imperial. It seemed as if his head were hewn from marble and like the head of a statue it was without movement. His eyes were intelligent. His whole face, in spite of its strength, had none of the coarseness of Skerrett's face. It was the face of a refined and civilised man. His skin was bronzed. Although of fine proportions, he looked clumsy owing to his shyness. He kept toying with his hands, stroking one with the other. His fingers were very long and white, with thin white hairs growing in little bunches on them.

63

" It's on account of Michael's death, I suppose," said Skerrett.

" Not altogether," said the doctor. " But that was the last straw."

" I see," said Skerrett.

The two men looked at one another.

" See that she takes the medicine I left for her," said the doctor. " But the important thing is not to annoy her in any way. Let her have her own way as much as possible. I think she . . ."

He paused and then added with difficulty :

" She is afraid of something."

Skerrett opened his mouth ; like a fish that has just expired. Then his face flushed. He cried out :

" What is there left for me any more than for her ? Is there to be no pity for me ? "

" I pity you," said the doctor hurriedly. " Don't misunderstand me."

" What does it matter whether I take to drink and end up in the madhouse like the man that was here before me ? I did my best. I worked like a slave and this is all the reward I get."

" There is no use looking at it in that way," said the doctor, getting to his feet. " We all have our troubles. I can assure you. The best thing is to expect nothing."

He put his hand on his breast.

" It's in here a man must look for happiness," he said. " Don't rely on others."

" But when a man wears himself to the bone . . ."

" Oh ! Well ! I suppose virtue is its own reward.

The great thing is not to surrender. Either you believe in God or you don't believe. If you believe in God and I daresay you do——"

" Of course I believe in God," cried Skerrett in surprise. " That's a queer thing for you to say, Doctor Melia."

He got to his feet. They looked at one another intently. The doctor shrugged his shoulders and said :

" Then what have you to grumble about ? It's quite plain to you. You have to do your duty and accept whatever God sends you. You'll be rewarded for it. As long as you believe in God you're lucky. Only you must remember that charity begins at home. Look after your wife. I'll call around to-morrow to see how she is."

He took Skerrett's hand.

" I must have a long talk with you some time," he said, as he pressed the hand. " It's lonely here for both of us, I think."

" God bless you, Doctor Melia," said Skerrett fervently.

" Thanks," mumbled the doctor.

Skerrett stared after him as he went down the path. The doctor's tall body slouched awkwardly. His head, the back of his strong neck and his wide shoulders were all square and erect. Then the rest of his body slouched, as if weary of life.

" What does he mean ? " thought Skerrett. " Do I believe in God ? "

The servant came back from the tavern. She had a pint of whiskey in a bottle. They had no brandy there. Skerrett took the bottle upstairs. He found his wife asleep. He put the bottle on the window-sill. Then he experienced a sudden desire to open it and swallow the contents. But he went hurriedly out of the room on tip-toe.

" Will you have your supper now, sir ? " said the servant to him in the kitchen.

" Supper ? " he cried in astonishment.

He remembered that he had eaten hardly anything since receiving news of the fatal accident. This worried him a great deal, for he was normally a man of powerful appetite, together with being concerned about his health, as is generally the case with strong men. So, although his gorge rose at the thought of supper, he forced himself to eat a great deal. He ate in haste, eggs, potatoes, cheese, bread and butter. The meal did him a lot of good. He said grace when he had finished and then, being exhausted, he fell asleep over the table. But he awoke almost at once, pursued by a horrid nightmare, in which he saw his son falling over the hill and screaming. He was shivering from head to foot. The nerves ached in the soles of his feet.

" I'm breaking down," he thought. " This must be stopped at once."

Going out to the shed at the back of his house, he took a sledge hammer. Then he stripped to the waist, tied up his trousers with a belt and took the hammer to the crags. He began to hack at a boulder. Night was falling and the air was extremely chilly, yet perspiration soon began to pour from his body. Rejoicing in his strength and in the liberation caused by the fierce exercise, he forgot his sorrow and began to grunt with satisfaction at each downward swing of the hammer.

He was still in his prime, although two years over forty. The muscles of his fine arms, that looked glossy with sweat, were still supple like those of a youth. His great chest, covered between the nipples with a thick, fair down, rose and fell without difficulty of breath. Along his broad back the muscles coursed in knots beneath the skin. Now and again he paused to stroke his luxuriant beard or to brush his hands through his hair. Then he would spit on his hands, grunt with pleasure and slash at the rocks with his hammer.

The moon came out. His body glowed in the moonlight. Sparks flew from the rock. His blows resounded far and wide throughout the silence of the night.

As it were, he was issuing the challenge of his strength to the rocky earth that had struck down his son.

CHAPTER VIII

As when the sun suffers an eclipse and the earth is covered with a horrid darkness, wherein the spectres of annihilation make havoc with all ordinary belief, and security becomes a sham, a brittle wall of glass behind which vainglorious man constructs the doll's house of his immortality, so did this death expose the unstable foundations on which he had tried to build his happiness.

Outwardly he remained a proud and undefeated man, but within his mind this terrible circumstance had invaded every stored experience of his life with doubt and disruption. He turned a bold face to the world, in all appearance defiant and stubborn, going about like a swaggering soldier, striking the road heels first, with his beard thrust forward, his head craned back on to his neck, swinging his arms from the shoulders. His hoarse guffaw was heard more often. In school he was more strict. At the chapel gate after Mass on Sundays he raised his voice with greater assurance to debate the affairs of the parish. When people condoled with him, he shrugged his shoulders and said brusquely : " It's God's will. Let His will be done."

So that they murmured at his callousness :

" There is no nature in him," they said. " Even death can't touch his pride."

They did not understand the struggle that was

going on within him or that it was his pride alone that prevented him from howling his sorrow to the moon like a lonely dog. Sometimes at school he found it extremely difficult to prevent himself giving way, when he heard the gay cries of the children at play-time and remembered how he used to feel his heart throb with pleasure at hearing the voice of his own son in the distance ; or else when he saw a boy in class look up into his face and the boy assumed the features of his lost one. Then indeed he would turn away, sigh and feel utterly helpless. A mist came before his eyes, a sourness rose in his throat and life became unbearably arid. Sometimes he was taken unawares by a pang of grief and it seemed to him that his heart would break unless he sought relief in tears, or drink, or in the outpour of prayers for comfort into a sympathetic ear.

Yet his pride prevented him from seeking outside himself for comfort. Trying to strangle his grief by main force, he became stronger, but at the same time poisoned in his outlook on life. The old faith which he had taken to his bosom on his conversion died without as yet making way for a new faith. Behind the mask of his arrogance, there was only ignorance and loneliness and a sour sort of impotent rebellion against the power that had defeated his purpose. The zeal with which he continued to perform his duties was merely a shield to prevent people from seeing that he felt defeated.

Were it not for his concern about his wife he might have fallen under this blow. As it was, the extraordinary change that had taken place in her prevented him from thinking too much about himself. His strength found work in trying to save her, not so much through affection for her, as to save himself from the shame of a further defeat in the eyes of the people. For he regarded his son's death to a large extent in this light, as a defeat of his plans.

" Anything I put my hand to succeeds," he used to say.

From the evening that he returned from the funeral and tried to sympathise with his wife without success, she had become a complete stranger in his house. She barely answered when he spoke to her ; and then, at the most odd moments, she developed a habit of nagging at him in a bitter fashion. He could not understand this at all, as she had hitherto been so meek and submissive. Now it seemed that his body had become repulsive to her, for she either suffered his embraces without movement of any sort, or else denied herself altogether, offering the condition of her heart as an excuse. She avoided his company as much as possible, talking in preference to the servant. When he pursued her and tried to make conversation, she would say : " Am I to have no peace, then ? You might at least have pity on me now, David, with my heart in this state. Now that I've lost everything." Then she would burst into tears. She shed tears in a manner that irritated him. She never sobbed aloud, but her mouth would quiver, tears rolled down her cheeks and then she gradually began to shake all over. If she were at all annoyed, even by an attempt at sympathy, while she was weeping, she went into a severe fit of hysterics. These fits so terrified him, that he soon stopped making any attempt to control her. Thenceforth she ruled in the house. A few times, he tried to establish control, by angrily abusing her when she was particularly offensive without cause. He even once raised his hand to strike her, but she made such a scene on that occasion that he never attempted it again. She had shrewdly realised that his solicitude for her was occasioned more by a regard for his own respect in the eyes of the people than by any real love for her, or remorse for his former negligence. So she ran screaming into the garden when he upbraided her. She kept shouting at the top of her voice : " Help. He's going to murder me. He'll kill me." After some time, he discovered that this fear and hysteria were almost entirely artificial, but he could do nothing about it.

" She has me cornered," he said to himself. " My God ! What a state I'm in now ! "

The doctor was no great help to him.

" What am I to do with her ? " Skerrett would say to the doctor, when the latter came to visit the sick woman.

" I really don't know," the doctor would answer. " It's very difficult for me to say. She feels she has a grievance against life and she puts all the blame on you. It's very extraordinary."

" But is there anything serious the matter with her heart ? "

" Nothing that I can find. Nothing serious, I mean. It's not very strong, but there's nothing to worry about. It's just that she has lost faith in life completely."

" Do you think it would do any good if she went away for a while to see her relatives ? "

" Yes. That might do her good."

But when Skerrett tried to persuade her to go away for a holiday that summer, she refused point blank. She began to blubber and said that she would die if she missed visiting her boy's grave every Sunday. She walked over to the graveyard at Kilchreest every Sunday afternoon, wearing her little black cloak and her feathered bonnet, with her eyes on the ground and her rosary beads in her hands. She looked such a pathetic little figure, fat, distraught and uncomely, praying along the road, that passers by stopped to commiserate with her ; and she was nothing loath to pour her troubles into their ears. And so cunningly did she manipulate the recital of these woes that people began to murmur about the foul way Skerrett was making her life a misery.

When she walked with him to Mass, she did her best to attract the attention of the people on the road. She would halt suddenly, lean against the fence and groan with pain. People gathered about her and then, when she had sufficient of an audience, she would continue her journey, saying in a plaintive tone : " Oh ! Then ! Oh ! Then ! What have I done to deserve all this pain ? " Or else, when she came in sight of the congregation, who were all gathered on the walls outside the church, waiting for the bell to ring as a signal that Mass was about to begin, she would begin to walk at a snail's pace, so that Skerrett might be embarrassed. Indeed, this was a great agony to him, for all eyes were fixed on the couple and he could imagine the people whispering to one another : " God help the poor woman. She is in great suffering."

At her work in school she became utterly feckless and incompetent ; so that the inspector that Summer reported that she was unfit for her position. It was in connection with this report that Skerrett had his first tussle with Father Moclair. About a week after the inspector's visit, Father Moclair came to the school and called Skerrett out into the little porch.

" I'm sorry to have to say this to you, David," he said, " but your wife'll have to resign unless she can improve on her teaching. The inspector has complained that she is altogether unfit for the position."

Skerrett stroked his beard and said nothing.

" I'm very sorry to have to say this," continued Moclair, " but they are getting more strict and we have to keep moving with the times. In fact, he complained to me that you yourself aren't keeping to the curriculum."

" I see," said Skerrett.

" Of course, I explained to him all you had done," said Moclair, " but there it is. They want things done in a certain way and we have to do what they think right. Then, somehow, you didn't manage to make a good impression on him while he was inspecting you. He complained to me of your arrogance. You contradicted several remarks he made.

74

That is no good to you. He's a nice man, Inspector Fitzsimmons, but he's very touchy and——"

Suddenly Skerrett cried out :

" I'll see them all in hell first. I have worked the flesh off my bones. I have——"

He struck his chest with his clenched fists and spluttered with rage.

" I'll see anybody in hell that dares meddle with my school. I made this school and my wife helped me to make it. We found these children a lot of savages and we have civilised them. We made this school what it is. Hands off us, then. Why don't they let us alone ? I'll fight to the last breath against any interference from anybody. If I'm put to it, I'll take the scholars out of this school and teach them on the road same as was done long ago. Why should I bother with every damn fool that's sent down from Dublin to interfere with my work ? I know what's useful to the scholars and I teach them what's useful."

" You had better control your language when you are talking to me," said Moclair in a menacing tone. " Lately I've noticed that you're getting a little too big for your boots. Don't forget I'm your manager. You'll run this school in the way I tell you, and you'll behave yourself when you're talking to me."

" You may be the manager," said Skerrett, " but I'm master in this school."

They looked one another in the eyes. Skerrett's shoulder muscles stiffened and the priest's hand closed about his riding whip. Father Moclair's face flushed and his eyes became very cruel. But he smiled and said :

" This is a new tone you're adopting, Skerrett. You used not to be like this. I've noticed you're very sour of late. You have changed for some reason. While things were going well with you, you were friendly, but at the first stroke of bad luck you turn to bite the hand that fed you."

" I've given in return," said Skerrett proudly, " a pound for every shilling."

" You were on your back when I found you," said the priest quietly. " I put you on your feet. But you had better realise in time on what side your bread is buttered. Otherwise there'll only be room for one of us on this island. I may as well tell you that in time. I hear everything that goes on in this parish and a little bird has been whispering in my ear that you've been keeping bad company lately. You've been having long conversations with Doctor Melia. He's not the best company you could keep."

" I'll keep company with whoever I please," shouted Skerrett.

The priest turned away and walked towards the gate. At the gate he paused, looked back at Skerrett and said in a low voice :

" The company you're keeping now is worse for you than when you were the drunken companion of coastguards AND THEIR WIVES."

" What's that you say ? " muttered Skerrett, taking a pace forward.

But he halted and went limp. He watched the priest mount his horse and ride away to the East,

rising and falling in his saddle. Then he rubbed his
forehead with his hand and said to himself :

" And that's the man I have worked for like a
slave. Now what am I to do ? "

Now, indeed, he felt menaced most dangerously
and all his anger against the unknown power that
had brought disaster on him became concentrated
on Father Moclair. Since the day he had seen the
priest's eyes look greedily at the silver coins on the
table of offerings, he had grown suspicious of the
priest's integrity and goodness. He had begun to
criticise in his own mind the priest's every action
and although he remained outwardly friendly as
before, he had lost faith within himself. He listened
to the gossip that was beginning to become current
on the island about the priest's growing avarice.
" He has a hand in everything," the people said,
" and wherever he puts his hand a penny is sure to
come out with it. He hoards his money like a miser
and nobody gets the benefit of it. He does not give
in charity. He only lends to the poor and like a
money-lender he has to be paid on the nail." Indeed,
there had recently been a grave scandal when Father
Moclair thrashed with a stick a poor woman to whom
he had lent money and who was unable to repay
him at the time appointed.

All these rumours fed Skerrett's suspicions and although he was reluctant to depose the hero he had
set up in his imagination, he could not resist dis-
liking the way Moclair concerned himself with
money, how he had a regular network of spies scattered over the parish, how he busied himself with

every tittle-tattle and private scandal, the pettiness with which he sought revenge for the least insult to his dignity, his suspicion of the simplest act that might be construed into hostility towards himself.

Now all this smouldering anger suddenly took flame and the priest became a demon in his eyes, which changed into evil what had formerly appeared most good and joy-giving ; particularly all those out-ward charms that had been the magnets of an almost sensual love. And he hated Moclair for his royal carriage, his magnificent eyes, his endearing smile, his subtlety of speech. He sought out his defects with the lust of hatred and fixed on that pimple which had grown on the priest's cheek, like a beacon of indulgence.

He felt outraged by the priest's assurance, by his immunity from suffering. He saw how Moclair stood alone and impregnable, with the powerful structure of the Church standing behind him like an army, placing him beyond reach of all attack. His priestly clothes seemed to have magic in them, making him inhuman and occult, for all bowed down in rever-ence before them and yet, within their shelter he was free to exercise all the human passions, except con-cupiscence of the flesh.

And Skerrett felt outraged now particularly by this concupiscence of the flesh from which Moclair was immune ; since he saw in it the basis of his own downfall ; this child on whose future he had placed such hopes ; this wife who after being a thorn to his senses had become a strangle-rope about his neck.

"Very well, Father Harry," he muttered to himself, as he threw out his chest, "I'll fight you, by God. I'm in the right. I've done my duty. I'll fight you. I'll surrender to no man."

And he returned to his work, so white in the face with anger that the scholars trembled. As soon as he arrived home, he took his wife into the sitting-room, closed the door and began :

"From now on I'm going to stand no more nonsense from you. You've got to settle down to your work and stop all this nonsense about your heart, or I'll be the death of you. You are making me a show board before the whole island with your goings on. You're doing your best to make my life a misery. Do you hear, woman ?"

Her lips began to tremble, but he shouted at her :

"Stop that. I'll flay the back off you if you start any of that nonsense. Do you hear now ? If I get any more of your whining, I'll be the death of you."

Her lips stopped trembling and she looked at him in terror. Then she wrung her hands, screamed and threw herself to the floor. Skerrett immediately forgot his resolution about bringing her to heel. He knelt beside her and began to whisper endearments.

"Oh ! Kate, what ails you ?" he cried. "I'm sorry I shouted at you. Speak to me, won't you ? Oh ! Stop shaking. You'll break my heart if you go on shaking like that."

For a while she lay on the floor trembling like a leaf and then she began to beat him with her hands and screamed :

"Help ! Help ! He's going to kill me."

79

The servant ran into the room.

" Bring something for God's sake," said Skerrett. " She's in a fit."

" What'll I bring ? "

" Tell him to leave my sight," wailed Mrs. Skerrett. " Take me away from him. Hide me from him."

" Take her up to her bed," said Skerrett.

He hurried from the room, took his hat and went out.

" I must go to the doctor and ask him what I'm to do," he said, as he hurried down the path.

CHAPTER IX

THE DOCTOR'S house was on a hill at the western entrance to Ardglas, some distance back from the road. An English gentleman had built it some twenty years previously, intending to end his life as a recluse on the island, which he had discovered during a yachting trip. He had built a cottage in the English style, with a long roof reaching to within a few feet of the ground on the north side, a tall outside chimney at one gable and latticed windows. Around it he began to grow a hedge. He planted rose trees and made beds for various other flowers. In a few years it looked a strange oasis of sweet growth among the surrounding desert of bleak crags. But the Englishman died after eight years, being devoured by the island before his hedgerows or rose trees had reached maturity. Succeeding owners had none of his taste for gardening and prettiness. A whitewashed stone fence took the place of the hedgerows. Potatoes and cabbages ousted the rose trees and the flowerbeds. The house became bedraggled and just as desolate as the surrounding crags. The island had swallowed it up, forcing it to conform to the savage dignity of the rocks.

Doctor Melia made no effort to improve its bedraggled condition since coming to live there. Although very enthusiastic in his work as a doctor, being prepared to go to the farthest end of the island at any hour to visit the sick, he seemed to have no interest in his own comfort, or indeed any sort of ambition in life. A taciturn man, he avoided people as much as possible, choosing to make contacts with the lowliest and most obscure persons and to spend his spare time studying the historical ruins on the island, or else in reading. From the beginning he refused to have any woman in his house and procured a disreputable fellow called Tom Fennett as his servant.

Fennett had for years been a by-word on the island and he was known as " the pagan," since he never went to Mass or the sacraments ; not because he did not believe in God, but simply because he felt an outcast from society. He had lived in the house of his married sister, who had taken his land on her marriage, because he did not want to get married or look after it. Instead of feeling grateful to him for this gift, for he had received no payment for the land, the sister treated him with shocking cruelty, often denying him food and locking him out if he happened to come home late. So that he lost all sense of self-respect and drank whatever money he could earn by casual labouring and doing odd jobs for the more prosperous people of Ardglas. He was now middle-aged, a round, fat man, with a black beard that covered his throat from ear to ear and yet left his chin exposed.

It was thought very odd that the doctor should choose such a man as a servant, but the doctor knew his own business and paid no attention to the gossip of the people. And in fact, a marvellous change had taken place in Fennett since coming into his new position. He stopped drinking and became as much a recluse as the doctor himself. So that people said in Ardglas that the doctor was also a pagan and that there were very queer things happening at the Englishman's house. Father Moclair, who disliked the doctor as soon as he saw him first, helped to spread these rumours, no doubt with the idea that they might help when the time arrived to get rid of the doctor. After the first month or so, the priest and the doctor ceased to be on speaking terms. Yet the doctor was a Catholic and attended his religious duties regularly.

When Skerrett arrived at the house this evening, Tom Fennett was digging in the garden, rooting up the stumps of old cabbages. He barely raised his head in answer to Skerrett's salutation.

" Is the doctor at home ? " said Skerrett.

Fennett spat on his palm and then said after a long pause :

" Gah ! He's at home all right, but he's talking to his duck. Best not go in unless you want him special."

" What did you say about a duck ? "

" I said he was talking to his duck," said Fennett. " That's what I said."

" What duck ? "

" The wild duck."

" What wild duck ? "

" The wild duck that came."

Skerrett frowned at Fennett and said :

" You're getting very short in the tongue lately. You were civil enough when you wanted the price of a pint or a chew of tobacco."

Fennett leaned on his spade, spat and said :

" Every dog has his day, Mr. Skerrett. Maybe the day'll come yet when no man'll have a tongue of any sort for you. Go about your business quietly, then, and leave well enough alone."

Skerrett went on into the house. He found the doctor sitting on a chair in the yard at the back of the house, watching a duck which stood by the far wall of the yard.

" Don't move," said the doctor excitedly on Skerrett's appearance. " I'm trying to make it eat while I'm watching it."

Skerrett looked in wonder from the doctor to the duck. There was a platter of food near the bird, which had got very excited at seeing Skerrett. It bent down its breast and stretched its neck several times, as if to fly away, but there was something the matter with its left wing, which trailed a little. It looked very beautiful, especially the bright coloured feathers in its grey wings. It resembled a tame duck, except that its plumage had a finer sheen and its movements were much more rapid and vital.

" That's too bad," said the doctor at last, as he got to his feet. " It won't eat at all now. You frightened it. I thought it was going to eat just before you came in."

" I'm sorry to disturb your duck," said Skerrett, " but I wanted to talk to you about something important."

The doctor paid no attention to what Skerrett said. He continued to watch the duck intently.

" It's very odd," he said, " how it won't eat while I'm watching it and yet as soon as I turn my back it will eat. If I could make it eat while I'm looking at it, I know I could tame it. Then it would make friends with me."

He scratched his chin and continued :

" There must be some deep meaning to that. Why won't it eat while I'm watching it ? I've had it for a week here now. Tom Fennett found it one morning on the crag. It was nearly dead with exhaustion. Its wing was hurt. I've nearly cured that. I suppose it will fly away when it gets all right. It's a pity."

" I wish you could cure my wife," said Skerrett.

" Your wife ? " said the doctor absently. " What's the matter with her ? "

" It's this way——" began Skerrett.

But the doctor interrupted him.

" Wouldn't it be nice if that duck got fond of me and came to see me now and again, even if it flies away ? I made friends with a wild goose once. It used to fly away and then come back again. Then it stayed away altogether. Some scoundrel shot it, I suppose."

" I want to talk to you about my wife," said Skerrett, beginning to be irritated by the doctor's lack of interest in his affairs.

" All right," said the doctor. " Come inside."

They went into the doctor's library. There was hardly an inch of vacant space all round the walls, which were entirely covered with full bookshelves.

Even the floor was crowded with books and there was barely room to sit down. Skerrett looked around him with suspicion and he became a little embarrassed. He always felt embarrassed in the doctor's house, as in the presence of one who was infinitely his superior in information and intellect.

" Well ! What's the trouble now ? " said Doctor Melia after they had sat down.

Skerrett described first of all his quarrel with Father Moclair and then his wife's hysterical fit. He had begun a tirade against Father Moclair's ingratitude, when the doctor cut him short with a sudden gesture.

" I don't like it at all," said Melia. " That worries me a great deal. I don't want any trouble here."

He looked very disturbed.

" Why should he say I'm bad company ? " he continued. " I've done him no harm. I don't want any trouble with him or with anybody else."

" I wouldn't mind that, Doctor Melia," said Skerrett. " He just said anything that came into his head. He has a mean, spiteful nature."

" I'm afraid there's more in it than that," said the doctor, in an agitated fashion. " He took a dislike to me from the very beginning. I came to this island to get away from all that sort of thing. I want to live quietly and to have no trouble. Skerrett, you mustn't make this priest an enemy of mine. You mustn't do it."

Skerrett was astonished by the doctor's fear of Father Moclair.

" Surely you're not afraid of him," he cried

arrogantly. " I'm not afraid of him and I'm in a more dangerous position than you are. He can harm me, but what harm can he do to you ? "

" Yes," said Doctor Melia, " he could do me a lot of harm. I'm not afraid of losing my job. I have money of my own and I can live without working as a doctor. But it's the worry of feeling that I have an enemy that I don't like. He could turn the people against me. I hate feeling that people are hostile to me. I've had enough of that."

He looked quite distraught and Skerrett wondered what had been his history, what great trouble had brought him to this pitch of nervous tension, at the thought of people becoming hostile to him as they had been at some other time. He was, too, very disappointed at this show of cowardice on the part of the doctor.

" I didn't expect you to look on it like this," he said gloomily.

" Yes. Yes," said Melia, " I'm afraid you've put your foot in it. You must go to him at once and apologise. You must say I didn't influence you in any way against him."

" I'll see him in hell first," said Skerrett. " I never apologised to anyone in my life and I never will."

" Don't be foolish," said Melia.

" I'm not foolish," said Skerrett. " I have my rights and I'll stick to them. I told him to his face that I'll have no interference. Neither will I. I told him I'd take the scholars out on to the road and teach them there. I have the people behind me."

" He'll soon turn them against you."

" Let him try."

" I see you won't listen to reason," said Doctor Melia. " But for God's sake leave me out of it. Don't drag me into this affair. If you intend setting yourself up against Father Moclair you must keep away from this house."

" I didn't come here," said Skerrett angrily, " to ask for your help to fight him. I came to ask about my wife. It's your duty to help me about her in any case, priest or no priest against me."

" That's true," said the doctor. " Excuse me. I had forgotten about her. I'm very sorry for you and for her, but I think you're not going about the whole thing in a proper way. Will you take my advice now, or at least give it a trial, that is, if you want to save your wife ? "

" Well ! " said Skerrett. " I'll hear what you have to say."

" Have some whiskey."

" I don't drink," said Skerrett.

" Maybe you're better off. I think I'll have a drink myself. I feel so worried about all this."

He went to a corner of the room and poured some whiskey into a glass. He drank it hurriedly. Skerrett was surprised and slightly displeased to see him drink ; rather was he displeased that the doctor should need drink to give him courage. He began to despise the doctor a little and it was with lessened respect that he listened to what the doctor had to say.

" There he is," he thought, " with all his learning and all his books. Yet he is a cowardly sort of man."

88

" You must learn to be humble," said the doctor.
" That is the important thing for you to do. I might
as well tell you the truth. I think you are too selfish.
You are not content with being a schoolmaster.
You want to be something more, a sort of king in
your district."

" Ha ! " said Skerrett. "You think that, do you ? "

" I do," said the doctor. " You and Father
Moclair are like one another in that respect. Each
of you wants to be king of the island. And I think
it's foolish for you to set out to fight him, so you had
better give in to him and be content with your
position as a schoolmaster. Try to do your work as
best you can and expect nothing in return except
your salary."

Skerrett moved restlessly in his chair and said
almost insolently :

" I thought you were going to tell me how to save
my wife."

" I'm coming to that," said the doctor. " You
must humble yourself before her too. Then she won't
be afraid of you. That's what's making her ill,
because she's afraid of you."

" It's not, then," said Skerrett. " It's how she
hates me."

" Well ! That's the same thing. Hatred always
comes from fear."

" I don't know what you are talking about, doctor
Melia," said Skerrett. " Don't I know my own
wife ? "

" I don't think you know very much," said the
doctor, beginning to lose his temper. " If I must tell

you the truth, you and Father Moclair are a damn nuisance on this island. Why don't you leave the people alone ? You are both meddling with the lives of the poor people and you do a great deal more harm than good. You have done a great deal of harm already and now you are quarrelling like a pair of thieves."

" Thieves ? Eh ? " cried Skerrett. " What the hell do you mean ? "

" Don't be offended," said Doctor Melia. " I'm speaking my mind and I don't care who knows it. I see you're too headstrong to do what I asked you to do, so it's no good trying to keep out of it. I'm going to be dragged into it with you. I can see that. This is what I mean. All these improvements that are being made, roads, fishing boats, grants from the government, all this new education and new habits of life that are being introduced into this island are only breaking up the peace and happiness of the people. Here in this village of Ardglas, I notice that the people are more degenerate and less happy than anywhere else in Nara, because they are more dependent on money and therefore less free. There is a pier and the steamer comes three times a week. There are three public houses and four shops. Middlemen are getting money together. The people have given up depending on the soil for their living and they are cadging about, becoming demoralised by this greed of money. Whereas in the remote villages, like Cappatagle, I notice how fine and self-reliant the people are. In that village they live as in a commune, all helping one another and hardly seeing a coin from one end of the year to the other. You and Moclair, if you had your way, would like to put a public house and a huckster's shop into that village, make them give up their way of living and become cadgers like the Ardglas people."

" Huh ! " said Skerrett. " That talk doesn't come well from you, with that glass of whiskey in your hand. I don't drink. I'm dead against it. I've done my best to put down poteen drinking in the villages and I preach against the public houses too. But you don't practise yourself what you're telling me. I'm trying to introduce public houses into the villages, am I ? "

" You're right in what you're saying," said the doctor. " But it's too late for me, I'm afraid, to become simple like an islander. I know too much, unfortunately."

" It's all very well for you to talk," said Skerrett. " You live comfortably here with a servant. You have money in your pocket. You can go away when you please. You have books to read. You have a wide knowledge in your head to give you the comfort of thought and speculation. And then you pretend to envy the unfortunate people who live in places like Cappatagle, without any of these comforts, living a life of ignorance and hardship from the day they are born until the day they die. Of course, I want to change their life, because it's a cruel and ignorant sort of life."

" How do you know ? How can you prove it ? "

" Well ! You go and ask themselves. They'll tell you quick enough they want to change it."

" They don't know what's good for them."

" Well ! Then if you think that life is good why
don't you go and live like that ? "

" Because I've been poisoned by my upbringing.
I'm now a slave to my habits. But I wish I had been
born an islander. Or I wish I had the courage of the
ancient saints and hermits that came here, to live a
life of solitude, silence and contemplation, with
birds and beasts as my companions. And that's why
I don't want any trouble with Father Moclair or
with the people, because some day, perhaps, I hope
to reach the state of mind of those saints."

" Well ! I believe differently to you," said Skerrett, " and I'm going to go on acting accordingly.
Neither you nor Father Moclair can stop me from
trying to improve the condition of the people. I'm
surprised that a man of your education, doctor
Melia, wouldn't have a greater sense of your duty
to your country than to talk like that."

" How do you mean ? "

" I mean that it's work like what I'm trying to do
is going to make Ireland a free and a great country
as it should be. It's only by educating the people and
improving their condition of life that we can help
Ireland to become free."

" What is freedom, might I ask you ? " said the
doctor.

" Eh ? " said Skerrett.

" I sometimes think that I did wrong in giving
Tom Fennett a job," said Doctor Melia. " He's beginning to get ideas of respectability."

Skerrett became more and more irritated with the

doctor's attitude. He felt very sorry that he had come and yet he did not want to go away without vindicating himself and proving to the doctor that his ideas were right. He had now completely forgotten about his wife's trouble, being caught up by the doctor's antagonism into the greater ambition of his life, to make himself a leader of the people in the march towards freedom and prosperity.

" You talk," he said, " like a man who believes in nothing. Neither in God nor in your fellow man."

" Maybe you're right," said the doctor, " and that I am indeed wrong, but time will tell. Maybe I don't really believe in anything. But did the saints believe in anything ? "

" What saints ? "

" The hermits that came here in ancient times to get away from the sorrows of life."

" They came here to save their souls."

" Well ! That's only a figure of speech, to save their souls. It doesn't mean they believed in anything."

" That's queer sort of talk," said Skerrett, feeling very shocked.

He began to feel afraid that the doctor was really a pagan.

" Now, look at it this way," said the doctor. " You see all these ruins around here. Some of them are three thousand years old. That's before Christianity was thought of. There are ruins of old druidic institutions. There are stone forts, built by unknown people. Then there are ruins of Christian churches. There are ruins of forts built by Cromwellian soldiers. There are ruins later than that of other institutions.

All these have passed away and so would your free Ireland, no matter how great, pass away, even if it became a world Empire greater than Rome or England. This island seems to me a blessed place, because it has survived until now all the changes that have racked Europe. The people have remained the same, living in freedom on their rocks. So I think it's a crime to try and change them. Even what you are doing is a contradiction, because if you are patriotic you shouldn't teach them English, thus taking away their old speech, which is so beautiful in their mouths, a storehouse of their folk poetry, while the bastard English they are learning from you is so ugly. It's all wrong, it seems to me."

" And what do you think we should do ? " said Skerrett. " Live in a barrel like Diogenes ? "

" Maybe so."

" You're a coward," said Skerrett. " You spoke your mind, so you won't be insulted if I speak mine. You're a coward."

The doctor's dark face flushed but he said nothing. Skerrett got to his feet and said :

" You are a better educated man than I am, so I can't argue with you. But I think you are a coward and you are saying all this because you are afraid to go in the open and help the people. You are afraid of Moclair. He has some hold over you. Well ! I'm not afraid. I'll see everybody in hell before I give in to man or devil."

The doctor got to his feet and said :

" Please don't be angry with me. I didn't want to argue with you. I know you're in trouble and I want to help everybody in trouble, but I don't agree with your ideas."

"Very well," said Skerrett, "I'll fight my own battles. I've lost my son. My wife seems to be going mad. Father Moclair has turned against me. You think I'm an enemy of the people. The inspectors are complaining that I can't run my school properly. I didn't want to come to this island. But I'm here now and I'm going to stay here. And, by God! no man can drive me out of it. I know I'm right and I'll fight to a finish. I put great faith in you, Doctor Melia, but I can do without you, too."

With that he clapped his hat on to his head and strode out of the house. The doctor followed him out, begging him not to be angry.

"Don't do anything foolish," he said. "Take my advice and go to the parish priest and make friends with him. Apologise. That's the best thing you can do."

Skerrett stood at the gate, shook his fist at the village of Ardglas and said :

"In future, I'm going to treat that village as the enemy's camp."

Then he threw back his shoulders and marched westwards to Ballincarrig, striking the road fiercely with his heels. The doctor looked after him until he disappeared around the corner of the road.

"What could I do for him ? " he said to himself. "Such a man is bound to be destroyed in the battle of life. How odd that he should have become a schoolmaster ! "

Then the doctor went indoors. He felt oppressed and lonely.

CHAPTER X

On his way home from the doctor's house, Skerrett went to see the Kearneys, with whom he had remained on terms of intimate friendship since he had lodged with them. They now had five children and they were finding the struggle for existence consequently very hard. Barbara had lost all her fresh beauty. She had become haggard and thin with work and worry. Lack of care in confinement had spoiled her figure and there was a constant expression of vague fear in her eyes, the expression of a young peasant mother who stands always in awe of famine. Her husband also had lost his suppleness. His back had begun to bend. His limbs were getting stiff and heavy. He had the same look of vague fear in his eyes. Yet they continued to be a model couple, never complaining of their hardship, nor slackening in their work. Their house was the neatest in the village. Their crops and cattle were excellently tended. There was never an occasion for the least breath of scandal concerning their behaviour. Skerrett always found peace at their hearth and in return he gave them every assistance in his power, for which they looked upon him as a benefactor; with great reverence.

Barbara was sitting on a low stool by the hearth, giving suck to her youngest child, as he entered the kitchen. She smiled at him shyly, showing her wonderfully white and even teeth, but she did not make any effort to conceal her breast. The infant turned a lazy eye towards the intruder and then gripped at the teat afresh with its toothless gums, kicked at his mother's belly and gurgled with pleasure. She fondled its little rump with one hand and with the other held her milk-swollen breast to its mouth. The other four children had been playing near the door, but they took shelter behind their mother, like startled chickens beneath their dam's wings. Two of them were boys and two were girls, but they all wore the same dress, a sort of petticoat, made of thick blue frieze. The eldest boy wore a cap. They became as silent as mice and just peeped now and again slyly at Skerrett from behind the arms that they held up to shield their faces.

" God bless you," said Skerrett.

" And you too," said Barbara. " Won't you give a chair to the master, Johnny ? "

Johnny was too shy to fetch the chair.

" I won't sit down," said Skerrett. " I thought John might be in."

" Indeed," she said, " he's only gone out this minute. The cow is ailing and Michael Ferris is come to look at her. The people are gone down to the red field to help catch her."

" God between us and harm," said Skerrett. " I'm sorry to hear that. I'll go down to the field. 'Faith, that's going to be a fine child."

He came over and fondled the baby's toe. And then suddenly he remembered with a pang of grief how he had fondled his own son's toes in this house.

He straightened himself and looked around at the familiar walls, the earthen floor, the dresser with its shining delf, the fireplace. All had got older and yet it seemed but yesterday. At that time the house had been newly built for the young couple. Now the arch of the chimney was becoming yellow with smoke. There were hollows in the earthen floor. Up above at the roof, the long slabs of turf, laid earth inwards against the rafters, had begun to sag. And there was the young wife, whose dazzling beauty had sent him wandering over the crags in despair, now become haggard and quickly losing the lustre of her eyes and cheeks. And as she eagerly told him about the infant, how she had less trouble with it than with any other of her babies, he became bitterly conscious that the years were passing rapidly and that there was a terrible loneliness awaiting his old age.

" They have all these children growing up about them," he thought, " and I have an empty house. Sure, what does their poverty matter to them ? "

He went down the lane that led from the back of the house to the red field, where he found a group of men gathered around the cow. They were preparing to catch the animal as he climbed over the fence. There had been a heavy drought now for three weeks and the heat of summer had parched the thin soil of the field, so that in spots the red clay, to which it owed its name, showed through the scarce and worn grass. The sun was low upon the western horizon and its red-gold rays came over the calm, white sea like a shining road. Upon the land broad shadows moved, as if drawing a smooth thin cloak

over the still crags, the parched glens and the little
stone-walled fields where the full-grown rye was
turning pale and slanting at the tips through weight
of seed. The air was so clear that the eye could dis-
tinguish the houses on the mainland ten miles away
and of such a soft delicacy that the act of breathing
became a sensuous pleasure. Up above there were
white clouds, standing here and there like cliffs of
ice, slowly shifting their form, lit with the sunlight
to a dazzling splendour. All round there was bird
music in the fullness of late summer, when the newly
fledged are opening their throats for the first song of
youth.

The terror of the sick cow stood out in sharp
contrast against this sweet scene of gentle beauty.
She had calved but lately and there being no proper
nourishment for her in the grass, whose sap had been
drained by the heat, she was unable to recover from
the labour of giving birth. Her sides were slack and
so thin that the ribs showed through her shabby dun
hide. The hide hung in loose folds from her great
hip bones down over her hollow flanks. Her eyes were
bloodshot. She moaned and fled when the men
approached her. Her muscles creaked as she ran and
a thin stream of saliva dripped from her jaws.
When she tossed her head it dropped on to her side,
where it lay like a worm. In the next field her calf
kept running up and down along the wall with its
tail in the air, excited by its mother's moaning.

At length they got the beast into a corner and a
young man jumped for her horns when she tried to
escape. He took the horns strongly in his hands and

turned her mouth sideways. Another took her by the tail. Another put his fingers in her nostrils. They all crowded around and pressed against her, until she ceased to struggle and stood panting, blowing loudly through her half-choked nostrils.

Then Michael Ferris sharpened a large claspknife on a whetstone he took from his waistcoat pocket. He was a very handsome man of fifty or so, still in the prime of life, although his hair had turned white. He wore a close-trimmed beard. His blue eyes were of an extraordinary brightness. The others held him in great respect, watching his every movement. He was the great authority on cattle in the centre of the island and acted as a veterinary surgeon, although, of course, he never received any payment. When he had sharpened his knife to his satisfaction, he approached the cow's head and ordered them to pull back the lid from one of her eyes.

" Ha ! " he said. " Look at that. She's rotten with it."

They all looked at the eye and agreed with him. Then he took a needle and pierced some greyish matter that had grown under the eyelid. He pulled it out and then cut it away with the knife. The cow writhed with pain, but they held her firmly. Although his fingers were quite stiff and coarse from hard work, his touch was marvellously sure and delicate. He worked with great speed, never making the slightest error with his knife, just like a clever surgeon. Skerrett, watching him, was astonished at his skill.

" You'd make your fortune as a doctor, Michael," he said.

Ferris made no reply, but taking some salt from a paper which Kearney held out to him, he rubbed it into the wounds.

" Let her go," he said.

They loosed the animal. She wandered about with her head to the ground, moaning with pain, from the wounds and stinging salt.

" She'll be all right now, John," said Ferris, as he wiped his knife on some grass.

" Yes, she'll be all right now," said the others.

" May God spare you, Michael," said Kearney.

None of them paid any attention to the cow's suffering. Almost at once they began to discuss something else ; and this was not through any coldness of heart, but because they regarded pain as a normal aspect of life.

" What news from Ardglas ? " said a little man called Finnigan to Skerrett. " I saw you going east along the road. Did ye hear anything further about the County Cess from the big priest ? "

" I didn't go farther than the doctor's house," said Skerrett gruffly.

He didn't like Finnigan, who was a sort of spy for Moclair. The little man did a slight business as a butcher, killing a sheep or two every week and hawking the meat all over the island in a donkey's creels. He also trafficked secretly in poteen, which came in a boat to him now and again from the mainland. Even though Moclair inveighed against the use of poteen from the altar, Finnigan was one of his most staunch supporters on the island ; neither did the priest ever take him to task for his transgressions, finding him too useful as a source of information. For Finnigan was a fine example of that " useful " type of scoundrel which is so prevalent in peasant communities, at first sight and to a stranger giving the impression of being neat, honest, industrious and intelligent, but on closer acquaintance turning out to be utterly untrustworthy and malicious, except towards the single individual whom he always picks on as his mentor, usually some person whom he regards as a sort of god because of " cleverness." The attitude of the people towards him was curious, for the nickname of " trickster " which they bestowed on him showed that they were in no doubt as to his real nature and yet they treated him with respect because of the cleverness with which he earned his living without tilling the soil, or " scalding his thighs with brine." Although Finnigan got half of his father's land on his brother's marriage, about sixteen acres, he eschewed getting married, which he said, " only led to a long family, hunger and hardship." " To live without women," he said wisely, " is to live without worry." And there he was, always neat and dry, following his sheep over the crags, or driving his donkey with mutton in creel, or sneaking about the lonely creeks at night, waiting for the poteen boat to land her sly cargo. His cheeks were rosy and well shaven. He was always even of temper, leisured, agog for every sort of pastime. The people envied him, even though they called him trickster.

" He's a strange man, that doctor," he said in the slow, significant mode of speech which he affected, in order to give his simplest words a deep and almost sinister meaning. " They say that he and the big priest don't get on well."

" That's none of my business," said Skerrett.

" Well ! If they levy this County Cess in the autumn," said Kearney, " I don't know what'll happen to the poor people. It's going to be a bad winter. With this drought the crops are certain to fail. Where are the poor people going to get the money ? Pigs have fallen in price and they say there's going to be no price either for kelp this year."

" Well," said Finnigan. " We had seven years of plenty, so we can't complain. Seven years of famine come after seven years of plenty, or so they say in the good.book."

" The people should stand together against this County Cess," said Ferris with sudden passion.

" Hear, hear," said Skerrett. " They should stand together and then the soldiers or police can do nothing to them."

" That's easy talk," said Finnigan. " They could be evicted. Father Moclair is in favour of paying it."

" Well ! Then, I'm not," cried Ferris. " I've gone to jail during the Land League and I'll go again sooner than pay a cent."

" And more 'll go with you," said another man.

" Sorra good that 'll do either of ye," said Finnigan, " to be rotting there in jail and yer families starving."

" Shut up," said Ferris angrily. " You have too much gab."

A heated argument began among the men as to whether the County Cess should be paid or not. This was a fine imposed by the government for damages caused during the Land League troubles. Ferris strongly objected to paying it, as he had been one of the most prominent of the active revolutionaries on the island. It was he who organised the principal of the outrages, when twenty-five head of cattle belonging to Mr. O'Malley, Mr. Athy's father-in-law and at that time squire of the island, were thrown down over the cliffs and destroyed in the sea. He was also concerned in the burning of the land agent's office at Ardglas, as well as in several other minor outrages. While in jail on suspicion of being one of the culprits he had imbibed revolutionary ideas from his fellow prisoners and he had since remained an ardent republican.

And Skerrett, listening to the conversation, felt pleased at the violence of opinion and at the fact that considerable dissatisfaction was expressed with Father Moclair.

" He's turning against us," said Ferris, " or so it seems. He's becoming too friendly with the tyrants."

" Money is gone to his head," said another man. " Where does he think we are going to get money to pay this bloody Cess ? "

" And where would ye be without him ? " said Finnigan. " Hasn't he done wonders for the island ? "

" We'd be where we always were," cried Ferris, " free on our rocks, as Doctor Melia says. To hell with what he has done for the island."

"I wouldn't pay much attention to what Doctor Melia says," cried Finnigan. " He's an enemy of God."

" You'll be an enemy of every decent man on this island, huckster," cried Ferris, " unless you watch out for yerself. I'm saying, men, that the time is coming when bullets 'll be flying. Aye ! And they'll find a bed again in the guts of informers and traitors."

" Easy now," said Skerrett, afraid that the impassioned Ferris was going to attack Finnigan. " It's not one another we should fight, but the enemy."

" You're right there, Mr. Skerrett," said the gentle Kearney. " It's no good fighting one another. We should stick together."

Ferris walked with Skerrett on the road home. Still excited by what Finnigan had said, he talked all the time about freedom and the necessity " to fight the tyrants every step of the way." His energy, considering his age, was astonishing. His body was still like a lathe of steel, moving with an agility almost equal to that of the wild duck Skerrett had seen in the doctor's back yard. Altogether, he was a most attractive person, in his beauty, his energy and his varied talents. He was a noted horseman, oarsman and wrestler. His courage, endurance and wiry strength were held up to the young all over the island as a model of excellence. A fierce love of freedom and a passion for justice, even in his most trivial human relationships, set his moral character on as high an eminence as his bodily virtues in the people's eyes. Yet the man was discontented with life, improvident in his domestic affairs, eager for change.

" I must have this man on my side," said Skerrett

to himself, as he listened to Ferris's excited conversation.

However, he did not wish just yet to ally himself too openly with Ferris's creed of violence. His common sense told him that it was rash and useless.

" I don't know, Michael," he said, " but that it would be foolish, if they send soldiers and police, to offer any resistance."

" But why ? " cried Ferris, halting in the road. " Can't we die ? Are we afraid to die ? What's the odds whether a man dies one year or the next ? "

He struck his breast and cried :

" The man that dies in defence of his home and country goes straight to heaven."

" I don't mind dying," said Skerrett, " if the principle is worth dying for. But I prefer to win and live to enjoy my victory."

" Well ! " said Ferris. " In any case, you're one of ourselves. You know what we want and we have trust in you. But over there in Ardglas they are being bought over by the tyrants. The church has always sold the people to the tyrants."

He left Skerrett a little to the east of the school and turned up towards his village of Cappatagle along a footpath over the crags. In his raw-hide shoes he hardly made any sound moving over the flat rocks, that had been polished as smooth as glass by the impress of human feet for hundreds upon hundreds of years. He moved rapidly, tall, lean, erect, with sudden jerks of his shoulders as he lengthened his stride now and again to cross a fissure between the rocks. His walk was like a dance, a movement perfect in rhythm and significant of some mystic bond between this beautiful human energy and the wild earth over which it passed.

Skerrett, so heavy and solid compared to this lithe and deer-like islander, struck the road with regular thuds as he went west. He felt greatly cheered and excited by his meeting with Ferris.

"With such men behind me," he thought, "I could fight ten like Moclair. Let him do his damnedest now."

And he began to make plans for harnessing Ferris's enthusiasm to a policy that would make victory possible.

Still meditating on these plans and already seeing Moclair routed and humiliated, he entered his house. There he received a shock which was to send all thoughts of leading the struggle against the priest clean out of his mind for some time.

Right in the doorway of the sitting-room his wife lay prostrate ; dead drunk.

CHAPTER XI

HE STOOD for a long time, quite still, looking at her in wonder, hardly able to believe his eyes. Her condition was obvious to him at once, as she had dropped a bottle in her fall. It broke against the jamb of the door and some whiskey which it held was spilled on the floor. There was a heavy smell of whiskey from her. Yet, it seemed so horrible to him that she should be lying this way on the floor, incapable with drink, that he was unable to do anything except look at her in wonder. The horror that her drunkenness inspired in him was a form of remorse, in that he felt he had himself been responsible for her coming to this condition. Had she not often helped him to bed in the old days ? Had he not given her an example which she was now following in her misery ?

" Oh ! God ! " he muttered. " Have I brought her to this ? "

The annoyance she had caused him in the past few months, his anger earlier in the evening at the way she had humiliated him before Moclair through her negligence at school, now ceased to count and he only felt pity for her, together with a biting shame for her unseemliness. To our Irish people, nothing appears more shameful than a drunken woman ; no crime, no matter how heinous, can inspire such a feeling of shame at the degeneration of a human soul as the sight of a woman brought beside her virtue by the sick sleep of drunkenness. Even a poxed whore in drink, as she is fished from the gutter by the Guards, evokes instead of impudent laughter in the gaping mob, a whispering pity.

Half-numb with shame, he took her in his arms and carried her upstairs. He laid her on her bed, drew some covering over her and then stood watching. What was to be done ? He could not think. The first clear thought that came to him was that this must be concealed from outside knowledge. He must hide this shame within his own conscience. The servant ! Ha ! Where did this whiskey come from ? Who procured it ? Now he remembered how he had been surprised, on the evening of the funeral, that his wife should ask for brandy. And that bottle of whiskey that had been fetched from the tavern had disappeared at once. His wife's intimacy with the servant now assumed a sinister aspect. He had also noticed that his wife, of late, had been continually chewing cloves. When he remarked on it, she had answered that the cloves were to take away the taste of the medicine the doctor gave her for her heart trouble. Now it was obvious that she had been drinking unknown to him, right under his very eyes, ever since the boy's death five months ago.

He hurried downstairs, picked up the broken bottle and smelt it. It did not smell like shop whiskey. Now he searched the house carefully, but failed to find any other bottles. He searched the yard as well, but without success. And then he crossed over the wall of the yard onto the crag. There was a break in the wall and beyond it, a used path to a little hollow between the rocks, where refuse was cast. He searched around in this place and at last found the hiding place of the used bottles. He examined them. A few of them were stamped like those sold in the tavern, but the majority were without a label and had obviously contained illicit stuff from a sheebeen.

" She's been getting it from Finnigan," he said to himself. " I'll soon stop that rat's work."

He came back to the house. The servant, who had been to visit her people at Kilchreest, had now returned.

" Lizzie," he said, " I want to talk to you."

" Yes, sir," said the servant timidly.

" You've been getting drink for the mistress," he said. " Where have you been getting it ? "

" Oh ! No, sir," she said. " I haven't."

" You lie," he cried. " Come on. Out with it. Tell me."

He took her by the arm. She winced and began to blubber. For a while she continued to deny that she had procured any drink, but at last she burst into tears and told him everything. At first she had got whiskey from Corless's tavern, but later she had got poteen from Finnigan, that being much cheaper and stronger. He made her go on her knees and then he threatened to kill her if she ever attempted to fetch any more.

" I'll pull out your heart with my hands," he said.

She clung to his feet and begged for mercy.

" Look after the mistress," he said, " while I'm

out. Is there any more drink in the house except that bottle she broke ? "

" No, sir," she said.

" Are you sure ? "

" None that I know about."

" If you do, spill it before I get back. If I get another drop here I'll be the death of you."

He rushed over to Corless's tavern. He found Corless sitting by the fire in the large kitchen, drinking a half gallon of porter with two of his customers. The man had got terribly aged and bloated since the evening he had driven Skerrett from Ardglas. He looked still more disreputable and unclean. Skerrett called him outside and said :

" You've been selling whiskey to my servant."

" And what about it ? " said Corless impudently. " Haven't I got a license signed by the magistrate ? "

Skerrett took him by the chest and shook him.

" Listen Corless," he said. " License or no license, you'll sell her no more."

" Let go of me," said Corless. " I'll sell what I please to whom I please. I'm John Corless. I know my worth."

" You'll do as I say," said Skerrett.

With that he pushed Corless against the wall and strode away. Corless shouted after him :

" I'll have the law of you for threatening me."

" I've warned you," cried Skerrett.

" And I'm warning you," shouted Corless.

Skerrett walked rapidly past his own house, until he reached a small cottage that stood alone on a crag east of the village boundary. This cottage belonged to Finnigan. It was invisible from the road and was approached only by a path over the rocks. Night had now fallen and there was no moon, so that Skerrett stumbled crossing a low wall, knocking some stones which made a clatter. A dog barked and then came rushing out of the house, with bared fangs. The dog, a vicious black mongrel, jumped at Skerrett's leg. Skerrett kicked at it and struck it on the side. It yelped and turned somersault, but it got up once more and returned to the attack. He had to beat it off with stones. During this time, some people came out of the cottage and moved away stealthily by another path which led north from the house towards the sea-shore. Skerrett could barely see their shapes in the darkness, but he knew they were drinkers who were making their escape for fear of a raid by the police. He climbed over the style into the yard and knocked at the door.

" Who's there ? " came Finnigan's voice from within.

" Open your damned door at once or I'll knock it down," cried Skerrett.

" God save us, what's the matter ? " cried Finnigan. " I'm going to bed."

" You're a liar. Open, I say. Open at once."

Although there had been a light in the window on Skerrett's approach, now there was complete darkness. He heard a shuffling noise within and he knew that Finnigan was hiding something. Again he cried out :

" Are you going to open at once ? "

" For the love of God, have patience. I'm coming."

The door was unbolted and Skerrett entered the kitchen. Finnigan stood within the door with a lighted dip in his hand. Skerrett closed the door.

" Put down the dip, Finnigan," he said. " I have something to say to you."

Finnigan went slowly to the dressers and put down the dip. He kept looking at Skerrett. Skerrett buttoned up his jacket.

" Now," he said. " Where is that poteen you were just hiding ? "

" Poteen ? " cried Finnigan in pretended amazement. " I was hiding no poteen. Where would I get poteen ? "

" You damned scoundrel ! "

Skerrett rushed at the little man, caught him by the throat and bent him backwards against the dressers. Finnigan tried to scream for help, but he was choking and could not utter the words.

" Out with it, before I choke you," said Skerrett. " You've been selling poteen to my servant, you rat. You've been at this game now for years, poisoning and robbing the people. But now you're finished. I'm going to deal with you. Where did you put that poteen ? "

Finnigan's face turned livid with fear and he clawed at Skerrett's hands. Suddenly Skerrett let him go, picked up a broomstick, and broke off the broom with his boot. He threw Finnigan across his knee and raised the stick.

" Speak up, before I break your back."

" Don't strike," wailed Finnigan. " Don't murder me. I'll give it to you."

" Be quick then," said Skerrett.

Finnigan got a stool, stood on it and then pulled down a ladder that stuck out from the edge of the loft. He climbed the ladder, rummaged about on the loft and then brought down an earthen jar, which he handed to Skerrett. Skerrett uncorked the jar and smelt its contents.

" Ha ! " he said. " We'll soon put an end to this."

He hurled the jar with great force against the fireplace. It smashed to pieces and fell among the burning sods of peat on the hearth. The poteen immediately took flame and roared up the chimney.

" God Almighty ! " wailed Finnigan. " Don't burn the house on me as well."

" You'll burn in hell yet," cried Skerrett, " you rotten scum. Now show me the keg."

" What keg ? "

" The keg you have buried. Be quick, unless you want your back broken with this stick."

He seized Finnigan once more and raised the stick. Suddenly Finnigan showed fight in his desperation and put his hand in his waistcoat pocket reaching for his knife. Skerrett brought down the stick quickly, the hand went limp and Finnigan howled with pain.

" God curse and blast you," screamed Finnigan. " You murdering blackguard, you dirty bully, you're trying to kill me. I'm going to the big priest about you. He'll run you off this island like a rat. Don't blame me for your drunken wife. You drove her to it."

Skerrett cut him short by raining blows from the

stick onto his back. At last Finnigan was cowed and begged for mercy.

" Don't kill me," he said, " and I'll show you the keg."

" Alright then. Get up off that floor and show it to me."

" Oh ! Mother of God ! You have me killed. My back is broken. You have me disfigured."

" Disfigured you'll be," cried Skerrett. " Be quick now."

Groaning with pain, Finnigan got to his feet. Skerrett made him walk in front down the lane that led northwards from the house. After climbing over a fence Finnigan suddenly tried to escape, but Skerrett pursued him and tripped him up. Thence he took Finnigan by the shoulder, until they came to a tiny glen among the rocks.

" It's here," said Finnigan.

" Where ? "

" There, under your feet."

" Dig it up, then."

" How can I dig it up with my hands ? I brought no spade."

" Dig it up or you'll find yourself buried along with it before the night is out."

" Oh ! Mother of God ! "

Finnigan got down on his knees and began to paw about on the grass. At this spot the grass had turned pale and it soon became evident that a round hole had been cut in the turf, but the sods had been replaced in such a cunning fashion that the cutting was hard to detect except on close inspection. He took away the sods, rooted some loose earth and then lifted a flat stone. Finally he hauled up a keg.

" There it is," he said.

Skerrett raised the stone and brought it down with all his force several times on the keg. He broke the keg to pieces. The whiskey poured out on the grass.

" That's done for," he said, throwing down the stone. " Now Finnigan, watch out for yourself. From now on I have my eye on you."

Finnigan, almost in tears, muttered :

" Maybe it will be the other way about, master Skerrett.

" Watch out for yourself," thundered Skerrett. " If I ever find tale or tidings of your having any more of this stuff, you'll get worse than you've got to-night. I tell you I'm desperate. Go home now, you dog, and pray to God for mercy."

He strode away. Finnigan went on his knees and begged God with great fervour to destroy Skerrett, to leave him homeless, without food, without drink, an outcast from all human intercourse. Then he went to another little glen and dug up a fresh keg which he brought home with him.

Skerrett had made a deadly enemy that night.

CHAPTER XII

SKERRETT now definitely took the doctor's
advice in order to keep the scandal of his wife's conduct from becoming public. He humbled himself
before her, but without any success. Next day happened to be Saturday and therefore a school holiday.
She stayed in bed and he waited on her, treating
her with every possible kindness, but she gave no
sign of being sorry for what she had done ; neither
did she thank him for his services. Indeed, her
effrontery was astonishing. When he began to de-
plore in a gentle manner the unfortunate habit to
which she had become addicted, blaming himself
largely for having brought her to it, she turned on
him like a virago.

"What are you talking about ? " she said. " I
take a drop of whiskey to relieve the pain in my heart
and you call me a drunkard. Drunkard indeed !
When you were sick all over my bed I didn't turn
on you. I waited on you hand and foot for years
and you only gave me curses for it. Now I'm broken
down. I'm a sick woman. I've nothing left but my
grey hairs and my broken heart. And you call me a
drunkard. When I fall down and hurt myself you
say I'm drunk. Kill me and be done with it. I know
you won't be happy 'till you've killed me and put
the green sod over my coffin. It's no use you

pretending to be sorry for me. I know what's at the back of your mind."

She sat up in bed, shook her fist at him and screamed :

" You have the cunning of a madman. This is a new dodge you're trying on to torture me. Leave me alone. Why don't you leave me alone ? "

Skerrett fled from the bedroom, overwhelmed by her savagery. The only thing he could do was to take the servant aside and again warn her that the least sign of drink in the house would bring down a terrible punishment on her head.

" Don't let me catch a drop here," he repeated again and again.

During that day and the following day, Kate made several attempts to persuade the servant to fetch some whiskey, but the girl refused. Although on Saturday Kate had threatened " to end her days on her back praying for her lost darling," she got up on Sunday evening ; obviously because she could get no one to fetch her whiskey. She came downstairs wearing her funny black cloak and bonnet.

" Where are you going, Kate ? " said Skerrett.

He had not left the house since the previous evening, except to go to Mass. He felt that he must stand guard over her.

" Where am I going ? " she said querulously. " I'm going where I always go on Sunday, to visit my darling's grave."

" I'm going with you," he said.

" Stay at home," she said angrily. " I want to be in peace by myself."

" I'm going with you," he said with determination. " You're not going to stir out of this house without me."

In spite of her protests and threats to make a scene on the road and to call on the people to protect her from this persecution he went out with her. She made no scene, however, but she never spoke to him the whole length of the way, although he talked to her with great feeling, asking her to forgive him for whatever injury he had done her in the past.

" Let us start out now afresh, Kate," he implored her. " We have only the two of us. Let us struggle along together and see maybe if we can find some peace and comfort in our old age. Sure there's no good in hardening your heart against me. What's done is done ; but there's always a chance of making a good fist of the future, with the grace of God. Let's kneel down together by Michael's grave and ask God to help us live a better life. Michael would like us to be happy together. He'd like us to love one another."

However, when they were kneeling side by side at the grave, she suddenly burst into tears.

" Oh ! May God forgive me," she said aloud. " Holy Mother of God look down in pity on me."

Then Skerrett took her by the hand and they prayed together fervently with their eyes on the little narrow grave, which was now covered with grass and pretty sea-side flowers. And as they walked homewards, although she remained silent, he had great hopes that her attitude towards him had at last changed, that she had softened and that she was no longer a stranger to him. So he talked cheerfully to her about their future, making plans. At supper she talked to him in a friendly way. She seemed to become rapidly more kind towards him and even solicitous about his comfort. They said the rosary together and he offered it up for a special intention which he asked her to pray for with him. He judged by the fervour with which she made the responses that she understood what the special intention was and that she would do her best to conquer her craving.

Next day, however, his suspicions were renewed. In the morning, he caught her looking at him with hatred, in a very cunning fashion. As soon as she noticed him watching her, her expression changed ; and that only made him still more suspicious. She was pretending to be friendly towards him and yet she did not feel friendly. Had she some new plan ? That greatly worried him. During playtime, he went into the girls' side of the school to see her. He found her and the principal teacher deep in conversation. By their look of surprise and displeasure at his arrival, he felt that their conversation was not an innocent one.

The principal teacher, a woman called Mrs. Turley, has been in the school for a year. She was the wife of a police sergeant, who was not now stationed on the island. She was a handsome woman of thirty, with remarkably blue eyes and soft, plump cheeks, whose florid colour did not seem altogether due to a natural condition of the blood. Very intelligent and energetic, this woman was an excellent teacher, whose kindness and charm endeared her to her pupils. Indeed, her conduct of her school gave as much satisfaction to the inspectors as Skerrett's conduct gave them displeasure. Skerrett did not like her. He had tried to persuade her to learn Irish and to teach the children to read and write in that language, but she blankly refused. She had no interest in social ideas. It was for that he disliked her.

Between her and his wife, however, there had been of late a very intimate relationship, which now caused him to be suspicious, as he saw them whispering together. He got very angry and although he had come into the school with quite a different intention, he now reverted to the question of teaching Irish.

" I'm very sorry Mrs. Turley," he said, " that I can't persuade you to take up Irish. Mark my words, you're not being fair to the girls in your school. Now that the Gaelic League is started, Irish is bound to come into its own, as the proper language of the country. Look what an advantage it would be to clever girls from this island to have a knowledge of Irish, when the language comes into its proper position."

" That will never be," said Mrs. Turley.

She had a very soft voice. A large, voluptuous woman, of very marked sexual attraction, she had always a disturbing effect on Skerrett ; a fact that also prejudiced him unconsciously against her. When looking at her, or talking to her, he could not help being aware of her seductive, full bosom, her bright eyes and her curving rich lips.

" You're wrong there," he said. " It's certain to come into its own when Ireland is free."

Mrs. Turley shrugged her shoulders and said : " Ireland 'll never be free."

" As sure as the sun shines it will be free," said Skerrett, " and before I die."

She shrugged her shoulders again and said : " I don't care whether it is or not."

Skerrett got angry.

" That's a nice thing to say for a school-teacher in a Gaelic-speaking district. You should know it's your duty to God as well as to the people to do every-thing in your power to further the cause."

" What cause ? " she said shortly. " I know my business and I do it. You look after your own school. Take the girls and teach them Irish if you are so anxious about it. It's not a part of my duties as head of this school, so I don't bother about it."

" Huh ! " said Skerrett.

She turned away to attend to a kettle that was boiling on the fire. Kate was getting a tea-pot ready to make tea.

" Tea ! " said Skerrett. " I don't take tea at this hour of the day. I take milk. It's better for the health. Tea is bad for your nerves."

" For God's sake, David," said Kate, " can't you take whatever you like and let us take what we like ? "

The two women looked at him with scorn and indignation and they put him to shame. He returned to his own school and ate his lunch of milk and bread and cheese. He found it very unattractive. Life had somehow lost all its savour for him. He felt that complete ruin would at any moment overwhelm him.

For the next week he lived in constant expectation of this ruin, but nothing untoward happened. Kate, in fact, behaved much better in the house and there was no sign of any drink ; although he noticed that she still continued to use cloves. He was now very timid of her, afraid that the least annoyance might force her into another bout of drinking. The wretched man was unaware that her conduct towards him had changed for the better, simply because she was developing the cunning of the drunkard and she had found a more subtle way of satisfying her craving. But for the moment, he was too nervous of a fresh disaster to enquire too closely into her conduct, provided she remained outwardly sober.

Then he was surprised by a sudden change in Moclair's attitude, on the priest's next visit to the school. Moclair entered, all beaming with smiles and taking Skerrett out into the porch, cocked his head to one side and whispered :

" Skerrett, I'd like you to forget our conversation of last week. I had no idea of the trouble you were in, otherwise I wouldn't say what I said. I'm very sorry for you and I'll do my best to help you over it."

As Skerrett bridled, the priest put up his hands, palms outwards, in protest.

"Now don't be afraid or shamed to open your mind to me," he said gently. "I know all about it and I sympathise with you. You can rely on me to do everything in my power to keep this thing as quiet as possible. But something must be done, David. She can't go on like this. I must have a long talk to her. But you should have come to me at once, instead of going after Finnigan."

Moclair sighed and said :

"I'm afraid nothing can be done with Finnigan. The poor man has been too long at this awful business. All the same, you had no right to attack him the way you did."

"So he went to you," said Skerrett.

"Yes. He came and complained to me. I told him he should be ashamed of himself, to have the impudence to acknowledge what he had been doing."

"If I weren't ashamed of people thinking me an informer," said Skerrett, "I'd have gone to the police about him."

"No. No," said Moclair. "You must leave the police alone. Now is not the time to have any truck with the police. David, you and I must stand together now. Let there be nothing between us. There is going to be a lot of trouble and we must stand together, you and I. What we have done for the island is likely to be all lost unless we can find a way out of our present difficulty."

He suddenly took Skerrett intimately by the arm and said with force :

"There are some people that kindness is wasted on. There are some ungrateful people in the world. You felt angry at the way the inspectors grumbled about your school. But what about me ? Look at the way people are turning against me here in Nara. Against me that have given eleven years of my life working tooth and nail for them. Eh ? "

In spite of his suspicions Skerrett could not help feeling sympathetic towards the priest, especially as Moclair's voice had never sounded so seductive and his pose of humility and persecution would " draw tears from a Turk," as the people said. He was an adept at this kind of play-acting ; being the humble and persecuted man. In any case, at this moment Skerrett was only too anxious to have a truce if not a renewal of friendship.

" Have no fear, Father Harry," he said, " that I am one of these ungrateful people. I never forget any man that does me a kindness. Least of all could I forget what you have done for me. Besides that, I look at things in another way. It's not what you have done for me that I take into consideration, but what you have done for the island. If we had a priest like you in every parish of Ireland, she'd soon be a free country."

" I do my best," said Father Moclair, with a sigh. " I do what little I can ; but if the people don't take my advice now and if they side with that scoundrel Coleman O'Rourke, God forgive me for speaking ill of anybody, it won't go well with them. There's going to be a lot of trouble."

" Have no fear," said Skerrett once more, " that anything you said to me last week could turn me against you now, Father Harry."

"Thanks, David," said Moclair. "I'm more pleased to hear you say that than anything in the world. Our enemies were already clapping themselves on the back, thinking we had fallen out."

Then he began a mysterious conversation about "dark forces" that were plotting the ruin of the island; so that Skerrett could not help feeling carried away by his old enthusiasm. While the priest spoke, he thought : "Maybe I was wrong in finding fault with him. We all have our faults and can I blame him for having his ? Look at all he has done for me. It's all very well for men like Dr. Melia to be showy on the surface. But what did Dr. Melia do for me when I went to him about my wife ? Paying more heed to a duck. Maybe Father Harry is everything I thought him to be."

"I'll go now and have a talk to her, David," said Father Moclair. "And don't worry about this. Everything'll come all right with the help of God. You and I have hard work facing us this autumn. O'Rourke is going about among the people, telling them they should stand out against paying this County Cess. There are others as well. You want to be careful of that man Ferris of Cappatagle. He's no friend of mine. He's up to mischief. Doctor Melia is another man you have to be careful of. If I told you all I know about him you'd have nothing to do with him. I could get him stoned out of this island to-morrow if I wanted to raise a finger. I may lose my patience shortly with some of these people and then you'll see real trouble. But I'm biding my time. I'm waiting for the first blow to be struck. Then I'll strike with a vengeance."

The priest's magnificent eyes flashed and he shook his riding crop at his invisible enemies. Skerrett, watching him, felt torn between a feeling of intense admiration for the man's strength, cunning and passion and another feeling, which made him think ; " What he'll do to them, he'll do to me later when it suits him. He wants me now because he's in trouble. And he has me by the ear on account of my wife."

After the priest's departure he felt greatly worried.

" I'm cornered," he repeated to himself now and again.

That evening, on meeting his wife, he was still more worried. She turned on him and said with great bitterness :

" So you went to Father Harry and said I had taken to drink. Very well, then. We'll see."

" What'll we see ? "

" I might as well be hung for a sheep as for a lamb," she said.

Skerrett shuddered and thought :

" Why is it there is so much suffering in the world ? Why ? "

CHAPTER XIII

COLEMAN O'ROURKE, the man to whom
Moclair had referred as his chief enemy, was a native
of Ardglas and the most vital character in the
village. He was then about thirty-eight years of age,
a short, stout man of immense strength. He was the
bull-necked type of Irishman ; a type that is
extremely rare among us, though quite common in
England. He had all the characteristics of that type,
strength, ferocity, obstinacy, courage and unbridled
passion. In spite of his Gaelic name, he resembled in
no way what is generally accepted as a Gael, having
the short split nose of a Norseman and the Norseman's flaxen hair, together with the beefy neck and
body and the full belly of a Saxon. But in our
country, the confusion of bastardy through recur-
ring invasions and bloody civil tumult has made a
sport of race.

When Father Moclair arrived in Nara eleven years
previously, O'Rourke was in jail on suspicion of
being implicated in revolutionary outrages connected with the Land League. When he came out of
jail he at once became a close associate of the parish
priest. Father Moclair found his enthusiasm, his
strength and his energy very useful and in return he
raised O'Rourke above the status of a struggling
peasant, who was trying to scrape a livelihood from
twenty acres of rocky land. O'Rourke was the first

to receive one of the new trawlers and as the fishing was very lucrative in the years that followed he found himself enjoying a prosperity of which he had never dared dream. Not only himself but his relatives shared in this prosperity, as it is a rule among us that politics of any sort are never divorced from nepotism. His sister, married to a man called Anthony Bundoon, became agent for kelp buying to an English firm. Bundoon started an hotel and became in a few years even more prosperous than O'Rourke himself. Another sister, who had been left a widow with three children by the loss at sea of a fisherman called O'Hanlon, started a shop. She also did well and was rapidly becoming prosperous. At the outset she had only a ton of salt, which her brother brought from Galway in his trawler, as her sole capital. By the sale of this salt during a glut of fish she gathered enough money to stock a little huckstering shop, where she did a smart trade owing to the influence of her brother. Later she got a license for beer and spirits and was now becoming a rival of the principal shop in the village, owned by a retired English coastguard called Pigott ; a Protestant who was a henchman of the old régime disturbed by the Land League. It will be understood that both these sisters had relations by marriage and that family ties among us are very strong ; so that O'Rourke, apart from his personal qualities, was a great power, not only in the village but over the whole island. On his wife's death in child-birth he tried to improve his position by marrying the daughter of Pat Coonan the rate collector, that " half sized buck," whom

Skerrett had met on the hooker *Carra Lass*. Coonan was another of the parish priest's henchmen and together with being rate collector, he was also harbourmaster and contractor for road mending. By marrying Coonan's daughter, O'Rourke felt that he would hold a tight grip on " whatever was going in the place."

However, Coonan's daughter met with disaster in the summer of 1894, just when O'Rourke and her father were settling the match, during various bouts of drinking in Mr. O'Hanlon's bar parlour. It became public knowledge that she had conceived of a policeman called Twig, a tall handsome fellow who was a menace to the virginity of the island maidens. On learning of his daughter's condition Coonan behaved like a madman. Carrying a reaping hook, in his bare feet, he ran up and down the road before the police barracks, screaming at the top of his voice : " Send me out the raper Twig, 'till I tear his guts out with my hook. I'll castrate the scum that raped my daughter. Out with him, the anointed son of Beelzebub." It proved, however, that it was no case of rape, but of willing passion between the young couple ; for when the police authorities took the case in hand, Twig expressed his desire to marry the girl and she was no less willing when approached. The father gave his consent on the advice of the parish priest, after Twig had declared it his intention to become a Roman Catholic. O'Rourke got furious at this. " She's a whore," he said to Coonan. " Your blasted daughter is a whore. Turn her out of doors. Send her to

America. Let her be stoned out of the island. She has dragged my name in the gutter. The dogs of the island are yelping my disgrace in my face. I'm stinking like a dog-fish dead in summer on a strand in the noses of the people." One evening, he cut loose in the village with an old blunderbuss, threatening to murder Coonan, who took refuge in the police barracks. O'Rourke was arrested, but owing to the desire of the police to keep the whole affair as private as possible he was released without prosecution. Twig and the young girl went away and O'Rourke locked himself indoors for a week, unable to face the public, owing to the contumely which he felt he had suffered. Then, in a fit of pique he collected his relatives and made a match with a woman of Ardcaol, bedding her within a fortnight.

He began at once an attempt to ruin Coonan, but in this the parish priest refused to see eye to eye with him.

"Coonan does his work well," said Father Moclair. "He's a good man and respectful in every way. I have nothing against him."

"Well! Father Harry," said O'Rourke, "it's either him or me. Let him be thrown out of his jobs as harbour master and road contractor and rate collector, or the devil a sight you'll see of me again anywhere you want me. And what I say goes on this island for any man that's worth his salt."

"Oho!" said Father Moclair. "So that's your tune now, Coleman O'Rourke. Get down on your knees and apologise."

"On my knees, is it?" cried O'Rourke in a fury.

" On my knees to a beggarly priest from the County Mayo. May the devil scald my guts with boiling vinegar if I do."

Whereupon Moclair struck him, and O'Rourke had to be held by some men who were present ; otherwise he would have committed " the sacrilege of striking the sacred body of a priest." Thwarted of finding relief for his hurt feelings in blows, O'Rourke set out to "destroy that stinking Mayo beggar," as he called Moclair. He found the situation favourable to his purpose. After years of plenty, prosperity had suddenly forsaken the island. Fishing had failed that summer. The markets were stagnant, so that cattle, sheep, pigs and kelp, in a word everything the islanders had to sell, fetched wretched prices. As a final calamity a drought came, ruining the crops and the grass, on which the live stock had to rely for sustenance. People had begun to mutter about a famine in winter.

Even before O'Rourke started his rebellion, murmurs against Moclair had begun to be prevalent in the hamlets from east to west of the island. A peasant's memory is short when it has to deal with benefaction ; more especially in a place like Nara, where the struggle of life was terribly intense. There, not only extreme poverty, but the very position of the island, foster in the human mind those devils of suspicion and resentment, which make ingratitude seem man's strongest vice. The surrounding sea, constantly stirred into fury by storms that cut off communication with the mainland, always maintains in the minds of the inhabitants a restless anxiety, which has a strong bearing on character, sharpening the wits and heightening the energy, but at the same time producing a violent instability of temperament. The fear of hunger becomes an evil demon, whose horns are emblazoned on the bright face of the sun as well as on the drooping bellies of the thunderclouds, that belch a blight upon the meagre soil, washing from the half-clad rocks the budding seeds and throwing a barricade of mountainous waves over the sea's rich treasure. So it comes to pass that a good catch of fish can send a whole village into a frenzy of excitement, while an outbreak of swine fever may cause a panic comparable to that caused by an earthquake among people differently placed on the earth's crust. This instability, in the same manner, turns friends into foes and foes into friends with startling suddenness. It corrupts the dictionary of human qualities, making the stolid neurotic in their spleen and showing by fits a ghoulish barbarism in natures ordinarily of sweet temper.

Thus they listened eagerly to O'Rourke's denunciation of Moclair and they said to one another : " He has become a tyrant like the landlords. Ho ! Ho ! We threw the landlords off our backs and there is this beggar priest riding us instead. He has brought a curse on the island. Before he came we were at peace and God was kind to us ; but now the sea herself has turned against us and the earth has gone barren." Signs were seen in the sky by the credulous and from day to day rumours of destruction spread from end to end of the island, passed quickly from mouth to mouth, by whispering women.

O'Rourke rode about on a horse, followed by his cronies, holding meetings in the hamlets.

" Don't pay this Cess," he shouted from his horse. " Let them come and take it. We'll pelt them with stones from the land God gave our fathers."

The anger of the people centred against the exaction of the County Cess, which they had hitherto paid with meek submission. Now it seemed to be the last straw that would break their backs. When the writs for payment were served, everybody obeyed O'Rourke and his friends. The writs were burned. So violent was the general feeling at first that nobody dared oppose O'Rourke, although the more sober element was not at all enthusiastic.

On the first Sunday in October the agitation reached a crisis. On that day the church at Tobar Milis was crowded to the door, as practically every able-bodied person on the island attended Mass, it being known beforehand that an important meeting would be held afterwards at the chapel gate. O'Rourke, accompanied by a large force of his friends, did not enter the church for Mass, but stood outside the door. As soon as Mass was over, he posted his men all round the church, to prevent anybody getting away. The whole congregation, men, women and children, except those who still remained indoors for special prayers or the learning of the catechism, all gathered on the sloping grassy plot that led from the church door to the road below. There were at least eight hundred people there, about half the population of the island. Although it was a raw windy day, there was a bright sun and the people made a quaint picture against the green grass, the white walls of the yard and the grey rocks beyond. Down below the church, the land fell steeply to the sea, which was torn by the wind, with row upon row of white gashes in its green back. The sky looked very fierce, its blue dome speckled with wisps of white cloud that raced before the wind. The wind came in sudden rushes and crookedly, whining as if in pain and curling on its tracks like a demented thing which can only vent its anger on itself. The people were in keeping with the shrewish temper of nature. The women, with their red petticoats and bright shawls, patched the green with blood, a colour symbol of the passion latent in their brooding eyes. They stood in silence, peeping modestly through the slits of their cowled shawls, moving now and again suddenly in common, as the murmuring of the men broke into a passionate cry, bringing fear of swift and dangerous action. The nervous movements of the men were in marked contrast to the passivity of the women. Their colouring was more sombre, all being dressed in blue or grey, except for their knitted belts of rainbow green and red and saffron. They moved like dancers, making no sound in their rawhide shoes on the silken grass, now here, now there, now on a bended knee, listening, now erect with arms waving in gesture. Their faces, blood red with wind and rain and sun, were of a sudden slit with white, as their teeth showed in the outrush of their passionate speech.

Like a burly cock on sentry go before his startled

hens, O'Rourke strutted up and down the road before the chapel gate, taking counsel with his friends about the coming discussion. He looked quite foreign to the people on the grassy slope above ; a stout cudgel of a man, from whose squat, full belly the short legs hung like posts. His strut was typical of the short heavy man, for he remained rigid as he walked, moving only the arms from the elbows and the legs from the knees, except for a rapid jerk of the chest, rather similar to the jerking of an angry swan in paddle. He was dressed differently also, in a rig becoming fashionable at that time among the native middle class of Ardglas, half-way between island dress and that of a " gentleman." This rig consisted of a blue swallow-tailed coat, a grey frieze trousers, boots, a starched shirt, a cravat and a broad-brimmed, black felt hat. He wore a sprig of heather in the band of his hat and he carried an ash plant.

The men with him on the road were also character-istic of the social changes that were taking place on the island, by their dress, speech and deportment. His friends from Ardglas, all fishermen, spoke a bastard English. They wore blue jerseys and heavy boots to which the white scales of fish still clung. They were slow of movement and clumsy in their gestures, as is common with sea-faring men on shore ; but they were more full about the body than the peasant islanders and their ruddy faces, well-fleshed, gave signs of better living than the lean hungry faces of the peasants. Furthermore, they had a swagger about them, which showed that they thought them-selves superior to the Gaelic speaking " slaves of the rocks," as the peasants called themselves. Yet the peasants of the western villages, especially Michael Ferris, had a wild beauty in their carriage, and in their rich language, which the Ardglas people lacked. There was something pure and complete in their whole bearing ; like that of a noble Zulu, in his war paint, compared to a wretched knock-kneed English trader, whose borrowed cunning serves to build an Empire on the bent backs of defeated but magnificent warriors.

Standing apart in a small group were the police, very slim, tall, erect and silent ; somewhat sinister, like guards in a jail, their blue-green uniforms well creased and adorned with shining buttons ; representatives of the distant and unconscious imperial race that held the island in subjection.

Still farther away, Doctor Melia sat on a fence, watching.

" What way is Skerrett going to go ? " said O'Rourke to Ferris.

" It's hard to say," said Ferris. " He blows hot and cold. I was talking to him yesterday. His heart is with us, but I think he daren't go against the parish priest."

" He'll come with us," cried O'Rourke, " or 'twill be the end of him on this island."

" Hear, hear," said O'Rourke's cronies.

" I'll go over and have a word with the doctor," said O'Rourke.

He strutted past the police, with his head in the air, to show the people how much he despised them. He halted in front of Doctor Melia and said :

" Will ye say a few words at the meeting, Doctor Melia ? We'd like to have an opinion from you. You're a good friend of the Nara people."

The doctor became very embarrassed and said :

" Oh ! No. I couldn't possibly. I have nothing to say, really."

" 'Tis a great pity, then," said O'Rourke, walking away.

He did not expect the doctor to speak and merely went over to that gentleman, in order to show the people how well connected he was with the gentry. As he passed the police on the return journey, he spat with great force. The sergeant, standing in front of his men, smiled contemptuously after O'Rourke. Then he walked calmly to where O'Rourke had spat and rubbed the spot with his shoe. A wag, among the people on the slope, whispered to his neighbours : " 'Tis no good him spitting on the doorstep, for Twig has pressed the button long ago and gone inside the house."

This remark spread rapidly through the gathering, causing a titter everywhere and doing a great deal of harm to O'Rourke. All peasants, being themselves utterly lacking in political idealism, unless it happens to benefit them materially, or through pique at failing to benefit materially by the existing order, are very shrewd at finding holes in the patriot's splendid cloak. Now they realised that O'Rourke's patriotism was largely the result of Constable Twig's success with Coonan's daughter.

" Faith," said they to one another, " 'tis poor comfort for us to get evicted by the red soldiers, so that fat-gut O'Rourke can get satisfaction out of the peelers."

Had the meeting begun at that moment, the people would undoubtedly have gone against O'Rourke ; but chance again swung the crowd into a mood of rebellion. Just as Father Moclair was coming out of the sacristy after having finished his breakfast and the people became silent in expectancy, the sound of an approaching carriage was heard coming from the west. Presently, around the angle of the road, Mr. Athy's landau appeared, going towards Ardglas, where the gentleman attended divine service at the protestant church.

" Here comes the tyrant," cried O'Rourke.

An angry murmur passed among the throng. All eyes were turned towards the approaching landau. They looked at it with deep hatred ; the hatred of revolting slaves for their master.

Yet, properly speaking Athy was not their master, although he belonged by birth to the landowning class. His position on the island was a curious one. About the year 1810, a man called O'Malley came to Nara from the mainland and married a woman of Kilchreest. The woman had a considerable holding of land, to which O'Malley added by shrewd dealings, principally by grabbing farms for which other peasants could not pay the rents. His son Cormac, being a man of great ability and character, improved the position of the family, so that he became tyrant of the island during the famine period in the late 'forties. He became tenant of all the good land in Kilchreest, about three hundred acres. There he built a large house, surrounded by a considerable demesne and assumed the style of a country gentleman of that period, with the local peasants practically as his serfs. He seized a further three hundred acres in the far west of the island, by the same method of grabbing holdings, from which the peasants had been evicted for non-payment of rent. He got still another two hundred and fifty acres at the village of Ardcaol, east of Ardglas, by purchase from a widow called McNamara, to whom he paid a yearly sum during her lifetime. Thus he held all the good land in Nara, except the farm of one hundred acres held by the parson at Ardglas. He assumed the title of The O'Malley of Nara. He married a Dublin woman of good family and changed over to the Protestant faith. He bred three daughters from his wife, and six sons illegitimately, from six women of the island. Although he was by blood akin to the people, he allied himself entirely with the land-owning and governing class, regarding himself as the genuine feudal baron of the island, with all manner of such rights, including flogging and copulation. And he was well worthy of his position, by virtue of his manly beauty, his intelligence and his courage ; so that even though the people hated him as a land-thief, a traitor to his faith and his race, they held him in high respect.

He died during the Land League days, while the peasants were plotting to assassinate him. His eldest daughter married Charles St. George Athy, who became nominal lord of the island on the death of his father-in-law. Athy, however, had none of

O'Malley's character. Being a spendthrift, a hard
drinker and an idle fellow, he made no effort to
maintain the position set up by O'Malley's shrewd-
ness and splendid immorality. Nor had he any contact with the people either, being alien to them in
race and traditions ; so that, although he was of a
mild and generous temper, they hated him more
than his predecessor.

Now, as he approached in his landau, they regarded him as the evil demon who caused their
present misfortune, since the County Cess was
levied to pay for the outrages committed against
his property. The simple carriage, a trifle shabby,
drawn by a single horse, with a coachman in island
costume, seemed to them a royal chariot purchased
by the wealth unjustly taken from them.

His wife and two daughters were in the carriage
with Athy. The two daughters sat with their backs
to the coachman, two slim girls of sixteen and
fifteen years. Their gloved hands were joined on
their joined knees and they sat with bowed heads,
very stiffly, obviously very conscious of the people
who were staring at them, conscious of their enmity
and returning it, without knowing why they were
returning it, resenting the loneliness of their position
in the midst of a hostile people and yet pricked into
a state of vengeful arrogance by the drug-filled
needle of their paltry caste. Their gentle little faces
looked pathetic and timid in spite of the pride on
their tight lips. Their mother, sitting opposite, wore
a heavy white veil that concealed all her face. A
thin, tall woman, she sat as stiffly as her daughters.

There was no timidity or pathos in her arrogance, but a splendid fearlessness. Proud and cold, she revelled in her isolation.

Athy himself looked out of place and uncomfortable. He was a kindly and exuberant fellow of forty-seven, florid of countenance, with puffed cheeks and roving blue eyes, that always seemed on the point of shedding tears, either in sorrow or mirth. Although more genuinely of gentle birth than his wife, he found his isolation irksome and had he not stood in fear of her, he would long ago have become assimilated by the people, of whom he was very fond. But he had not the strength of character to assert himself, so that he now sat huddled beside her in his shapeless clothes, very awkward and shamefaced, scowling from beneath his shabby old hat and glancing now and again furtively at the people. As the carriage passed the chapel gate, Father Moclair was just taking up his position to address the meeting. Athy, who found the priest's company amusing, nodded his head and tipped his hat in friendly salutation. The priest bowed slightly and raised his hat. Mrs. Athy, without looking up, shifted brusquely and gathered her skirts closer about her, as if warding off an unpleasant contact. The carriage moved on. The coachman had been so intimidated by the scene that he forgot to raise his hat passing the chapel gate and did not do so until the horse had trotted on ten lengths farther. The police sprang to attention and saluted smartly as Athy went past.

"There ye are," whispered O'Rourke to his

cronies, who had now closed around their leader on the road. " See how they winked at one another, Athy and himself ? It's a plot between them."

" Bullets 'll' have to fly again," muttered the fierce Michael Ferris. " It's not cattle 'll be thrown by the cliff this time."

Then a hush fell over the gathering as the priest began to speak.

" I have called this meeting to-day," he said, " to let you decide what you are to do about paying this County Cess. I don't want to influence you in any way. I am your ambassador before the throne of God, but in the things of this world also it is my duty to advise you and then support you in carrying out what you decide to do, if you decide on nothing that is against the law of the church. Give unto Cæsar what is due unto Cæsar and to God what is due unto God. If you think this Cess is unjust and it may be unjust, there is still something you have to bear in mind, before you decide to resist paying it. You will lose, in my opinion, more than you will gain by resisting. For eleven years now I have worked to improve your condition and I will go on working in the same way if you stand by me. But if you refuse to take my advice now, you will tie my hands. If you refuse to pay this Cess you'll get no more grants from the government. The County Council will refuse to mend the roads. You'll lose your doctor. You'll be left without any help from outside. You'll have to go back to your rocks and your fishing lines."

" We'll be better off," cried out Ferris.

" Hear, hear," cried O'Rourke.

" Think before you leap," cried Moclair, " I have not finished yet. I say you'll lose all you gained and furthermore you'll have to pay this Cess in any case. For the soldiers are going to come and take your cattle and your pigs. They'll evict you from your homes."

" We'll meet them with stones," cried O'Rourke.

" To hell with the tyrants," cried a man.

" Down with the landgrabber," cried another.

There was a wild yell and several voices cried out in unison :

" To hell with the robbers."

The priest spread out his hands, appealing for a fair hearing ; but O'Rourke stepped forward and began to address the audience.

" Men and women of Nara," he cried out in a hoarse voice.

He was greeted by a loud cheer. However, when he tried to continue, words failed him and he merely repeated the same sentence over and over again in a halting fashion.

" We'll die before we pay it," he went on saying.

What he lacked in power of oratory he replaced by a profusion of gestures, swinging his stick about his head, stamping on the road and drawing his hand across his throat, in token of his evil intentions towards the enemies of the people. Indeed, in a very short time, the crowd in general took voice and there was complete disorder. The women got frightened and began to call on their men to go home. Some seized their men and tried to bundle them away by main force, but this only added to the excitement, as the men refused to budge and became violent. Soon there were numbers of little struggling groups all along the grassy slope of the yard. The police moved closer, fearing a riot. Their movement was noted at once and resulted in stopping the quarrels, for everybody began to shout insults at the government's servants. Finally the parish priest managed to make himself heard. He now spoke angrily.

" Remember," he said, " that if you refuse to take my advice you must rely on those whom you have chosen for your leaders. You must take the consequences. Don't expect any help from me."

" We don't want any help," cried O'Rourke.

" There was a time when you did," retorted Moclair. " There was a time when you came begging to me."

" I never begged from you," shouted O'Rourke. " That's a lie."

" How dare you call me a liar," cried Moclair. " You'll be sorry for this, Coleman O'Rourke, mark my words."

" I dare you and I double dare you," shouted O'Rourke, swinging his stick. " I dare any man that calls me a beggar to do his worst. Ha ! I'm man for any man, priest or bishop, God or devil. I don't give a damn for hell, book or candle light. Bare naked I'll fight any man on road or in field. Here it is.

He struck his chest.

" Here it is and there it lies," he cried.

The tumult began once more and now people were shouting at the priest asking him where he expected them to find the money for the Cess.

" We are starving," they cried.

" The winter is on us," they said, " and our little houses are empty."

" Is it the bread out of our children's mouth you want us to give the red soldiers ? " they said.

At that moment Skerrett came out of the chapel, where he had been teaching catechism to the children. The people cried out to him on his appearance.

" Let the schoolmaster speak," they cried.

" He is a friend of the people. Let him speak."

" Up Skerrett. He's the man for us. We'll follow his advice."

Skerrett stroked his beard and threw back his shoulders, proud of this ovation. His wife and Mrs. Turley came out after him.

" Now, David," said his wife, " don't say anything foolish."

" Silence woman," said Skerrett and then he looked towards Moclair.

For a moment, on hearing the cries he had thought himself indeed master of the situation and the leader of the people ; but his wife's words sharply reminded him that he could not afford to range himself against Moclair. He saw the priest watching him with a cunning look, which seemed to say : " Watch what you say. I have you by the throat." At once the applause became bitter to him.

" Well ! Speak up, Mr. Skerrett," cried O'Rourke.

" I'd rather not say anything," said Skerrett, halting near Moclair. " I'm only a stranger on this island after all "

" That's not so," several shouted. " You're one of ourselves."

" That's not so. He's a friend of the people."

" God bless you, sir. We'd be lost without you."

" Speak up teacher. It's yourself that has the learning for it."

" Well ! " said Moclair in a menacing tone. " Now is your time to show what you're made of. Why don't you speak ? "

" Very well," said Skerrett. " I'll speak."

" More power to your elbow," cried Michael Ferris.

Skerrett raised his right hand clenched and he was on the point of beginning his speech, when Father Moclair said in a voice scarcely above a whisper :

" I want to remind you of the promise you made the other day, before you begin to talk."

Skerrett dropped his hand and turned once more to Moclair.

" I promised you nothing."

Suddenly Moclair wheeled around and throwing out his arms wide, cried out in a loud voice to all the people :

" Men and women of Nara, don't be led astray by this plot hatched by my enemies. Are you going to hand over your priest that loves you and that has fought for you to his enemies ? Who are these men in secret plot against me ? Every one of them has been helped by me. The curs, they are biting the hand that fed them."

" Do you call me a cur ? " thundered Skerrett, leaning forward.

His wife screamed and rushed over to catch him.

" Out of my way, Kate," he muttered.

Moclair pointed a finger at him and said :

" It would be fitter for you to take your sick wife home and look after her than to be meddling in other people's business, Skerrett. Look after your work and leave my work alone."

" Let him speak," cried O'Rourke, rushing over with his stick upraised. " You stinking beggar from Mayo, why don't you let him speak."

" No man 'll stop me from speaking," said Skerrett in a loud voice. " I tell you all that this Cess——"

" Wife beater," shouted Moclair, " you are no fit person to tell them anything."

Skerrett plunged forward to strike, but the by-standers took hold of him. Then O'Rourke and his friends attacked the men who held Skerrett. In a moment there was a riot. Women screamed. The police drew their batons and rushed into the fight. The main body of the crowd fled in all directions. Moclair stood with arms folded, calm and motion-less, until the police had separated the two struggling factions. O'Rourke and Ferris, in spite of a fierce resistance, were put under arrest. Skerrett had received a black eye.

" You are responsible for this fight, Skerrett," said Moclair to him. " You'll be sorry for this yet."

" Do your best," cried Skerrett, " I'm not afraid of you."

" Traitor," shouted O'Rourke, as he was being bundled off by the police. " The peelers were bribed by you. I'll have vengeance for this."

Scattered about on the walls, the people began to boo the police as the two prisoners were led east to Ardglas, followed by their women and their friends. Father Moclair's horse was led to the gate and as he mounted, he also was met with a boo, although part of the audience cheered him. The priest smiled to himself as he trotted home. He had effected his purpose by having O'Rourke and Ferris arrested. He knew that the agitation would die down without their leadership. And as for Skerrett . . ."

" I'll see to him," said Moclair to himself, as he dug his heel into his horse's side.

Skerrett walked home followed by a large crowd. The people were very excited. They had been terrified by the outcome of the meeting and their mood of rebellion had changed to one of craven fear. Skerrett, on the other hand, was now determined on rebellion.

" He called me a cur before all the people," he kept thinking.

His pride was hurt to its very core.

Now and again he stuck out his chest farther and lurched forward.

CHAPTER XIV

ON THE following Thursday, O'Rourke and Ferris were sentenced to fourteen days imprisonment with hard labour by Mr. Athy at the Ardglas Petty Session. They were taken to Galway jail in the steamer Clochar. With their imprisonment, as Father Moclair had foreseen, the agitation against payment of the County Cess was without leadership and became impotent. The Cess was levied without resistance over the whole island. A few people here and there could not pay ; but Father Moclair made good their default out of his own pocket.

However, the feeling against the priest became more intense, especially after the release of the prisoners, who received a public ovation on their landing from the steamer at Ardglas. For a few weeks it seemed that the priest had suddenly become anathema on the island where he had formerly been regarded as an idol. His name was execrated in every village. Outrages were committed on those who had remained faithful to him. A large proportion of the people stayed away from church. At Ardglas O'Rourke make an attempt to beleaguer his house, cutting off even supplies of food and instituting a general boycott.

Then as winter advanced, hunger began to become widespread among the people. Every day, the destitute were coming into Ardglas begging relief from the authorities. A great many families were without fire. They scavenged among the rocks and along the sea-shore, for briars and pieces of wood thrown up by the sea. Even the dung of animals was collected in the fields, dried and used as fuel. Parents sold their clothes to buy food for their children. Even so, the children came to school often without food. Their pinched faces were a pity to the sight. The animals were in even worse condition than the people themselves. Lean after the summer's drought, they were unable to bear the cold, which was particularly severe. Many of them died among the rocks.

Now the tumult of revolt gave way, under the stress of hunger, to the silence of despair. And the priest seized his opportunity with remarkable skill. During the time when he had been cursed, insulted and boycotted by his flock, he never once allowed their conduct to force him into the least gesture of retaliation. Like a dignified man, at whose heels a little cur is barking, he never turned to kick ; nor did he take the least notice, but acted as if they still were faithful to him ; remaining proud and gently contemptuous of their anger. And then, when they came to him with hands stretched out in appeal, they found that he had plans ready for their succour. With Skerrett and Doctor Melia, he formed a relief committee. Mr. Athy, Mr. Willis, the Protestant parson, the police, the coastguards and the government officials, all contributed liberally to the funds of this committee ; but Moclair kept these " enemies of the people " in the background, lest too close association with them might give scandal to his

flock. And although Skerrett and Melia worked
harder than he did, going among the people to
relieve the sick and indigent, it was he himself
who, lordly on horseback, with his magnificent eyes
and his subtle smile which nothing could disturb,
attracted all attention.

When in January he received a bequest of five
hundred pounds from a group of charitable people
in Dublin and later in the same month a grant from
the government for building a pier at Kilchreest the
gratitude of the people knew no bounds. He again
became their idol. The bequest was spent on clothes
and food for the most needy. Others got work building the pier. Then he was able to say to those who
blamed the levying of the County Cess for the
hunger :

" There you are. What did I tell you ? If you
hadn't paid the Cess you'd get nothing. It was the
people who did the outrages who caused all the
trouble. In future have more sense. Trust to me and
I won't fail you in your time of need."

And lo ! when cruel winter melted in the exuberant passion of young Spring, it seemed his magic
wand had laid the spectre of famine. When the fishing
started the nets came full ashore and plenty once
more gladdened the hearts of the people. Again they
thanked God for having given them such a noble
and munificent pastor. His enemies dwindled to a
handful and even the violent O'Rourke was bought
over by the reception through Moclair's influence
of a fresh supply of trawling nets from the government authorities.

His power on the island had now increased ten-fold, as the outcome of this trouble. The wise manner in which he had used his victory insured him against a repetition of the rebellion.

Then he set about the task of getting rid of Skerrett ; the one thorn in his side ; that insolent schoolmaster who tried to set himself up as a rival.

CHAPTER XV

In the meantime, Skerrett's hands were tied by his wife's conduct. Otherwise he would assuredly have led the people against Moclair ; but the shame of having a drunken woman in his keeping kept him subdued.

During winter she had rapidly become a public scandal. She had either taught her principal, Mrs. Turley, how to drink ; or else that woman had come to the island a drunkard and been responsible for Mrs. Skerrett seeking relief in drink on the death of her son. At any rate the two women began to use the school as a drinking shop. Kate, being deprived of money by her husband, sponged on Mrs. Turley. The latter paid Finnigan to leave a jar of whiskey late at night in a hole at the back of the school and the two women kept going out to this hiding-place during school hours and having a tot. In the evening, each brought home a little bottle concealed in her clothes. Sometimes they got quite drunk during their work, terrifying the children, who complained to their parents. Skerrett lost all patience and beat his wife severely when she came home drunk one evening ; but this only drove her to further excesses

A little later, a peasant coming home from Ardglas after dark heard wild laughter in the school ; and being timid of ghosts, he reported the matter to Skerrett. The two of them returned to the school and

157

on entering found Mrs. Turley lying dead drunk on the floor, half naked. They had to carry her to her lodgings. This news got about at once and a deputation went to Father Moclair, asking for the removal of the two drunken school mistresses. Moclair was only too eager to effect the removal, which came about in April. Sergeant Turley came and fetched his wife. Mrs. Skerrett took to her bed and swore she would never again leave it. Their places were taken by two respectable spinsters, who gave satisfaction to everybody.

This affair did great harm to Skerrett's reputation among the people. The loss of his wife's salary reduced their income from one hundred and twenty to eighty pounds a year ; but even so, without children, they could live in comfort on that sum in Nara, together with putting a little away each year for their old age. It was the insult to his dignity that humiliated him ; and the knowledge that Father Moclair was gloating over his discomfiture.

He now conceived a deadly hatred for his wife, whom he regarded as the cause of all his misfortunes. For Moclair he developed an equal hatred. Yet instead of causing him to lose heart or slacken in his work, this hatred only made him double his efforts.

" If I can't beat him one way," he told Doctor Melia, with whom he was again becoming intimate, " I'll beat him in another way."

" Don't be a fool," said the pessimistic doctor. " He'll drive you out of the island."

" I'll see him in Hell first," said Skerrett.

The priest, in fact, did his best that year to drive

Skerrett out of the island ; but the man's position was
still too strong to allow him to be easily up-rooted.
First of all Moclair ceased to inspect the school,
giving out that Skerrett had grossly insulted him.
Instead he sent his curate to do the weekly inspection. Then he sent in a report to the education
authorities, suggesting that Skerrett was unfit to
conduct the school. A special inspector came down
from Dublin and put Skerrett through a severe examination. By good fortune, this inspector happened
to be a friend of Doctor Melia's and prejudiced
against the clergy. The doctor had a long conversation with him at Ardglas the evening before the inspection. He pointed out that Skerrett was an excellent man, who was most conscientious in his work
and extremely beneficial to the children ; but that he
had got into trouble with Father Moclair, who could
not brook any independent spirit within his sphere
of influence. Thus, even though Skerrett failed
lamentably to prove that he was sufficiently well-
informed on his duties as schoolmaster, the inspector
gave him an excellent report and the priest was out-
witted.

Moclair knew the cause of this report and Doctor
Melia became as hateful to him as Skerrett himself.
From then onward, a battle of wits began between
these three men. The priest became a nightmare to
the doctor, who being naturally of a nervous dis-
position, felt menaced in his liberty by the terrific
hold the priest was gaining over every aspect of life
on the island. Being timid of doing anything himself
he spurred on Skerrett.

" My God ! " he whispered to Skerrett. " It will soon be impossible to breathe on this island, except by that man's permission. People are getting afraid to talk to me, because Moclair has spread the report that I am a pagan. If I talk to a woman, no matter how old she is, the next thing I hear is that I'm leading a loose life. I'm getting afraid of that man."

" Well, then, I'm not afraid of him," said Skerrett.

He now tried to come closer to the life of the Gaelic-speaking peasants of the west, according as Moclair fortified himself more strongly in the anglicised village of Ardglas. It was ironical that he, who swore to make the Ballincarrig people learn English in a month, now ceased to use that language altogether, except when he had to do so in school. He even taught through the medium of Gaelic. The Gaelic League had been started in 1893 and a wave of enthusiasm for the language was spreading over the country, with the growth of militant republicanism. Scholars began to visit Nara and among these scholars Skerrett became known and respected. He contributed articles to Gaelic publications in Dublin and in a short time, he became somewhat of a national figure in scholastic circles. This, however, did not improve his position in Nara ; for the people were ready to believe with Father Moclair that " Irish would get them nowhere." And Skerrett became for them " a decent poor fellow enough, but a bit touched in the head."

The new gospel of love for their language and traditional mode of living, together with a longing for national freedom, which he began to preach to them, made no appeal to these peasants, who, like all peasants, were only too eager to sell any birthright for a mess of pottage. And Father Moclair, the man of progress and materialist, had the pottage.

Little by little Skerrett found that he was being regarded as a crank. People no longer listened to his advice with respect ; neither did they raise their hats to him in passing. Father Moclair and his curate were now the only two people on the island to whom hats were raised. In the school itself it became difficult to maintain discipline. The scholars began to play truant. When he chastised them with his old severity, they complained to their parents and these latter visited the school in a threatening fashion ; sometimes even coming to blows with the master.

But he was undaunted. The more fortune turned against him, the more obstinate he became in his curious conviction that good must always triumph over evil and that virtue must be rewarded. Under the doctor's influence he absorbed the doctrines of philosophic anarchism, which have been made popular in Prince Kropotkin's work. The doctor mixed this philosophy with a mystical worship of the earth and the old pagan gods of the island. Indeed, he worshipped the island itself.

" I don't believe in the occult," he said to Skerrett. "Indeed I don't believe in much outside visible life, but I feel myself being swallowed up by this island. I feel as if I were in love with it. And isn't

it odd how we all live here without women ? Mark
you, there is something queer in that."

A deep friendship developed between these two
men, who seemed to have so little in common ; the
one timid and monkish, the other arrogant and
passionate. The doctor, being unable to express
himself in action, drove Skerrett to action.

" The whole of life is based on love," he said.
" But there can be no love where men are scheming
to outwit one another in business. Every prophet the
world has ever known has preached this gospel of
mutual love and that it cannot exist where. the
pursuit of money corrupts human nature. This love
is only possible in a village community ; or at least,
as near as can be. It is only in villages that people
can live without money."

Their friendship became the talk of the island and
Father Moclair lost no time in making mysterious
references from the altar about pagans that were a
menace to the souls of the people. But Skerrett
countered this charge by increasing his outward
show of devotion to religion, praying loudest in the
church at the public responses, going to confession
and communion once a week, making pilgrimages
to holy wells in an ostentatious fashion. In the same
manner, the doctor, who had now entered into the
fight with almost equal zest, became fanatical in his
devotion to his duties.

The rivalry between the schoolmaster and the
priest became ludicrous in many ways. On learning
that the priest had bought a cow, Skerrett did likewise. When it became known that the priest had a

half share in a new trawler, Skerrett countered by investing most of his savings in a fishing curragh and nets. The people jeered at his fresh activities, likening him to a sand-lark, that bird notorious for its greed. " Yet," they said, " the sand-lark cannot forage on two strands at the one time." Indeed their prophecy proved to be true.

At first, both the cow and the fishing curragh prospered well enough. In the first year's fishing the curragh earned enough to repay him for his outlay. He also rehabilitated himself in the people's favour by accepting only a third share of the boat's earnings, instead of half, which had been the rule previously. Thenceforth, this became the general rule, so that the poorest peasants and fishermen once more looked upon him as their benefactor. Indeed for two years, in spite of his continued trouble with his wife, who was drinking on the sly and misbehaving herself in every possible way when she was not posing as a bed-ridden invalid, life became once more a source of infinite joy to him. He bought two fields near Cappatagle to feed his cow, one small grassy field and a large crag, where there was hardly any grass at all. In possession of these fields he felt himself a genuine peasant and on a footing of equality with the people in discussing everything that pertained to the management and exploitation of the land. In the same way, with his fishing curragh, he could pose as a fisherman. And in the close communion which these possessions and pursuits established between himself and the people, he felt safe from his enemy.

But ill fortune had not yet finished with him by any means. In the Spring of 1898, his cow, after giving birth to her third calf, drank a quantity of cold water and died in great agony. In the following autumn a still greater misfortune befell him.

CHAPTER XVI

ONE MORNING early in October, a group of fishermen were taking shelter in the lee of a high rock above the western end of the beach at Kilchreest. It was not yet dawn and there was a fierce wind. They were arguing with one another, as to whether it was safe to go out to take the nets they had set the night before.

" It should be dawn now."

" It should be. 'Twas four o'clock when we left our village."

" It's five now and I can't see my hand."

" It's pitch dark, surely. The wind is screeching like a stuck pig. There must be a heavy sea."

" There's no sea. Ye can't hear it break on the beach."

" Let's go out before it rises with the wind. Or else the nets'll be carried away."

" It's too dangerous, comrade, in this wild, dark wind. Let's wait for light."

" Aye ! And give our mackerel to the dog-fish. Let's out. Come on men."

It was the skipper of Sherrett's curragh, who spoke last, a young man called Daly, a relative of Corless the tavern-keeper. He strode down from the rock to the curraghs, which lay in a row mouths downwards, on the beach, beneath a sand bank.

He raised the prow of the boat and called to his crew.

"Get under her," he said, "and put her down. Let it not be said that a cap-full of wind can keep us on the shore. 'Twill be light when we reach where the nets are set."

"Yerrah! Will ye look at the fury of Pat Daly?" cried a man from the group under the rock. "Risking his neck for another man's share. If it was his own curragh and his own nets he'd be still in bed cuddling up against his wife's flanks."

Pat Daly, holding up the prow of the curragh against his chest, cried out loud against the screeching wind:

"Ha' 'Faith, there's fury in your heart Peter Culkin more than in mine. Two years ago I was fishing in your curragh for the eighth share. Now I'm fishing for the sixth share. Aye! and every poor man like myself, with little land and a long struggling family, fishing out of the island of Nara, is on the sixth share as well as me, since the noble friend of the poor took a hand in the fishing. He put bloody gombeen men like you where you belonged. Go and peddle his poteen for your lousy cousin, the trickster Finnigan."

There was a titter of laughter from the group under the rock; Culkin made no reply. Daly and his men hoisted the eight-oared curragh from her perch and began to make their way towards the tide. Three men carried her on their shoulders. The fourth man went in front with the oars, directing the way in the darkness. The curragh in the gloom looked like a black beetle on stilts, marching backwards, her square stern in front. They dropped her with a splash into the tide.

The group under the rock increased, as men kept coming from the villages. They renewed the discussion about the advisability of going out to fetch the nets.

" Who in the name of God are the madmen facing out in this windy darkness ? " said a new-comer.

" It's Pat Daly," said Culkin. " By Ganeys ! that man has become the greatest wind-bag on this island since he became hired man to Skerrett, the schoolmaster. It's all nonsense. Schoolmasters shouldn't mix in business they don't understand. It was the same during the time of the County Cess when he and the rest of them near ruined the island with a droughty famine. It will come to no good, his meddling, either in the fishing or in anything else. There is a curse on the man. He won't make a penny out of his curragh and he won't let any man else make a penny either. Can any honest man keep a curragh and nets on a third of the catch ? "

All the other men, even those who owned boats and nets, jeered at the greedy Culkin.

" If it were left to men like you, Culkin," said one, " it's little chance a poor man'd have to get a bite at all ! "

" That's true," said another. " Whatever faults Skerrett has, pagan or no pagan, he is the friend of the poor. He has his hand in everything that benefits the poor. Only for him the blight'd be on my potatoes this year. He wrote up and we got this spraying machine now in our village."

"Blast him and his spraying machine," said Culkin.

"Blast you, instead," said another man. "When my daughter was going to the hospital in Dublin last year, Lord have mercy on her she didn't last long, he came to me and gave me a hansel to pay her way."

"That's true, Peter Fahy," said another. "I remember it well. Sure many's a man's daughter has a good place around the country, in service with his friends of the Gaelic League. He's the greatest man ever came to the island bar Father Moclair himself."

"Yerrah ! Is it to Father Moclair ye're comparing him ? " said Culkin. It's like comparing a mongrel dog to a prince. Isn't this boasting bag of guts the worst enemy of that great priest, that puts bread in our mouths and miraculous unction on our souls, to give us a fair course on the road to Paradise."

" 'Faith, then, it's a misfortune sure enough they're enemies," said the last speaker, " and the queer nonsense that does be running through Skerrett's head is the cause of it. Out of books or somewhere he gets it."

"He gets it from the devil," said Culkin.

Just then there was shout from the sea's edge : "Stick her out now."

There was a dull rumble of oars falling on thole pins. Then came the creak and splash of rowing. Daly had put to sea.

" They're foolish to go out in this darkness," said a man from the group in the lee of the rock. " With the way the wind is blowing, they might get into a sudden swell of sea unknown to them. The strand is in shelter. That's why the waves are breaking smooth."

" Whist ! " said another. " Great God of glory ! What's that ? "

A wild shout had come to them from the dark sea. There was a moment's pause. Then another shout came from the same direction :

" She's on us. We're drowned."

The men ran at once from the rock, down the steep fall of the sandy beach, slipping and falling in their haste over the loose mounds of soft, heavy sand. The tide was out and it was some way to the sea's edge, according to their reckoning. But they halted half way, confronted by a huge wave that had broken at their feet, with a roar that drowned the wind. The curragh came rolling towards them sideways on the breaking wave. It was hurled on the sand and left there stranded when the wave retired. One man still lay in the stern. The others sat stunned on the beach, motionless where the sea had thrown them. When they were dragged to their feet and brought together they all began to babble. The man left in the stern was the only one who understood what had happened.

" I was standing up," he said, " pulling on my oilskin trousers. They hadn't much of a stroke on her, as they were wetting their oars. Before I sat down, I turned around to see could I get my bearings, so as to stick her up properly, when I saw a mountain of sea standing over us and coming like a race-horse. I couldn't see its top in the blackness. I shouted. We had two fathoms of water over us coming in."

" Bad cess to you, Coleman Kelly," said Daly. "You always bring bad luck wherever you go. You are a big, loose, awkward, senseless sort of an idiot. Why weren't you sitting in your seat? You turned her stern."

" We're better off as we are," said Kelly. " With that sea we'd be drowned for certain, for weren't we making for the Little Reef? It must be in breakers and we thinking it's smooth. You can't hear them in this wind and they breaking."

" We're nearly drowned as we are," shouted Daly. "Last week, you fool, you put your oar in a net and nearly drowned us too."

People laughed at the clumsy young fellow.

" It's as bad as the time he nearly blew himself up," said a man. " He threw a lighted match through a little hole there was in the side of an empty barrel of petrol. Then the fool sat down opposite the little hole to see what would happen. By Ganeys ! That iron barrel blew up like the end of the world. Blood in ouns ! It made a noise like the falling of a cliff. The houses rocked in our village, though the barrel as ye know, was lying half a mile away among the boulders on the shore. Not a bit of it was found within three hundred yards of where it blew up. And the devil a hurt came to the fool that was sitting by the hole."

Again there was loud laughter.

" 'Faith, I was hurt sure enough," said Kelly. " I had a pain in my guts for a week after it. I was as deaf as a stone as well."

" This is no time to laugh," said Culkin. " My advice to you men is to go home and leave this doomed curragh alone on the beach. It was a sign from God, that wave."

" The devil flay the marrow from your bones, you miserable, crouching mongrel," said Daly. " You better keep your tongue in idleness, or Skerrett'll hear of your gab and then you'll be sorry."

" Ho ! " said Culkin. " I'm not afraid of that bum bailiff. I double dare and damn him to it, him or his screeching, drunken wife. Ho ! Ho ! Is it Culkin afraid ? "

" Come on lads," said Daly. " Pay no attention to that sucking weasel. Down with her again. She's not hurt. Bail out that water. It's daylight now. Away she goes. Lay hold."

Again they pushed the boat into the tide and boarded her. The others also went to fetch their boats.

" What I said is true," said Culkin to his crew, as they brought down their curragh. " That wave was a sign that God is angry with this upstart school-master. Bring a goat to the church door and she'll try to pull the cloth off the altar. Setting himself up against Father Harry ! 'Faith, that's a hairy proposition."

The sky had broken in the east. Dawn spread quickly over land and sea ; a wild, October dawn, frosty and grey, without a bird to hail its coming with a song, except the wailing curlew and the sea-roving gulls. The barren island rose from the womb of night in austere majesty, its summits black against the sky, with drifting shadows passing over the crags and grassy glens, that fell uneven by low rock ramparts, to the white-scarred sea. In the tide-way on the beach, a line of gleaming weeds lay red. Clouds of sand whirled like twisting ropes among the sandbanks and then fell in swishing showers. Cocks were crowing in the villages.

One by one the boats were lowered into the tide. The oars were set in place. The stern men pushed from the shore, ran for a few paces through the tide and then jumped nimbly, landing on their knees in stern. With a merry rhythm, the oars dipped and rose, dripping with brine. The little black fleet made way to the nets, out between the two long headlands that bound the narrow harbour. The sun rose. The wind died down. The sea ceased to break. It's surface became covered with a lace-work of drifting foam. The dying wind passed over it quietly, as if lulling it to sleep, making dark frills on its blue-green back. In the distance the curraghs became dark blots ; sometime disappearing in the radiant sun, when only the upraised oars, like a struggling insect's legs flashed white each side a dark, low streak upon the water. Then the boats halted one by one and in each stern a man rose like a short mast to haul in the nets.

A crowd began to gather from all directions towards the little pier on the west side of the harbour.

Here there was a store for fish curing, fronted by a
sloping concrete square. About thirty youths and
maidens were waiting on this square when Harkin,
the fish agent, arrived on his bicycle from the village
of Kilchreest. As soon as he arrived, he called out :
" Come on, you devils. Line up here till I count
you."

He looked a fierce man in his top boots and drooping red moustaches. Opening a tattered note-book,
he called the roll of his work-people. There were ten
on his list of regular workers. When these had
answered their names he ordered them brusquely
to work. The others crowded round, begging to be
hired. They looked wild and famished, being
children of the very poorest people, without either
land or fishing boats. A few of the girls were bare-
footed in spite of the cold. Their clothes were in
tatters.

" God blast ye ! " shouted Harkin. " Do ye think
I can hire the whole population of this bloody
island ? "

Still they came running after him, telling him in
piteous tones of their desperate need. He unlocked
the store and shouted to his men :

" Roll out those barrels ready for the carts. Set
up the trestles. Get the salt ready. Jump now, you
pack of lazy bastards. Give that place a wash down.
Lay hold of that hose. Pump water one of you.
Look alive, you cod-fish."

There was a strong smell of pickle everywhere.
Streams of picked water had run down from the
concrete square on to the lower part of the pier,

where it mingled with peat dust, making a soft black mould that stuck to people's boots. Everywhere on the ground and along the slashwall there was a thick white rime of mackerel scales. The air was bitterly cold.

The young people, who were not yet hired, watched the boats from the end of the pier, hoping to get hired if there were a big catch. Flocks of sea-gulls, hovering about in the sky, also hoped for a big catch. Afar off, on high places, women going to milk their cows halted to watch the boats anxiously, shielding their eyes with their hands. There was a clatter of hoofs from the horses being fetched to cart the barrelled mackerel into Ardglas.

Then old people and children began to arrive with cans of tea and buttered bread, in readiness for the returning fishermen. The cans had cloths tied around them to keep the tea warm.

Suddenly, somebody cried out :

" There's Skerrett going for his swim. God ! He'll be frozen this morning."

On the opposite side of the harbour, about a quarter of a mile away, there was a little concrete slip, jutting into the sea. Skerrett appeared on this slip, carrying a large white towel on his shoulder. While the people watched him, astonished at his hardihood, he stripped off his clothes until he stood naked on the edge of the pier. Then he put his feet together, made the sign of the cross, raised his joined hands over his head, leaned forward and plunged headlong into the sea. " Ah ! " said one of the on-lookers. " There's a man for you ! He's as strong as a lion. He's now forty-six years of age and there's not a young stripling on the island with his guts."

" Easy for him," said Harkin, with a coarse snigger. " He doesn't use himself in his wife's bed. He hasn't slept with her they say this last two years. He can get up fresh. Lay hold, there, you pack of rotting dog-fish. Lay hold, I say."

In the bright, clear light they saw Skerrett swim strongly out from the pier, his bearded face rising now and again high from the water. It was now so calm that they could hear his hoarse splutters, as he spat the brine from his mouth.

" He's a damn fool," continued Harkin. " If I had his soft job, I'd be still in my warm bed, on this devilish morning."

Skerrett turned over on his back and made a foaming trough of the water with his feet. Then he turned again and swam hurriedly ashore.

" Heh ! you devils," they cried. " Look what he's at now."

Skerrett began to leap into the air, to bend, to twist sideways, to touch the ground with the tips of his fingers without bending his knees. When he had finished his exercises, he dried himself and put on his clothes. Then he marched at great speed westwards to the pier. By now the people had lost interest in him as the curraghs had begun to approach.

" That's Pat Daly in front," said a voice. " He looks loaded to the transom."

" He is, 'faith, loaded sure enough," said another. As the curraghs came nearer they called out :

" Was the night any good, Pat Daly ? "

Daly turned and shouted : " Praise be to the all-powerful saviour of mankind, we are loaded with a single net."

" A thousand praises to the glorious son of God ! " the people cried.

Just then Skerrett marched down the pier.

" Good morning, Skerrett," said Harkin. " There's your curragh coming loaded. It's nice for you and you not lifting a hand. It's fine to have money and to be able to buy the labour of others."

" Huh ! " said Skerrett. " I never ask any man to do what I'm afraid to do myself."

" True for you, sir," said an old man. " Hell to your lousy soul, Pete Harkin. You came here from Ardglas without a shirt and now you're getting cocky with the spoils of robbery. Only for that man," pointing to Skerrett, " it's five shillings a hundred you'd be paying for mackerel instead of nine. No wonder you have a bad word for him."

" You gelded old ram," said Harkin, " sure I pay what I'm ordered to pay and no more and no less."

" In two years you've got rich," said the old man.

" Rich do ye call me ? " shouted Harkin. " Didn't I work hard for the couple of bob I've earned? Ye are a proper lot of envious devils, ye are. Ye'd sell the hair off yer chests to best one another. They'll turn on you, too, Mr. Skerrett. So you needn't hold your head so high in the air."

He strode down to the edge of the pier shouting :

" Every man for himself in this world. Every man for himself. Damn the man that's down. He had no right to fall. Here's to the man that's up. Long life to him I say. Come on, sea scavengers. What have you got in your boat? Row, you devils, and throw out your fish."

"Well done, Pat," cried Skerrett as the curragh came alongside.

"God bless you, sir," said Daly. "It's glad I am to bring this fine load ashore for you."

Skerrett threw back his shoulders and stroked his beard with pride. His heavy body, becoming very fleshy around the neck and belly, stood out arrogantly among the crowd of lean, wiry islanders that surrounded him, looking down with greedy blue eyes into the loaded boat. His beard had begun to grow grey. Folds of flesh eddied over the collar of his raincoat. The rim of a bald patch on his crown showed at the rear of his cap. His thick sensual lips were opened outwards, red and moist, as if about to kiss.

They began at once to haul up the laden net. It was white with mackerel. It came up the side of the pier like a stream of molten silver. It brought a rich smell of the sea, mingled with the smell of bark. Stray fish fell into the water and children, with loud cries, tried to catch them with spears, before the swooping gulls seized them in their prodding beaks.

"Did the other curraghs get any?" said Harkin.

"They're all loaded," said Daly.

"Come on, then, all of you," said Harkin. "Sign on here. Lay to, my hearties. Look alive, you hungry sons of tinkers. Heigh ho! Heigh ho!"

The fish was hurriedly taken from the net and counted by the hundred into baskets, which were rushed up to the concrete square and there spilt on the long boards before the curers. The curers slashed them down the backs with their knives. They were washed in brine, rolled in salt and then packed into barrels. The curers began to sing. Here and there a fisherman, having drunk some hot tea from a can, did a caper of dance, exalted by his good fortune.

" We have to go out again," said Daly, when the net was ashore. " We have three more nets to take."

" Praised be the glorious son of God ! "

This cry rang out again and again along the pier, as the other curraghs came alongside, loaded with fish. All hardship was forgotten in the joy caused by the rich ocean's bounty. Daly and his crew again put to sea, shouting a song as they rowed. Skerrett walked up and down the pier, ankle deep in the soft, black mould. His trouser legs and the skirt of his raincoat were speckled with the white scales of mackerel. He felt exalted, not only by the good fortune that had come to himself, but also by the feeling that the people again revered him as a noble benefactor. He noted how the young girls looked at him with shy interest, from under the cowls of their little black headshawls and their regards stirred his blood with a memory of youth's passion. He watched their lithe bodies move to and fro with the ease and grace of wild animals ; their rosy cheeks, their magnificent young eyes ; and he thought if his wife died he might mate with one of them.

Then life would begin once more in all its exuberance and joy ; the life of a fisherman and peasant ; free and noble on this wild island ; with children at his knee and a young fair bosom to enlace in his strong arms.

It was already time to go home and have breakfast before opening his school, but he stayed on, unable to leave this scene of common joy. And then, when he was on the point of leaving, a cry came from the sea.

It was a cry of anguish that brought a death-like silence to the pier. Then the people looked to sea. Three curraghs were rowing furiously towards a black dot that lay motionless. Just before the leading curragh reached it, the black dot disappeared and there was another shriek.

This time the cry was taken up on the pier. Skerrett's heart stopped beating. A voice within him said :

" That's my boat. Oh ! God ! Why do you pursue me with your hatred ? "

CHAPTER XVII

A very extraordinary thing had happened. Coleman Kelly, that clumsy young man who was always pursued by ill fortune, was standing in the stern of the boat, hauling in the end of the last net, when he suddenly lost his balance and went overboard. The boat was very deep, carrying much more than she should, owing to the wish of the crew to take all the remaining nets on one trip. When Kelly went overboard with a cry of fright he held on to the net-rope, which came with him and gave the boat a slight jerk. The second man shifted his position in order to clear himself of the out-rushing net, with the result that the boat canted over the other side, the far board went under water and down they went. All except Kelly were entangled in the nets, which, laden with mackerel, sank to the bottom, hauling the men and the boat with them. Kelly dropped the net and grasped a floating oar, with which he managed to keep himself above water until he was rescued. The other three men were never found. They were devoured by sharks or by some other sea-monsters, before their galls burst.

This disaster caused a great sensation on the island, affecting Skerrett very deeply. The search for the corpses went on for many weeks, as the islanders considered that a soul could not rest unless the body were buried in consecrated ground. So they refused to give up hope of finding the lost ones. It was terrible for Skerrett to see the women go along the shore day after day, crooning the death wail, searching among the rocks for their lost ones. Sometimes a shoe was found, or a cap, and then the whole agony was renewed, as people mourned these articles in lieu of their owners. Although the accident could not possibly have been his fault and although he did everything in his power to help the bereaved relatives, there were some who placed the responsibility on Skerrett's shoulders. I must say that the majority of the people, considering that the loss of a boat and nets on such a poor island equalled the loss of three human beings, sympathised with him as much as with the relatives of the deceased ; but Culkin, Finnigan and others, parasites of Father Moclair, quickly spread the rumour that " the curse of God " was upon Skerrett. This accounted, they said, for all his bad luck, the loss of his son, of his cow and of his boat, as well as his wife's disgusting drunkenness.

"Everything he touches is cursed," they said. " 'Tis best to keep clear of him."

Culkin, in particular, took great delight in telling everybody about " the sign from Heaven " that was sent on the morning of the disaster ; and he felt very proud that he had warned the crew not to put to sea in the doomed boat. The superstitious minds of the people were not proof against these rumours ; although those friendly to Skerrett were inclined to think that the curse was not of God but of the Devil, who injures the Good, whereas God merely injures the Wicked. A violent controversy went on in the hamlets about this question. Nor was Father Moclair above playing a rather suspicious rôle in the argument. Coleman Kelly had suffered a great nervous shock as the result of his experiences, especially as the relatives of the drowned men blamed him for the accident. So he took to his bed, at first through the debility brought on by fear, and later, when he found that he was attracting general attention, for the pleasure of notoriety. Then his relatives were persuaded by Culkin and others to go to the parish priest and ask that a Mass be said in the house, in order to drive out the evil spirit that had taken possession of Kelly. This the priest consented to do. The mass was said in great secrecy and immediately afterwards Kelly got out of bed, went about his work and appeared to enjoy excellent health. This convinced even Skerrett's most ardent supporters that there was something occult in the matter. His enemies crossed themselves when they passed him on the road. All showed an increasing distaste for his company and they spoke to him in the timid and almost hostile manner that they would address a Protestant, a murderer, or an atheist.

Instead of ignoring this distrust, as Father Moclair had done during the time of the County Cess, Skerrett acted in a very foolish manner. Mob ignorance can only be countered by silent contempt. Instead of keeping silent, Skerrett went about saying in a loud and scoffing voice that the curse of God, or of the Devil, was nothing but a gross superstition. Accordingly, the people thought him still more accursed and they became still more distant ; and he only became more angry in insisting that he was not accursed. And so he was forced by his own lack of tact into the position of being regarded as an enemy of society.

Among those who attempt to improve society there are always two groups ; revolutionaries and reformers. The latter aim at leading the people towards the desired goal by reasoned and gradual progress. The former try to affect the change by violence, by sneering and an affectation of superiority, which is generally a token of defeated ambition or of some abnormal passion, akin to insanity. Skerrett had begun as a reformer and he was now forced by Moclair's cunning into the other group. And as there is only a thin dividing line between a revolutionary and a reactionary, in face of general popular hostility Skerrett soom became a complete crank, criticising every social activity and custom on the island.

The priest no longer took any active measures to get rid of him, reasoning thus : " He'll hang himself by his own folly, whereas, if I interfere too soon, he might get wise and defend himself." And in any case, Skerrett was no longer a menace to the priest's power, as he was fast becoming a laughing-stock. Gratitude for the great services he had rendered the people was lost in the laughter that his antics now inspired. And indeed, a great deal of his conduct was ludicrous.

It was especially ridiculous how he tried to show that his strength was still in its full vigour, even though he was well on the road to middle age. It was over a mile from his house to the jetty where he plunged into the sea every morning. He now began to walk that distance quite naked, except for a towel around his waist, just to show how hardy he was. This practice came to an end, however, when a woman of Ballincarrig, meeting him at dawn as she went to milk her cow, fled in terror from his nakedness and reported to the police that he had exposed his person to her. This, of course, was quite false, but it caused a further scandal. Then he spent three nights in succession within an old fort, which was supposed to be haunted by malignant fairies and where no one had ever dared spend a night before. He slept on a rock, protected by a single blanket. Although the people were amazed at his hardihood, in that he was not afraid, nor did he get pneumonia and die, they laughed at his folly. Neither did his sleeping there in security persuade them that the place was not inhabited by malignant fairies. Popular superstitions are always proof against alien experience that runs counter to them.

In the same way, when he preached Dr. Melia's hotch-potch philosophic anarchism to them, they shrugged their shoulders. He was now trying to turn them against the use of money and trade.

"Money is no good to you," he said. "Instead of selling your pigs, kill them, cure them and eat them. Kill your lambs and eat them. If you join together, you can have beef all the year round, by killing one beast at a time and sharing the meat. What good is the money to you that you get by selling these animals, or your fish ? You use it to buy

tea, sugar, flour, drink and tobacco. You don't need
these things and they are harmful to you. You
become slaves to the shop-keepers. You are in debt
all your lives. You can get all you need from the
land and the sea, without ever going to a shop.
You were free before shops came to the island. Keep
away from Ardglas. Ardglas is the headquarters of
the Devil."

" Huh !" said Culkin. " He had a different story
a few years ago. When he sees he can't make money
himself, he hates to see any poor person earning a
red penny."

And that was the general opinion of the people.
Although he proved to them again and again that
they were being exploited evilly by the shop-keepers,
they persisted in their mode of living. Even though
they admitted that they were just as enslaved by the
new-born gombeen-man class, " of their own flesh
and blood," as they had been by the landowners,
they went their way and shrugged their shoulders.
People do not go back to primitive communism
merely because it is proved to them that progress
towards capitalist civilisation is slavery.

When Skerrett complained to Dr. Melia about the
people's stupidity, the doctor shrugged his shoulders
exactly as the people had done.

" I've come to the conclusion," he said, " that
human beings are detestable. It doesn't matter to
me how they live, provided they leave me in peace.
The ancient hermits were the only people who
had a sensible idea of life. But then they believed in
God and I am very doubtful about God's existence ;

indifferent to it, in fact. I'd hate, in any case, to have to worship the same God as Father Moclair and Finnigan."

" What's the good of hiding your head in the sand like an ostrich ? " said Skerrett. " Why don't you take your coat off and fight against ignorance same as I'm doing ? "

" What's the good of it ? " said the doctor. " The only way to achieve happiness is to hope for nothing and aim at nothing. Are you happy ? "

" How could any man be happy the way I'm fixed."

" Well ! Then, you're not qualified to preach to others."

" You're preaching to me, but you're not happy."

" I soon will be," said the doctor.

" How ? "

" I'm going to give up my job and become a hermit. It's no good trying to live by good works. If an honest man brings himself into public notice by good work, he only gives scoundrels a reason for striking him down. Unless a man is a scoundrel he should hide himself. The mob loves only scoundrels. Being base itself, the mob only loves what is base. Being slaves they only love those who ill-treat and rob them. Look at Moclair. Look at Finnigan. Look at all the hucksters and publicans at Ardglas. Then look at yourself. You are queer in their eyes, so even though you work for them they scoff at you and think you a fool, because you are not hoarding money and trying to persecute your neighbours. They'll stone you out of the island because of your honesty. I've come to the conclusion that, wherever there is a priest, a policeman and a shopkeeper, there can be no justice and no peace."

" That's a cowardly way of looking at life," said Skerrett. " My opinion is that the majority of the people are all right, but they are led astray by that grinning devil Moclair."

" Are they ? " said the doctor. " He is no worse than they are and he is a great deal more clever. That's all. So he lives on them. No—Skerrett, have sense and leave them alone. Go and live in a hole like a hermit. That's what I'm going to do."

The doctor did not become a hermit, as he had threatened. In the following Spring, an interesting thing happened, that destroyed his pessimism and forced him to leave the island. During that winter, the fortunes of the Athy family reached a crisis, owing to Athy's debauchery and gambling. He had to sell his horses, his yacht and practically everything he possessed, in order to pay the most pressing of his debts. His farm at Ardcaol was taken by the Congested Districts Board and an islander who had made money in America took the farm in the far west of the island. Nothing was left to Athy but the farm at Kilchreest and that was absolutely naked of stock. All this happened with startling suddenness. Athy drank for a week on his last few pounds and then he was put to bed with delirium tremens. Melia was called in to attend him. The islanders were delighted at Athy's ruin and they thanked God heartily for having struck down " the monstrous tyrant." It was, in fact, thought indecent that Melia should attend him and that Father Moclair should go to pay a visit to the sick man.

"Now the land taken from our fathers will be divided among us," said the people.

As yet they knew nothing about the purchase of the farm by the returned American and they thought the Congested Districts Board had taken the farm at Ardcaol for immediate distribution. Moclair had always given them to understand that Athy's land would be divided among the dispossessed. Nothing of the kind happened, as might be expected.

First of all, the doctor created a public scandal of the first magnitude. It was noticed that from the first day he visited Kilchreest House he began to be more tidy in his dress. He became more cheerful and his manner underwent a complete change. For this, Athy's eldest daughter Charlotte was responsible. The doctor fell in love with her almost at first sight ; a passion which she encouraged. Although she was only twenty and the doctor was quite old enough to be her father, she was anxious to escape from the desperate position in which she now found herself. In a few weeks, Athy was cured of his delirium tremens, but Melia continued to frequent the house. Tongues began to wag. And then suddenly, in the month of May, the doctor and Charlotte disappeared from the island, as if by magic. They had embarked at Liverpool on a ship for the United States before tale or tidings were received of them.

Everybody on the island was astonished, except Father Moclair, who maintained that the doctor's

189

conduct was only what might be expected from such a ruffian. " He has a wife somewhere in England," said the priest, " living with an actor." Then the doctor's secret history, which had remained hidden so long, became public property ; how he had caught his wife with an actor and nearly horse-whipped the couple to death ; as a result of which he had to give up his practice in London.

All this caused profound astonishment to Skerrett. He regarded the doctor's conduct as a blow to himself. Indeed, he felt that Melia had deceived him quite as much as Father Moclair, preaching a worship of village life, ascetisism and self-containedness and then dashing off to America " with a foolish slip of a girl." There was jealousy, too, in Skerrett's irritation. There he was himself, cut off from all sexual pleasure, a prisoner on this rock among a hostile people, while the doctor was loose on the great American continent, with a pleasant young concubine to bed. Now he was completely alone and exposed to the " grinning devil's " hatred. His mind began to become slightly deranged under the press of these calamities. He no longer saw any hope of defeating the priest who began to stride away boldly to unquestioned dominion over Nara.

In the month following Melia's disappearance, Moclair began to build a new residence at Ardglas, on the site of his former cottage. It was a large and pretentious building, with a flat roof in the modern style. It was far larger than Athy's house at Kilchreest. Masons were brought from Dublin. The islanders gaped at its cost. Many of them scowled at its grandeur, especially as Skerrett pointed out that the money to build it had come out of the pockets of the poor.

" Now you see what he was after," cried Skerrett. " The miser is opening up his treasure-pillow and pouring out his gold to build this Tower of Babel. Ha ! No sooner has the old tyrant fallen than the new tyrant builds his castle."

Skerrett was beside himself with rage, as the new house began to rise on its foundations. In answer, he began to build a peasant's cabin on the crag he had bought near the hamlet of Cappatagle for his cow. When the people asked him why he was building this cabin, he answered :

" Shortly I may need a hiding-place from my enemies. When the tyrants begin to build fortresses to enslave the people, the just must prepare a hiding-place."

All this foolish talk did him no good. The people rightly thought that he was going out of his senses. Yet the undertaking saved him at that time from going completely insane. He hired nobody to help him in the work of quarrying stones ; but worked himself every evening with a crow-bar and sledge-hammer. Singlehanded he made slow progress but that did not concern him. In the liberation produced by the fierce exercise, his mind was relieved and he grew content. Indeed, there was method in his apparent madness.

" If Moclair gets me removed from the school," he thought, " I can live here. I'll get a few pounds a year pension and I can grow enough vegetables here, together with keeping a few goats. Then I can fish, too. I'll be far better off than I am now. I'll be more dangerous to the grinning devil, for I'll be free of him. I'll stay on this island and be a thorn in his side."

He would swing his hammer at a rock, grunt and say with glee :

" Oh boys ! won't I be a thorn in his side ? "

By November he had quarried enough stones and he was getting ready to build, when his wife put an end to the work for the time being. Since she had given up teaching, he had been able, more or less, to curtail her drinking, by refusing to give her any money and warning the publicans and potheen dealers against supplying her with whiskey. She had certainly managed to get drunk from time to time, by theft, or by selling her clothes. On one occasion she had even entered the church during Mass terribly drunk. She had thrown herself on the floor, screamed and uttered the most obscene accusations against her husband. Their relations during the whole of this time had been awful. All decent human intercourse between them had entirely ceased. Each hated the other bitterly. Each did everything possible to shorten the other's life ; Mrs. Skerrett out of pure hatred, Skerrett in the hope that he might be able to re-marry and beget children on his wife's death. Kate had grown into a most disgusting slut. She made no effort to keep herself clean. In fact she made herself look as unseemly as possible in order to madden her husband. With all the cunning of a perverted person, she made a science of baiting him, resorting to the most disgusting practices in order to annoy him. Being slow of wit, he was no match for her. He could only beat her, when driven beyond endurance. He did this very rarely, as he found out that she liked being beaten and used his violence to vilify him in public. The house got into a state of gross disorder, as Kate took pleasure in soiling whatever the servant made clean. She took especial delight in ruining Skerrett's books, burning some, mutilating others.

No doubt she was insane during the whole of this period, but although Skerrett would have only been too pleased to get her confined in a lunatic asylum, she was too cunning to give him an opportunity of having her certified. It was Finnigan that finally drove her completely insane.

One evening in late October, as Skerrett was coming home over the crags from his quarrying, he came across Finnigan in the corner of a quiet field. Finnigan was ill-treating a goat that he had found trespassing on his land. The people of Nara regarded trespass as a crime almost on a level with murder, owing to the scarcity of grass. They were prone to maim animals they found trespassing, instead of prosecuting the owners. Yet they were fanatically addicted to trespassing. Finnigan was notorious in this respect ; so he was also fond of maiming animals that sinned against him. Now he had the goat in a corner, in the shelter of a high fence. He was tying a cord on the brute's thigh, so tightly that it would immediately lose the use of the leg and eventually lose the leg altogether, unless the cord were removed.

This was a favourite method in use among the islanders for maiming animals.

Skerrett was wearing raw-hide shoes, so that he came upon Finnigan unawares. In any case the goat was shrieking frightfully. He caught Finnigan by the nape of the neck, threw him to the ground and then beat him until he was almost unconscious. He undid the cord and loosed the poor goat. Finnigan was afraid to prosecute for assault, as he himself might be more severely punished, under English law, for ill-treating an animal. The goat's thigh, and the cord which Skerrett was wise enough to put in his pocket, were there as evidence against him. He chose quite a subtle method of wreaking vengeance. He began to supply Mrs. Skerrett with whiskey free of charge. The wretched woman, after a fortnight's drunkenness, went completely insane one evening. She waited for her husband's return from school, standing behind the front door, with the tongs in her hand. When he entered, she struck at him as hard as she could. Although small and weak, she managed to hit him with considerable force above the temple. She knocked him out of his senses. Next she attacked the servant, who defended herself, however, and escaped without injury. Mrs. Skerrett then set fire to the house and fled. The fire was extinguished by the servant before it did much harm, although part of the staircase was destroyed.

An hour later, Mrs. Skerrett was found by two people who chanced to pass, as she was about to throw herself, stark naked, from a rock into the sea. It was a tragedy for Skerrett that the two people arrived in time to prevent the woman putting an end to her useless and disgusting life. Under the circumstances, she was taken by the police, certified insane and removed to the county asylum.

The blow on the temple which Skerrett had received did not seem very serious at first. Although it pained him considerably while it was healing, he did not take much notice of it. At the time, he was so relieved by his wife's confinement in the asylum, that the small matter of his injured skull appeared to be of no account. During the winter, however, he began to have severe headaches. He suffered from loss of sleep and his strength diminished greatly. When he resumed work on his house, he found that he got easily tired and perspiration came profusely after the slightest effort. His sight also failed. In the following January he had to go to an oculist at Galway and get fitted with a pair of spectacles. This mortified him greatly, as he was proud of his appearance. Indeed, people remarked that he was breaking up very rapidly. His hair was now quite grey and the bald patch on his skull was spreading. Loose folds of flesh appeared on his body. His thighs lost their firmness. He could no longer hide from himself the knowledge that he was getting old.

Childless, without a wife, tied to a lunatic, unable to remarry, a failure at his profession, scoffed at by the people, watched at every step by an implacable enemy who never let slip an opportunity to wound, he again became surly and brutal in his treatment of the school-children. At the beginning, this brutality had been salutary in that it helped to civilise young people, who could not be suborned by any other means. Now it was merely the vicious snapping of a wounded creature. The children answered by torturing him at every opportunity. They no longer feared his strength and they did their best to turn the school into a bear-garden. With the exception of Kearney and Ferris, none of the parents took any notice when he complained of the children's naughtiness. With all his old obstinacy, he persisted in his rude methods of trying to restore order and meeting with no success he threw all idea of following the prescribed curriculum to the winds, turning his school into a platform for Republican nationalism, anarchism and the cult of the Irish language.

Lo! Things were again almost what they had been at the beginning of his career on the island. He was almost in the position of his predecessor, that weak drunkard who ended his days in a lunatic asylum. There he was, in spite of his force, conquered by the island which he had tried to dominate. Like a malicious sea-monster, the island had at first toyed with him, giving him promise of greatness. Now it was crushing him into a weak, defeated thing, a subject for the most common man to mock.

CHAPTER XVIII

WHEN Pontius Pilate handed over Jesus Christ to the Jewish priests for crucifixion he was acting in accordance with fixed imperial procedure ; which is, to govern subject races through their priests. In the same way, the British government handed over the people of Nara to Father Moclair, if not for crucifixion, at least to do with them what he willed.

By this time, he was the undisputed ruler of the island, having silenced all opposition in his own flock and sucked the power of those outside his spiritual domain. With the fall of Athy there was nobody on the island of any consequence other than Moclair. The government officials made no pretence of trying to govern the people except through his mouth. And he had become a prosperous man. Indeed, it was remarkable how rich he had become in twenty years on that barren island, seeing how he arrived there in penury. The islanders prospered with him, but on a far lesser scale, excepting perhaps the tradesmen and boat-owners of Ardglas. But the arrogant severity with which he ruled more than balanced the material benefits of his rule. His avarice, especially, both made life unpleasant and set an evil example to these simple islanders, who were quick to imitate their pastor's character. Indeed, great though the beauty of a march towards civilisation may be, whether on a gigantic scale like that of the

Greeks and of the Elizabethan English, or on a small scale, like that of this handful of islanders, the beauty is always stained by the demons which the advance lets loose. It seems a people cannot progress without losing their innocence in the cunning necessary for ambitious commerce ; and that avarice brings in its train dissension, strife and manifold corruption. By now the islanders were constantly at war with one another, in their eagerness to procure the money which their priest so loved.

Indeed, he encouraged their internal strife ; for it was only by setting them at one another's throats that he kept their eyes from looking at his own increasing corpulence with jealousy. His subtlety was never more in evidence than in his management of their dissatisfaction at his failure to have Athy's land distributed. He pointed out to them that as far as the farm in the west was concerned, it was " the greed of their own flesh and blood " that prevented the land being distributed. Yet, the returned emigrant who had purchased the farm had paid the priest a good sum for his good-will in effecting the purchase. Even so, Moclair hinted privately that he had opposed the deal, but had been unable to prevent the purchase. The enraged peasants in the west of the island committed all manner of outrage against " their own flesh and blood," loathing him much more than they had loathed Athy, who after all had been " a gentleman." Father Moclair was able to earn a pound or two in bribes for protecting these outrageous peasants from the law. He also accepted further gifts from the returned emigrant in respect of sermons which advised the peasants that " to live and let live " was the correct interpretation of the Christian religion.

In regard to the farm at Ardcaol, he pursued the same policy of getting dog to eat dog. By right this land should have been divided among the landless fishermen of Ardcaol, especially as these fishermen were descendents of Cromwellian soldiers abandoned by General Ireton and therefore deserving better of the British Government than the islanders of un-English origin. The Government deserted them at Moclair's suggestion, just as Ireton had abandoned their ancestors. Father Moclair pointed out that these landless fishermen of Ardcaol, although descended from English Puritan warriors, were a worthless and immoral set of scoundrels, who would be too lazy to till the land if they got it. This was mainly true; although the priest's antagonism to them was largely caused by their failure to pay him any dues. They were even in the habit of contracting marriage by their own natural devices, without troubling to get the priest's sanction, since that cost money.

At the same time, all the tradesmen and owners of trawlers in Ardglas wanted to purchase the land, with the result that the whole village soon got into a state bordering on civil war. Mark you, the good priest made a considerable sum out of this general land hunger ; since each pretender to the farm greased his palm, in hope that Moclair would " put in a good word " for him with the Government officials. Moclair did nothing of the kind. He had his own plans for the disposal of the farm.

A little time previous to this, a retired district inspector of constabulary, named Davin, had come to live on the island. Moclair intended that this Mr. Davin should marry Miss Kitty Moclair, a spinster of forty, who had been keeping house for her brother for some time. It was also his ambition that Davin should buy the Ardcaol estate and make a good nest for Miss Kitty, who was becoming rather a problem. There was a fine lodge on the farm and the land was good; and it would be decorative to have a retired district inspector as a brother-in-law. In the meantime the grass on the farm was let to whoever was willing to purchase it. A man named Thomas Griffin was installed as bailiff.

This young man was very ambitious and greedy, quite of the priest's own kidney ; so that, at first, they got on very well together. Griffin was a brother of Barbara Kearney. He had been Skerrett's pet scholar as a boy. As he showed remarkable intelligence, Skerrett had done everything in his power to further the lad's advancement. Having fixed antipathy to commerce of all kinds, considering it socially immoral, he encouraged Griffin to learn a trade.

" Thomas ! " he said, " the most noble callings are those of the farmer and the fisherman. After that come the priests and doctors and school-masters, who teach the people to lead good and wise and healthy lives. Then come the artisans, the carpenters, the weavers, the tailors, the smiths, the masons. The man who buys and sells for profit is a robber. He is a parasite, like the louse that feeds on flesh and blood.

Many of the world's greatest men have been carpenters, but no great man ever sold things from behind a counter for profit."

At Skerrett's instigation, Griffin served his apprenticeship to a carpenter at Galway. On his return he proved to be an excellent worker at his craft. Skerrett felt very proud of the young man. Shortly, however, Griffin got married to a girl from Ardglas, the daughter of a former revolutionary called Fitzgerald. With his wife's dowry and his own savings, he opened a public house at Ardcaol, much to Skerrett's disgust. Thenceforth, Skerrett cut off all communication with him, calling him a scoundrel and a mean cringing ruffian. He, on his part, forgetful of all Skerrett had done for him, was as mocking as the next in his references to " the bladder," that being Skerrett's nickname, owing to his habit of " blowing " his opinions on every conceivable subject.

Now Griffin, becoming bailiff of the Ardcaol estate through Father Moclair's influence, suffered his ambition to develop into a mania, like the frog that tried to swell into an ox. He wanted the estate for himself. First of all, he went to Father Moclair and asked the priest to speak to the Board official on the matter.

" Are you mad ? " said Moclair, astonished at the young man's ambition. " Where would you get the money to buy it, even if it were for sale ? "

" I thought you might be able to guarantee me at the bank," said Griffin.

Father Moclair got furious.

" This is too much altogether," he said. " Get out of my house."

Griffin went away in a temper and became the priest's enemy. He wrote to the bishop, complaining of Moclair and suggesting that the bishop should do what Moclair had refused to do. The bishop sent the letter on to Father Moclair, asking him to answer the charges made against him. Moclair then denounced Griffin by name from the altar at Tobar Milis. Griffin countered by occupying Ardcaol Lodge and giving the grazing only to his friends and relatives. Moclair called in the Board officials. Griffin was ignominiously ejected from the lodge and from his position as bailiff. A brother of O'Rourke's was made bailiff instead. Deeply mortified by his defeat, Griffin now employed himself and his friends in writing letters to the bishop and to the public press, complaining about the priest's conduct of the parish. Some of these complaints were serious and well-founded ; particularly an instance where Moclair had flogged a young adulterer so severely that the man had to be taken to hospital. Finally the bishop, then an infirm man, was forced to send his administrator to enquire into the charges on the spot.

This happened in the Spring of 1902. The administrator, a choleric little man called James Mongan, came ostensibly to perform the ceremony of confirmation ; but he lost no time in collecting every jot of scandal about Moclair at Ardglas, although he was Moclair's guest at the parochial house. Mongan expected to be the next bishop and he was jealous of Moclair as a dangerous rival. Moclair had become

famous of late in the diocese. " Here is a chance,"
thought Mongan, " of putting him out of the running." The bishop, having a weak heart and a dis-
eased liver, through excessive whiskey drinking and
other unhealthy practices, was not expected to out-
live the year. There was no time to lose, therefore,
if Moclair were to be disgraced in time for the
election.

But Mongan was no match for Moclair. On the
evening before the confirmation, he primed Mongan
with good whiskey and then told his own story in the
most humble manner, taking a good deal of blame
for the unrest on the island, but apportioning the
chief blame to the machinations of his arch-enemy,
David Skerrett. He said, with tears in his eyes, that
he had raised this schoolmaster from the gutter and
yet the man was his most bitter enemy. For many
years he had been plotting, trying to drive Moclair
from the island. " I hoped to end my life here," said
Moclair, " among these people that I love so much
and for whom I have worked day and night. If I'm
removed now it would break my heart."

" Why haven't you complained about this man
Skerrett," said Mongan.

" I did complain," said Moclair. " But he has
the Board of Education on his side. The new school
inspector is a Freemason, I'm told. He always gives
Skerrett a good report, although the school is going
to rack and ruin. What can I do ? If I take any
action, people will be only too ready to say I'm
persecuting him unjustly."

He put his case so well and so humbly, and he

convinced Fr. Mongan so adroitly that he had no designs on the bishopric, and finally the whiskey was so good, that Mongan staggered into bed firmly resolved to vindicate Moclair's honour.

" I'll see to-morrow what can be done to this ruffian Skerrett," he muttered. " Protected by Freemasons is he ? I'll give him the boot."

CHAPTER XIX

Until quite recently, in remote parts of Ireland, the ceremony of Confirmation was not in general use among the faithful. In each hamlet there were quite a number of Christians, who evaded passing "under the bishop's hand," after proving in examination that they were conversant with the dogmas of our holy faith. The rapid spread of the English language in these remote parts towards the end of the last century, together with the establishment of national schools, coincided with an equal spread of Catholic dogma ; so that the number of unconfirmed Catholics grew less according as the knowledge of Protestant English increased. Until Republican Skerrett's appearance at Ballincarrig school, a great number of grown people remained unconfirmed in the centre of Nara, having no English with which to read their Catholic catechism. By his strenuous efforts the number of the unconfirmed had been very considerably reduced. It may sound ridiculous that Gaelic, supposedly a Catholic language, should be inimical to the spread of Catholic teaching, while English, eminently a language hostile to our holy faith, should have the opposite effect. Such, however, seems to be the truth. It is equally ridiculous that Skerrett, a noted enemy of the clergy and a nationalist, should foster both English and Catholicism. Indeed, it is astonishing how paradoxical life is.

Unfortunately for Skerrett, there still remained in his four hamlets a dozen or so of old men, who had managed to escape being confirmed. These were all between the ages of sixty and eighty. Then there was a score of unconfirmed persons between the ages of twenty and sixty. Now Father Moclair rounded up all these delinquents for confirmation, not because he was troubled by their ignorance of the Christian mysteries, but in order to get Skerrett into trouble. They were all men, as the unconfirmed women lied so cleverly that he was unable to prove they had not passed under the bishop's hand. Thirty-two men, all illiterate, of varying degrees of stupidity, attended the night classes, at which Skerrett coached the children for confirmation. It was impossible to teach the old people anything, both because they did not want to learn and because their minds were incapable of absorbing knowledge even if they wished to do so. Skerrett was exasperated by their stupidity, lost his temper continually and as a result was unable to teach either the children or the old people.

The priests, even though it was manifestly their own business and not Skerrett's, gave him no assistance with this work. Indeed, nothing in our national life is more odd than the manner in which our large army of priests relegate to the school-teachers the business of expounding Christian doctrines. Our large army of priests costs the country many millions a year for maintenance, yet the school-masters are forced to do their work. Of course, in this instance, it was farthest from Moclair's wish that Skerrett's charges should learn anything about God, or about the Catholic catechism. And Skerrett fully realised the plot that was being laid for him. On the morning of the confirmation ceremony, he put his candidates through a trial at the school. Without exception, they all failed lamentably. The old people, to a man, were unable to say who had made the world. Some of them thought there were six gods, others favoured the theory that there were only three. One old fellow modestly insisted that he was not so foolish as to enter into a dispute about theology with his betters.

" I'm in for trouble," said Skerrett to himself, as he marched over to the church that afternoon, at the head of his ignorant scholars.

However, he was undaunted. He had just finished building his house at Cappatagle. The roof was thatched, so that he was ready to retire at any moment on his fortified position, should he be dismissed from his school. In order to show in what contempt he held the administrator and Father Moclair, instead of wearing his best clothes, he wore island costume, which he had tailored himself. He had been wearing these clothes while working on his house and they were patched in many places and none too clean. His raw-hide shoes had long cowhair sticking out from the sides. In fact, he looked quite disreputable. It was a general holiday and large numbers of the parishioners had gathered to watch the ceremony. There was a roar of laughter when Skerrett appeared, dressed in this curious manner.

It was the beginning of May and the weather being very fine, the administrator had decided to hold the examination on the sloping lawn before the church. The curate, Father Timmins, had come in advance to arrange the candidates on this lawn, in ranks, under their respective teachers. At previous confirmations, Skerrett's pupils had always been placed in the front rank as a mark of honour to his position of leading teacher on the island. Now, however, they were placed in the extreme rear. Skerrett grew indignant when he came aware of this.

" What do you mean, Father Timmins," he said gruffly, " by putting my school last? It's always been placed first."

" The first shall be last and the last shall be first," said the curate impertinently.

" What do you mean ? " said Skerrett, still more gruffly.

" I'm following my instructions," said the curate.

" Whose instructions ? "

" That's my business, not yours."

" I'll soon show you whose business it is," cried Skerrett. " Move back there."

Whereupon he marched his school from the rear rank to the front, lining his candidates across the church door. The curate was too timid to offer any resistance, beyond saying that Father Moclair would have something to say about this refusal to obey his orders.

" Let him say what he pleases," growled Skerrett.

A chair had been brought from the sacristy and placed in front of the church door for the administrator's use, while he was conducting the examination. Skerrett boldly planted himself on this chair, crossed his legs and began to stroke his beard. The people watched him in horror, as it was considered indecent that he should incontinently use a convenience destined for the administrator's seat. Then the curate, going among the ranks to see that everything was in order, noticed that Skerrett's candidates had catechisms in their hands.

" Who gave you these catechisms ? " he cried. " You know you shouldn't have them here."

" Leave them alone, Father Timmins," cried Skerrett jumping from his chair. " They'll keep those catechisms."

He turned to his scholars and said :

" Open your catechisms under his nose and read out the answers. Don't be afraid of him. Those of you who can't read had better ask him to read the answers for you. Don't be ashamed if you don't know the answers. Knowing the catechism makes no man a better Christian. You will grow up in the love of God more by learning to till your land well, to be good fishermen and good heads of families than by learning these answers like parrots. Those of you that are on the road to the grave have already earned or lost the right to Heaven, so anything you learn now won't help you. In any case, the catechism of a good man can be written in a dozen words. Let him do his worst."

The curate, now a little terrified, went away to the rear and talked with the other teachers, who were gathered there in a group. Skerrett returned to his chair. A little boy in the front rank became so terrified by the scene between Skerrett and the curate that he went into hysterics and had to be taken aside by his mother. The other children also were on the verge of hysterics. In fact, a scandalous scene had developed. The people crowded near, some denouncing Skerrett on the plea that his conduct was blasphemous, others jeering at the old men in his rank. Indeed, they looked ludicrous among the children, some leaning on sticks, crippled by old age and rheumatism. One of them now saved the situation by his humour.

He was an old fellow called Paddy Grealish from Cappatagle, sixty-five years of age and yet in splendid health. Of great size and strength, he stood in the centre of the rank, leaning on his stick, with one leg thrust forward. A thick, black beard covered his cheeks and throat. His head kept moving from side to side, like a listening bird.

" Arrah ! Will ye hould yer whist ? " cried Grealish. " Sure what harm is it to give me this little book ? I don't know a word of what's written in it, but in my opinion it's all nonsense. Isn't it well known, Mr. Skerrett, that God knows everything ? Tell me that now and tell me no more."

" That's true," said Skerrett.

" Well ! Then," said Grealish, " as He knows everything, what's the need for this little breeches of a bishop's mate putting us under an examination ?

Doesn't God know well that we're ignorant peeple and that we know nothing, so what's the good of asking us ? "

The people roared with laughter at this sally. Delighted at the attention he was attracting, Grealish continued.

" Now this is the way it appears to me," he said. " And I out alone in the field, sowing or reaping, and a lark sings all of a sudden in the high sky, or maybe a rainbow comes to circle heaven with its pretty hoop, I take off my hat and I cross myself and I give thanks to the almighty and the all-merciful Father of men for the gladness in my heart. I know well what I am doing and why I'm doing it and I see with the eye of my mind the powerful king of Heaven, all glorified in a gold waistcoat and he drinking with his angels on a diamond stool. But ... Holy Jakers ! If this little breeches of a bishop's mate asks me who God is, I can't remember what I saw in the field, or what I'm telling ye now. That's the trouble with me. The same way, when I'm going to confession, I can't remember my sins and I have to stand a while at the gable of the confession house, cursing and blasting, so as I'll have something to tell. And then again, when I go into the confession room, I can't remember how many times I cursed at the gable."

Again there was a roar of laughter, until somebody called out :

" Here they come ! " All looked towards the east. A jaunting car, drawn by a smartly trotting black horse, came round the corner. On it were four

priests behind the driver. Other jaunting cars followed, carrying the principal citizens of Ardglas.
Then there was a procession of horsemen.

" Stand your ground now," said Skerrett to his
candidates. " Don't be afraid of him."

" Holy Jakers ! " said Grealish. " I'd give a great
deal now to be sitting on a rock, fishing, far away
from here."

All the people took off their hats as the priests
began to mount the steps leading to the lawn. The
curate ran down to meet them. He said something
to Father Moclair. The latter whispered to the
administrator. Mongan puffed out his cheeks and
said something in an angry tone. Then he continued to mount the steps. He was extremely short
and fat, with a face of a carrot colour, very thick
white eyebrows and bulging blue eyes. He was not
by any means sober, as Father Moclair had taken
good care to prime him well at lunch with
whiskey.

" Make way there," said Father Moclair.

The ranks parted to give the administrator passage.
He walked straight to the chair on which Skerrett
was sitting. Skerrett had taken off his hat but he
had not risen.

" Get off that chair ! " cried Father Moclair.

Skerrett did not move. Astonished by this effrontery, Moclair took a pace backwards and stared at
Skerrett, as if to make sure that the man was really
sitting there.

" Are you gone mad, Skerrett ? " he said. " You
come here dressed like a tramp and you remain

sitting after I tell you to stand up ? Are you out of your mind ? "

" I'm not out of my mind," said Skerrett, " and I dress as I please. I also sit where I please and when I please."

" Well, you won't sit on my chair at the door of my church," cried Moclair, raising his stick.

The administrator caught Moclair's upraised hand. " Don't touch him," he said. " I'll talk to him."

Whether gifted with a curious sense of humour, or simply because he was a little drunk, the administrator took a pace forward, bowed low to Skerrett and said :

" I bow before thee, Lord Straw."

The people looked in amazement at the administrator's obeisance to Skerrett, not knowing the meaning of the insult that had been offered to the schoolmaster. For the title of " Lord Straw " was one given, as a mark of contempt, by the Irish to those usurpers raised by the English in place of the dispossessed Irish noblemen. The administrator wished to infer that Skerrett was being set up by the Freemasons of the Board of Education as the Pagan Lord of Nara. Skerrett knew nothing of the Freemasons, whom Father Moclair had invented, but he understood the meaning of the phrase " Lord Straw." He stood up and said with great dignity :

" Most Reverend Sir, you have to deal here with no man of straw, but with a man who has never been unfaithful to his race."

" You have a short memory, you ruffian," said Moclair.

" Hush ! Father Harry," said the administrator.

" We'll deal with him later on. Let's get the examination over first. I'll deal with his lordship afterwards. Keep your seat, my lord. Come along, Father Harry. We'll begin at the bottom of the yard and work our way up to his lordship's level."

He marched to the rear rank, which he proceeded to examine first. Thus he put Skerrett's pupils last. Skerrett resumed his seat and began once more to stroke his beard, just as if nothing had happened. The people whispered among themselves in awe. They looked at Skerrett as if he were a monster. They had been prejudiced against him by his continual bad luck and the hostility of Father Moclair. Now they saw the whole force of the Church ranged against him. They would not be surprised if he had suddenly been turned into a goat before their eyes, or if the ground had opened up and swallowed him. The atmosphere became very tense. Skerrett's children, who had been nervous before, were now almost terrified out of their wits. The older candidates were equally nervous. In fact, one of them took fright and bolted from the rank. He was away over the church wall in a flash and then fled along the crags, before he could be stopped by any of the priests. However, no great attention was paid to his disappearance, owing to the tension.

The administrator examined the children in the rear very casually, asking them the simplest questions, hardly waiting for an answer, patting them on the cheeks, praising their teachers in a loud voice. When a child became confused, Mongan answered the question himself, making the child repeat the words. He passed from rank to rank in this way, until he came to Skerrett's candidates.

" Now for it," said Skerrett to himself.

Until this moment he had remained calm and self-controlled, sustained by the feeling of being a martyr ; a feeling which enables even weak men, if they believe firmly, to suffer the greatest trials with dignity. Now, however, the nearness of his enemy and the insolence of little Father Mongan disturbed his calm. His breast began to heave. His heart beat more quickly. His blood mounted to his head, filling him with rage. He wanted to rise up at once and shout his defiance.

" Look at them," cried the administrator, standing at the far end of Skerrett's rank. " Where did these old men come from ? "

" They haven't been confirmed yet ? " said Father Moclair.

" This is a nice state of affairs," said Father Mongan. " I was told the Ballincarrig school was the best one on the island, being in charge of Lord Straw, a famous Gaelic Leaguer, Republican and know-all. He is supposed to be a first class teacher, according to the reports of the inspectors sent down from Dublin. And what do I find ? Can you explain this, my lord, how these men haven't been con- firmed yet ? "

Skerrett got to his feet and approached the administrator.

" It's not my business," he said arrogantly. " I'm not the priest of this parish."

" Oho ! " said Mongan. " And will you explain

to me why these children have got their catechisms in their hands ? "

" So that they can read out any answers they don't know," said Skerrett still more arrogantly.

The administrator shook his fist in Skerrett's face and cried out : " You're turning this examination into ridicule. You're doing it on purpose. You're insulting your holy faith. If, indeed, you have one. Now my man, you've come to the end of your tether. I'll make an example of you."

" Do your damnedest," shouted Skerrett. " Too long have I put up with persecution from your cloth. I'm ready for you. Do your worst."

" Silence," cried Moclair. " Stand back, you impertinent ruffian."

Skerrett glared at Moclair, but he remained silent. He wanted to strike his enemy, but he suddenly felt strangely weak and even helpless to stiffen the muscles in his arm. A humiliating sense of impotence overwhelmed him and he wanted to cry aloud like a woman in despair, against all the shame and suffering of his life. He became aware of the futility of his gesture of revolt, of the unassailable power of his enemy. He shuddered as he heard the administrator question the first child.

" What is the Mass ? Come on. Speak up."

Mongan spoke sharply, in a loud voice, so that the child got afraid, stammered for a few moments and then burst into tears. Skerrett could keep silent no longer.

" You should be ashamed of yourself," he cried, " terrifying a child in that way."

"How dare you speak to me like that?" cried Mongan. "Madman, do you know who you're talking to?"

"A man as I am."

"Liar, I'm not a man as you are. I'm your superior."

"I have no superiors before God," said Skerrett.

"I won't stand any more of this," cried Mongan, dancing up to Skerrett in a towering rage and shaking his little fist. "I'll have you excommunicated by bell, book and candle-light."

Skerrett folded his arms on his bosom and stared at Mongan with lofty contempt. The little man didn't know what to do under the circumstances. Although normally shrewd, he had been confused by the whiskey he had drunk and by the unexpected independence of Skerrett. After staring at Skerrett for a few moments, as if he were going to scratch the man, he turned away again and took revenge indirectly by exposing the ignorance of the scholars and deploring in a loud voice their misfortune in being under the control of such an abominable teacher. When he came to Grealish, he cried:

"Where was this child found?"

"God save you, noble priest," said Grealish pleasantly. "Faith, I was found in bed by the midwife, same as any respectable son of a married mother."

A roar of laughter from the crowd greeted this remark.

"Well! What do you know about your religion?" said Mongan.

" Noble priest," said Grealish in a fawning voice, " sure it's not to you, that's maybe been to Rome and kissed the Pope's foot, I'd dare talk about religion. 'Faith, I believe everything I'm told by Father Harry, God bless him, and that's enough religion for me."

" How many Gods are there ? " said Mongan.

" By Gorries ! " said Grealish. " Your reverence must be making fun of me. Sure it's not from a poor old fool like myself you'd be likely to find out anything."

Here the people laughed once more and Grealish beamed genially.

" None of this impertinence," cried Mongan. " Or else you'll die a pagan. Didn't Lord Straw teach you anything ? "

" Who did ye say ? "

" Your teacher, Skerrett."

" Ah ! Now you've said it," cried Grealish eagerly. " There's a fine proper gentleman and no doubt about it. He's the poor man's friend."

He turned to Skerrett and added :

" Aye ! Brother, I'd say behind yer back what I say to yer face."

" Speak to me," shouted Mongan. " Did your teacher teach you anything about your religion ? Or did he just teach you to insult your priests ? "

" God between us and all harm ! " said Grealish, " sure he did nothing of the kind."

" Nothing of what kind ? "

" It was about my son that had the fever," said Grealish.

" You're a fool," cried Mongan. " You're a stark, raving lunatic. You're a disgrace to this parish. Who made the world ? "

" Well, now," said Grealish, " I couldn't say for certain. I was told last year by Paudeen Flynn, while he was putting a shoe on a horse I had, that it was how . . ."

" Silence ! " said Mongan.

He turned to Father Moclair.

" No effort at all has been made to teach this man. In fact, all these people are no more nor less than pagans."

" Like teacher like pupil," said Father Moclair.

" Pagans ! " sneered Skerrett. " According to you, a pagan is any man that dares to question the authority of men like yourself. It's you and priests like you that are the pagans."

" Now you're coming out in your true colours," said Moclair. " At last we know how we stand."

" You've long since shown your true colours, as far as I'm concerned," retorted Skerrett. " I'm a sinner like the next, but I'm more Christian than you, Father Harry. You've turned this island into a Hell. Now you're trying to destroy me, the only man that stands in your way. Strike tyrant. But I'll escape you. Strike, I say, but the last blow will be mine."

" The first is mine," cried Moclair raising his stick, " and the last will be mine too. Take that, you scoundrel."

The stick came down on Skerrett's head, near the spot where he had been struck by his wife. The stick was a mere cane and the blow, though sharp, had no force behind it ; yet, to everybody's surprise, Skerrett collapsed at once. He staggered back against the wall and then sank to his knees, like a pole-axed bull. Then he made an effort to straighten himself. He brushed his spectacles from his eyes, in order to sight his enemy properly. But the effort was useless. He fell in a heap to the ground ; Grealish ran forward to help him.

"Stand back, you ! " cried Moclair. "Stay in your place."

Mongan was a little worried by this unexpected brawl. He realised that it added nothing to his own dignity. Being a timid man, he felt nervous of the way Skerrett lay, as if dead.

"Is he badly hurt ? " he whispered to Moclair.

Moclair was unmoved. He was quite used to the exercise of force in maintaining control over his parishioners.

"He's all right," he said carelessly. "That will cure his insolence. Take him away, somebody."

John Kearney came over quietly from the crowd of onlookers and raised Skerrett in his arms.

"I'll give you a hand, John," said Grealish, leaving the rank once more.

"Stay where you are, Grealish," snapped Moclair.

"Ah ! Hell to my sowl ! " shouted Grealish, making pretence of hauling off his waistcoat and addressing the people instead of addressing the priest. "Sure I wouldn't let a sick dog lie on the ground without lifting a hand to help him. No man is going to stop me either."

" Are you threatening me ? " cried Moclair, raising his stick once more.

" Let there be no more disturbance," said Mongan nervously. " Control yourself, Father Harry. It's scandalous enough as it is."

" I'm finished with your catechism," cried Grealish, now giving vent to the anger that had been caused by the administrator's bullying questions. " My father and all my ancestors were born on this island and they're buried here too, and they were all honest men, so, by Gorries ! I'll take impudence from no foreigner, bishop or tinker, or beggar from the County Mayo. Up Skerrett ! "

He uttered a wild yell and then ran forward to help Kearney, who was carrying Skerrett over to the wall. Other men also crowded round Skerrett. They took him into a house near the church and laid him on a settle in the kitchen. For the moment, popular sympathy had swung over to his side, owing to the brutal manner in which Moclair had struck him down.

" It's a shame," they said, " to strike a lonely man like that."

After drinking some water, Skerrett revived and asked what had happened. He had been almost unconscious. He was still very groggy, like a boxer who has been knocked out severely. When they told him what had happened, he shuddered, drew his palms down his cheeks and said in a tone of bitter sadness :

" God pity me ! My strength is gone. I'm a toerag and a show-board before all comers. This is the end of me."

"Have courage, brother," said Kearney.

"Where are my spectacles?"

A man handed him his spectacles. He put them on slowly and then peered around him at the people. All the old arrogance and brutality had left his countenance. He looked helpless and in the power of some vague terror that made his dim eyes furtive. And then, he seemed to remember something that roused him, for he suddenly jumped to his feet, straightened himself and cried:

"A blow for a blow."

"Where are you going, brother?" said Kearney.

"I'm going to face him," cried Skerrett.

"God between us and harm," shouted the woman of the house. "Don't let him raise his hand to a priest."

"Let me go," cried Skerrett, as they took hold of him.

And then again he went limp and had to be laid back on the settle.

"You had best take a little rest," said Kearney, "and then make the road home with me."

"Yes," said Skerrett. "I'll go home. I'm not well. Give me water."

After drinking some more water, he was able to rise again and leave the house. Kearney tried to assist him, by taking his arm, but Skerrett refused assistance. Even though he felt dizzy and weak, he did not wish to be seen by his enemy, leaning on another's strength. The enemy, however, had by now entered the church and there was nobody in the yard other than a small knot of people who stood whispering near the door of the sacristy. They were Griffin and his friends, who were waiting to present a petition to the administrator. Skerrett's followers now deserted him to join this group. Grealish went also, although he took good care to stay at a safe distance from the church door, lest one of the priests might come out suddenly, catch him and force him to say who had made the world.

" You had better stay here, John," said Skerrett, when he and Kearney reached the road. " Moclair'll only get his knife in you if you come too far with me."

." I don't care about that," said Kearney gently. " I'll see you as far as your house."

" I'll be able to make my own road, John," said Skerrett. " You go back and see what happens. Come over to the house afterwards and tell me what they say."

Kearney agreed to do this and Skerrett strode out boldly, swinging his arms from the shoulders, with his head thrown back. He maintained this quick pace by an effort of will, until he was out of sight. Then he halted and leaned against the fence. He felt very faint. Then again he went on, walking on the grass by the fence, putting out a hand now and again against the fence to steady himself. There was a stabbing pain in his temple and his stomach convulsed as if he were about to vomit. Yet he did not feel uneasy about his condition. Such men, of little imagination, are gifted with a courage which enables them to concentrate all their force on combating a present danger, without wasting any on speculation about the future. For this reason, they can take an extraordinary amount of punishment without thought of surrender. Indeed, instead of being worried about his condition, Skerrett felt rather pleased that the battle with Moclair had begun in earnest.

" I have driven him into the open at last," he thought. " Let him drive me from my school now if he wants to. I'll not go, though, before I'm made to go. And then I'll go to Cappatagle. I'll go to Cappatagle and fight him from the rocks. Huh ! "

Yet, when he reached his own house and sank into his easy chair in the sitting-room, a horrible melancholy took hold of him. There was nobody to receive him, as the servant had gone to the well to beetle some clothes. There was dead silence ; the silence of an empty house which, to a man in pain and needing comfort, terrifies the mind with presages of death. Now he thought bitterly of all the years he had spent here, the joy of those years when his little son was running about and later the misery that followed his son's death. Then, indeed, it seemed to him that his life was under a curse, as he remembered how everything had gone wrong with him, how he had been stripped, little by little, until he was now alone and helpless, a subject for derision and contempt.

His hatred of Moclair roused him at last from this feeling of depression. The blood rushed to his head. He got to his feet, clenched his fists and cried aloud :
" I'll kill him ! "

The words re-echoed strangely through the empty

house, but they left no determination in his mind. On the contrary, he shuddered at the thought of what he had said. His hands fell to his sides, he bowed his head and began to pray God for help. Then he sat down and fell asleep.

When he awoke, Kearney, Harkin the fish buyer and the servant were in the room.

" Are you feeling bad ? " said Harkin. " That was a bad blow you must have got. It was a cowardly thing to hit a man undefended. You should take the law of him."

Skerrett felt refreshed after his sleep. His arrogance had returned. So he looked at Harkin and said gruffly :

" Did you come here to persuade me to go to law with him ? "

" Bloody woes ! " said Harkin. " Don't turn on a man that came to visit you in a civil way."

" I know well why you came," said Skerrett. " I only want men friendly with me for the sake of justice. You have something else at the back of your mind. You are against Moclair because your brother didn't get a trawler this year as he expected."

" Have it your own way," said Harkin. " But if I were you, I wouldn't be uncivil to a man who wants to be a friend. You may need all your friends shortly."

" I have all the friends I want," cried Skerrett. " Leave my house."

Harkin went out muttering.

" You had no right to send him away like that," said Kearney gently. " I think, by the looks of things, there is trouble coming and it's best for you to have as many of the people on your side as you can."

" What did Father Mongan say from the altar ? " said Skerrett.

" I think it was about my brother-in-law he said most," said Kearney. " He said it was no good people writing to the bishop with complaints and that Father Moclair was running the parish well and doing great good to the people. So the people, he said, should obey Father Harry, and not be fighting one another, nor trying to grab land that didn't belong to them."

" What else did he say ? "

" Well ! " said Kearney. " He said there was a man on the island sold to the Free Masons and that the people should beware of him, until such time as he could be removed. Everybody said it was you he was driving at."

" It was," said Skerrett. " And what did the people think of that ? "

" They are in two minds," said Kearney. " You won't mind my talking to you as man to man."

" Go ahead."

" Well ! They think you had no right to say what you said to Father Mongan. But then again, they say it was a cowardly thing for Father Moclair to hit you with a stick. They said that if you went to law with him, you'd have plenty witnesses on your side."

" I doubt it," said Skerrett. " Not many would give evidence for me."

" Well, I'll give evidence for you," said Kearney.

" Thanks, John," said Skerrett, " but I'm not

going to law. I despise a man that would go into a court in order to get satisfaction for a blow. I'm in the right and I'll fight my own battle without any help."

"All the same," said Kearney, " 'tis best to protect yourself as well as you can. They'll try to drive you out of your school."

Skerrett struck his chest and cried :

"Let them do it. But they can't drive God out of here. They can't drive the courage out of my heart either. Oh, God ! If I were only as strong as I was, I'd defy the whole tribe of them and beat them to their knees, as I was beaten this day, to my eternal shame."

He put his hand to his temple and said :

"This awful pain keeps stabbing me."

"Hadn't I better go for the doctor ? "

"No. I'll not have him in the house. I'll have neither priest nor doctor. I never had a doctor in my life. I always was my own doctor. When my time comes I'm ready to die. I'll die as I have lived, without any man's help. Let it be written on my tombstone, that here lies a man who never of his own free will bowed his knee to another. I'd rather die in my prime than live a slave. And in any case, I have no great wish to go on living like this, a half cripple, too blind to see the rising sun."

CHAPTER XX

THE ADMINISTRATOR's visit, instead of settling
the trouble in Nara, merely accentuated it. He reported to the bishop that Skerrett was the cause of
all the trouble and that the rebellious school-teacher
was a menace to the faith of the islanders. Whereupon the bishop had a strong letter sent to the Board
of Education, demanding Skerrett's removal. He
sent another letter to the people of Nara warning
them against entering into secret association for the
purpose of procuring land that did not belong to
them. This letter, being read by Father Moclair
from the altar at Tobar Milis, was regarded by
Griffin and his friends as a personal indictment.
They went so far as to say that the bishop had sent
no letter whatsoever, or if he had sent a letter that
Moclair had corrupted it for his own benefit. Their
hostility to Moclair now became really dangerous,
as they realised his cunning prevented them getting
redress for their supposed grievances by legal means
and that their only hope for revenge lay in adopting
desperate measures. Feeling ran so high in Ardglas
between the rival factions, that the principals on
either side went about armed with sticks.

Skerrett had a footing in neither of these camps,
for he inveighed against both parties, calling them a
gang of ruffians who were quarrelling over their loot.
He refused to canvass in any direction for support,

and at this moment, when he stood most in need of public sympathy, he did his best to alienate even his few remaining friends by his conduct. On the morning after his scene with the administrator, he arrived at his school a little earlier than usual, even though he was feeling so ill that a less obstinate man would have stayed in bed and sent for a doctor. Of late there had been a certain section of his pupils who played truant in the morning, failing to arrive at school until close on noon. He birched them severely, but without any success, as they had ceased to be afraid of him, both owing to his loss of strength and the constant ridicule of their elders. This morning he decided to make an example of these scholars ; but it turned out that nobody at all appeared at school. The rumour had got about that Skerrett was in bed sick and that there would be no school that day, so all the scholars gathered together in a field among the crags and amused themselves at hand-ball. He waited in his empty school-room until nearly eleven o'clock, marching up and down with his cane in his hand, getting more and more distraught. Then he set forth to look for them. Standing on the top of a fence, he heard loud cries from the playing field and hurried in that direction ; but before he came near his approach was noticed by scouts whom the scholars had set to watch. There was a loud warning whistle and the boys scampered away over the crags, shrieking defiance. He followed them in this manner from place to place until he was utterly exhausted and he had to return to his school. During the afternoon he went around from house to house threatening the parents of the defaulting children, but he met with civility from very few. Even people who had benefited by his past kindness closed their doors in his face, or else told him impudently to go and complain to the parish priest. In the evening he went home feeling very disheartened.

Next morning, however, he determined to punish his scholars with such severity that they would never again dare play such a trick on him. Therefore, according as they arrived, he set upon them all with great cruelty and without any discrimination, lashing them from head to foot until he was exhausted. One of the children, a rather delicate boy from Tobar Milis, received such a severe stroke on the head, that he fell ill on arriving home that evening. His mother came over to the school on the following day, stood out in the road and cursed Skerrett at the top of her voice. She barged at him with such violence that a crowd gathered and Skerrett was forced to come out and argue with her. Even then, if he had been tactful or apologetic, he might have saved the situation. Instead he adopted an arrogant attitude, thus infuriating the poor woman and the other people present. It made matters worse for Skerrett that the lad in question was an intelligent and industrious scholar, who had merely been forced to play truant by the others. Ferris, who happened to be in the crowd, came over to Skerrett and advised him that he was acting in a foolish fashion.

"You mind your own business, Ferris," said Skerrett.

"You say that to me," cried Ferris with indignation. "You turn on me that has always stood by you."

"I don't want any man to stand by me," cried Skerrett. "I can look after myself."

With that he marched back into his school. That evening all the windows of the school on the side facing the road were broken by stones. Next day not a single child from Tobar Milis came to Ballincarrig. With Moclair's permission the parents decided to send them to Ardglas. Skerrett reported the outrage done to the windows, but the police could secure no information that might lead to the detection of the culprits.

"Ha !" said the people. "He's going to the police now. He's turning into an informer."

They began to shout insulting remarks as they passed his house in the evenings. When he rushed out to retaliate by throwing stones after them, the people merely jeered at him. They took advantage of his failing sight by tying a rope across a path along the crags where he was in the habit of taking a stroll. Then they lay in wait for him. When he fell over the obstacle they whistled in derision. At the end of a month, more than half the scholars had stayed away and a number of those who remained only came to annoy him. His whole time in school was practically occupied in useless chastisement. The desks were again mutilated as they had been in Scanlon's time. The whole school got into a filthy condition. The scholars grew so wild that their behaviour became a scandal on the island. On leaving school every evening they engaged in battles with stones, one village challenging another. Very often some of them received serious injuries in these battles. At length, in the middle of June, a deputation called on Father Moclair, asking for Skerrett's removal.

" He's worse than his wife was," they said. " He has turned the children into savages. We are in danger of our lives if he's allowed to go on like this any longer."

Father Moclair sent an urgent message to Dublin and the school authorities promised to send down an inspector immediately. Being notified of the date of the inspector's arrival, Father Moclair went to Galway to meet him. This time, he wished to make sure that the inspector would be properly prejudiced against Skerrett. And then, on the night before Moclair's return with the inspector, an extraordinary thing happened.

CHAPTER XXI

A T MIDNIGHT on the twentieth of June, a coast-guard named Jonathan Smallbotham, while marching back and forth on duty in the station yard at Ardglas, heard a strange sound which brought him to a halt. He had drunk several pints of Guinness's porter during the evening, so that his mind had been, previous to this noise, confused to the point of somnolence. In fact, he had been dreaming of his home in Poole, Dorsetshire, and cursing the evil fate that had marooned him on this barren island, among a community which he found alien to his tastes.

For this reason he took no particular notice of the sound at first, being inclined to think it was a faint peal of thunder, as there had been some earlier in the day ; but then, as he got fully awake, his curiosity was aroused, for he saw that it could not possibly be thunder, as the moon rode full in a clear and blue sky. In fact, he grew slightly afraid of an attack, a feeling only natural in those days for an armed servant of the British Crown, lodged among a subject people whose allegiance was very doubtful. Of late, the attitude of the people of Nara towards the coast-guards and police had been almost menacing.

He looked over the station wall towards the point whence the sound had come. About sixty yards away, in the middle of a considerable garden, stood Moclair's residence. Although it was on a slightly

235

lower level than the station and was therefore partly in shadow, he could see it distinctly in the clear light. Everything seemed at peace there. He was about to turn away again, when he heard a slight sound to the right of the house. Glancing in that direction, he saw a dark figure disappearing over a stone wall. The fugitive had dislodged a small stone in his crossing. Smallbotham shrugged his shoulders.

" Some other plot that blooming priest is hatching," he said to himself.

His general dislike of the islanders, as " a lot of bloody Irish," was centred particularly on Father Moclair ; for Smallbotham was a bigoted Methodist and he detested any priest wearing the uniform of His Holiness the Pope.

" Clever bloke, that Moclair," he said, as he stretched his arms and yawned. "He's made a damn good thing out of this island, though it beats me how he's done it. It does straight."

He looked with jealous indignation at Moclair's fine house and remembered that there had been only a miserable cottage there six years ago, when he himself came to the island. He thought it was grossly unjust, that he, a member of an Imperial race, should be forced to lead a paltry existence, while this priest, almost on a par with an Indian or a Kaffir, should amass wealth and dignity.

" It's damn low," he thought, " the way he goes scrounging off the poor devils here. They're half-starved and he has all the best. He has a regular little demesne here, flowers, walks and everything, just like a proper gent. God strike me stiff, but these blokes get away with it all right. It ain't right, the way they're let boss the show. They're all a gang of rebels at heart. That's the way I look at it."

The back door of Moclair's house now opened and a woman appeared. He saw her distinctly in the moonlight. She wore a long coat over her night-dress. She looked about her nervously and then hurried to the corner, stepping carefully over the gravel in her bare feet. She looked around the corner and then ran quickly back into the house, as if overcome by a sudden fear. She closed the door after her with a bang.

Smallbotham wondered what had happened. For a moment, he put a lewd construction on the affair, as he remembered that Father Moclair was away and that Miss Kitty was alone in the house with the servant ; but he dismissed this explanation, on recalling how unapproachable he himself had found the island women. And in any case, Miss Moclair was too plain to tempt even the most lust-ridden man. Five minutes later, when his comrade James Pritchard came to relieve him, he reported the whole incident. Pritchard, being quite sober, was much more disturbed by the sound.

" It might have been a burglary," he said.

" Nonsense," said Smallbotham. " There ain't been no burglary on this island since I came here six years ago."

" True enough," said Pritchard. " There's nothing to burgle but the rocks. What did it sound like ? "

" It might have been a pot flung against a door. It sounded like thunder at first."

" What ? Thunder ? Go on. Was it that loud ? We best go over and see."

" No," said Smallbotham. " Leave 'em alone. No use getting mixed up with these blooming islanders. It's none of our business. Any day I expect to see them start murdering one another."

" All the same," said Pritchard, " you might run across to the police barracks and tell the sergeant."

" No fear," said Smallbotham. " I'll have nothing to do with them. You can take it from me, the less you have to do with these people the better. I knew a bloke once on another island off the County Mayo and he got chummy with the local people, drank with them and so on. A proper, decent sort he was too. Bloke called Woods from Plymouth. What did they do ? I ask you. They stole his bleeding rifle. Then he gets brought up and court-martialled, there being some trouble on at the time with these here rebels, they were sore about his losing the rifle ; so they packs him off to another bloody island. An awful place it was. He bore no ill-feeling. He was that sort of a chap. Happens there's a fever on this other island short time after that and he goes into a house where they were all sick, nurses the blooming lot until they got better. Then he caught the fever himself. I'm telling you straight that he lay there with the fever until he died and not one of these bastards would come near him. Year or two after that just before I came here, I was over on that island and there I saw his grave. A bleeding shame it was. There was only an old wooden cross put up but even that had fallen down. Not a soul came near it to look after it. There was the grave, right on the edge of the sea, with the sand creeping up towards it, and this old wooden cross fallen down. They'd buried him outside their regular graveyard as he wasn't a Papist. I damn near wept looking at it. There was poor old Timber Woods, gave his life for these bloody people, and they wouldn't put his wooden cross straight. I said to myself ' Look here, Jonathan, my boy, let this be a warning to you.' And so it has been and damn well right. I have nothing to do with them since. I'm here and I got to stay here until I'm moved. But my motto is, while I am here, they can murder one another for all I care and I shan't raise a hand."

" You're probably right," said Pritchard. " It's my idea that the sooner we English get out of this country the better. Hand the lousy country over to the priests. Then the bloody Irish'll soon be sorry we left."

" You're right there," said Smallbotham. " A dog couldn't piss against a post without their permission if these priests had as much power as they're looking for. And they soon will have it, way things are going. Look at that poor fellow, Skerrett, over there. About the only man on the island worthy of being a British subject. Might even be taken for an Englishman in many ways, except for his silly bloody notions. Look how they treat him. Listen to me, Jim. The only way to treat these people is to kick them and keep on kicking them."

The two coastguards forgot all about the strange sound, in the pleasure they derived from grousing about the vices of the islanders.

CHAPTER XXII

ABOUT eight o'clock next morning, Molly Kelly, Father Moclair's servant, rushed into the hall of Togher's Hotel, where Father Timmins had lodgings.

"For the love of God, Father Timmins," she cried, "come at once. The house is destroyed by a bomb."

Father Timmins ran out of the dining-room where he had been having breakfast.

"What did you say?" he gasped.

"A bomb," she said. "It was flung through the window."

All the occupants of the house, including a government official, the agent of an English kelp-buying firm, a cattle dealer and a foreign gentleman studying ancient monuments on the island, crowded around the distraught servant.

"A bomb was flung through the window," she cried. "The house is in tatters, but there's nobody killed or wounded. It was the grace of God saved me and Miss Kitty. We haven't slept a wink all night. We were afraid to come out, for fear the murderers might be waiting for us with a gun. I just ran over now, but I must hurry, as Miss Kitty is shivering with fright."

In a few minutes the village of Ardglas was in an uproar. All those who were already out of bed ran at once to the parochial house. People were shouting

241

on all sides to those afar off, crossing themselves, rushing to and fro as if in panic, begging God to strike down those who had committed this dreadful outrage. Men ran into the street out of their beds, clad only in their shirts. Curiously enough, the police were the last to hear of the outrage, although the barrack was no more than two hundred yards from the parochial house. When at last the sergeant and two of his constables arrived on the scene, the house was surrounded by a great crowd of shouting people, who abused the police for their incompetence.

" Blood and turkeys ! " said O'Rourke to the sergeant. " It's little ye have to do in that barracks, but carve yer names on the flagstones of the yard, when ye are not annoying honest people and yet ye can't keep the priest's house from being bombed into small pieces."

The police sergeant, a man called Devitt, glared in silence at O'Rourke, who had once spat in front of him. Then he shouted :

" Clear the way there ! "

He strode up to the house, delighted that such a terrible thing had happened. He was a man of splendid physique and although an arrant coward, gave the impression by his carriage that he was an unconquerable giant. He seemed to carry something huge and heavy under the breast of his tunic, which looked like a bird's stuffed gullet. He swung his great arms like clubs. He brought his heels to the ground furiously as from a great height, drawn by a magnet. When he entered the house he was led by the curate into the drawing-room on the left of the hall.

" Look at that, sergeant," cried the curate. " The place is a wreck."

" Stand back there now," said the sergeant, " and touch nothing."

" Nothing has been touched," said the curate, dropping a piece of burnt fuse to the ground.

The sergeant looked suspiciously at the curate and then proceeded to examine the room. While he did so, Miss Moclair, in a hysterical voice, went on describing the events of the night before. There was no great damage done to the room. All the glass had been blown from both windows. The mortar had fallen to the floor from part of the ceiling. There was a crack in the wall over the fireplace. The furniture had been upset and there was a quantity of small debris lying about, including two torn window curtains, a portion of an iron pot, some sacking cloth, a piece of yellow twine and the burnt fuse, which the curate had dropped. The sergeant took all these latter articles " into custody," as he said himself. Then he took a statement from Miss Moclair and from everybody present.

When he had finished he said gravely to the curate:

" Father Timmins, I'm inclined to come to the conclusion that an infernal machine was thrown through one of these windows, with the intention of causing grievous damage to the house or the occupants or both."

" Sure every damn fool knows that," said O'Rourke. " Don't stand there. Go and find who did it. Every one knows who did it. Go and arrest the scoundrel."

" Don't you interfere with me in the execution of my duties, Coleman O'Rourke," said the sergeant. " Otherwise, you might get into trouble. This is a very serious business."

Whereupon he began to measure the room and afterwards made an examination of the grounds, picking up pieces of glass and measuring them also. The people, however, were indignant with his methods and demanded in loud voices that he should go at once and arrest the culprit.

" It's Tommy Griffin did it and no one else," they cried on all sides.

By ten o'clock practically the whole population of the village had gathered outside the parochial house, where the priest's chief supporters, led by O'Rourke, held a public meeting of protest. O'Rourke finished his speech by saying :

" If the police don't want to arrest the scoundrel let's go and do it ourselves."

" Hurrah ! " cried the crowd. " Bravo, Coleman ! Let's pull him out of his house and tear him to pieces."

Whereupon the crowd, armed with sticks and stones, set out in search of Griffin. Information was received that he had been seen a little while previously entering the house of his brother-in-law, Fitzgerald.

" Fitzgerald is in it, too," cried O'Rourke. " We'll take the whole crew."

" We'll take them all," cried the people.

Fitzgerald's house was on the sea-front, a building of two storeys, bound on one side by a large shed. Griffin and his brother-in-law were in this shed, when the people came along shouting and waving their sticks. The two men closed the door of the shed on seeing the people's agitation and hearing their cries. O'Rourke halted before the door and shouted :

" Come on out, Griffin, you murderer. You come out here and answer the charge."

" I'll see you in hell first," came Griffin's voice from within.

" All right then," said O'Rourke. " Break down the door, men."

Suddenly Fitzgerald stuck the barrel of a shot-gun out through the little window of the shed and shouted :

" If any man comes near this door I'll fire ! "

The crowd yelled.

" Don't be afraid of his gun," said O'Rourke. " He won't fire. He's afraid to fire."

" I've fired before," said Fitzgerald, " and I'll fire again."

" Pelt him with stones," said O'Rourke.

Then somebody cried :

" Here come the peelers ! "

" Stand fast," said O'Rourke. " Face the peelers."

The crowd hung back, however, as the police came up at a run, accompanied by Father Timmins.

" Move on now," said the sergeant. " What's all this about ? "

" There are the criminals, barricaded in that

shed," said O'Rourke. " Go on and arrest them. They're armed and they're going to shoot down the people."

Fitzgerald withdrew his gun and called out to the sergeant :

" I only pointed the gun in self-defence, when they threatened me."

The sergeant went over to the shed and ordered the door to be opened.

" Show me your warrant," said Fitzgerald. " I'm in my own house. You can't come in here without a warrant."

" Hear that now," cried O'Rourke. " Doesn't that prove it to you, sergeant ? They're doing away with the evidence of their guilt in there in that shed."

" Be quiet now," said the sergeant. " Come on ! Be off home all of you, or there's going to be trouble. I'll attend to this myself."

Father Timmins now stood on a low wall and addressed the crowd, begging them to keep the peace until Father Moclair arrived on the steamer.

" All right, father," said O'Rourke. " We'll be quiet, but devil a man we'll let escape out of that shed until they are arrested. Sure the sergeant there has all the evidence he wants. Why doesn't he go and get a warrant ? "

" Let him go and get a warrant ! " shouted the people.

Finally the sergeant placed two policemen on guard outside the shed, to prevent any violence on the part of the crowd. Then he went to the magistrate for a search warrant. The crowd shouted abusive epithets at the two men in the shed. The women were most fierce in their abuse. After some time Griffin's wife, accompanied by her two young daughters, arrived from Ardcaol. She began to barge the other women and called on her relatives to come and defend her husband and father. A riot seemed imminent and the police drew their batons. Then again Father Timmins mounted the wall and asked for peace.

" It would be fitter for us," he said, " to make up a collection for Father Harry than to be making a disgrace of ourselves in this way. Let us take up a collection and hand it to him as he steps off the boat and say it's the least we could do to make amends for the damage done to his house. This mark of our love for him will help to heal his break-ing heart. We can show him in this way that the people of Nara condemn with all their souls the terrible outrage that has been committed.

" Bravo ! " cried O'Rourke. " No sooner said than done. Lads, gather round here."

A committee was formed at once for making the collection. Followed by the greater part of the crowd, O'Rourke and the other members of the committee went from house to house, receiving money everywhere, as all were anxious to divert the least taint of suspicion and disloyalty by a liberal contribution. They went down to the pier and collected from those working at the fish curing station, as well as from the crews of the trawlers, which had returned from the night's fishing. In all, the sum of thirty pounds was collected, about twice as much as the amount of damage done. Moclair had made money even by the bombing of his house.

In the meantime, the sergeant had arrived with his warrant and on the shed being opened to him by the beleaguered couple, he made very important discoveries. He found sacking cloth, twine and fuse, similar to those found in the priest's drawing-room, together with a small barrel of powder. Although Griffin was able to explain that all these were used for blasting purposes, the sergeant placed him under arrest, to the delight of the people. He was brought to the barracks and locked in a cell.

When the steamer arrived at one o'clock in the afternoon, the pier was crowded and as Father Moclair stepped ashore, a deputation of the most important people in the village read him an address which the curate had drawn up. Indeed, everything was done in such an efficient manner by the curate that Moclair's enemies afterwards said the whole business had been concocted by Moclair himself. In any case, he appeared to be overwhelmed with grief as he stepped ashore. Tears rolled down his cheeks when O'Rourke handed him the money and he leaned on the curate's arm as he walked away. He said nothing, but his silence impressed the people far more than the most eloquent speech would have done. At the moment the people would have died for him to a man.

All along the pier and up the road to the town, men took off their hats and asked for his blessing.

Some women even knelt in the road and asked God to protect him in future. He passed along like a Pope, with his hand raised, giving blessing. However, when he reached his house and he was alone with the curate, O'Rourke and his closest friends, his tears gave place to a violent outburst of anger. He marched up and down the drawing-room, looking at the damage that had been done, crying angrily :

" This is my reward for nursing that snake in my bosom. To think that a man could be found on this island, among a people I have given my whole life to make happy and prosperous, to try and blow up my house and murder my sister, because he couldn't get this farm. Was it mine to give ? I have helped him in every way I could and then he turns on me, just like that damned Skerrett whom I saved from the work-house and put in Ballincarrig school. Ha ! There's the man that's at the back of it all. Griffin is only a cur that has learned well from his teacher. But Skerrett is at the back of it. The police'll deal with Griffin. My friends, we must find another way of dealing with Skerrett. I'm going to root them all out, the whole pack of them. Stand by me and we'll put the finishing touch to the whole crew of them. Let not a man escape our vengeance. We'll make them curse the day they were born. We'll hound them out of this island like the dogs that they are. I'll have no mercy. By God ! I'm roused at last and woe to him that crosses my path from now on. Here in this room let us band ourselves together in solemn league, to punish in every way we can anybody that lifts a hand or a voice to help Griffin or Skerrett, or their relatives or their friends."

" I swear to do whatever you say, Father Harry," said O'Rourke, raising his hand.

The others swore likewise.

CHAPTER XXIII

AFTER a hurried lunch, the inspector drove over to Skerrett's school on a jaunting car. He was quite a different type of man from the inspector who had been influenced in Skerrett's favour by Dr. Melia some years previously. He was named Coonan, a middle-aged and pious fellow of the true faith. He had been deeply impressed by Father Moclair on the journey from Galway. Moclair had received news of the outrage by telegram before leaving port and he was therefore able to play the rôle of a persecuted man with great success. Mr. Coonan, only too ready in any case to take a priest's part against that of a man who was suspected of republican and pagan tendencies, felt horrified by the outrage, which, Moclair insinuated, was entirely due to Skerrett's evil influence. Before the boat touched the pier at Ardglas, the inspector had practically decided to condemn Skerrett in his report, as being unfit to conduct any school in a Catholic parish.

On the way to Ballincarrig he had a talk with the driver, a man called Reilly, who always acted as Moclair's jarvey and was an enthusiastic admirer of the clergy, as he relied on them principally of late for his livelihood.

"Oh, indeed," said Reilly, "this man Skerrett is up to every sort of devilment. Some say he's out

of his mind, but I say he's sold to the devil. Arrah !
Sure, he teaches the children nothing in that school.
They are half wild for want of control and yet he
beats the heart out of them. I'd rather send my son
to a bird's nest than to a school like that."

" Is that a fact ? " said Mr. Coonan.

When he saw the broken windows of the school
and the disorder of the school yard, he was still
more shocked. Pieces of mortar had been torn from
the walls. The door had lost half its paint. The
gate would not shut properly. Several slates were
broken on the roof. Nettles grew along the bottom
of the walls. Three scholars, looking very wild, had
been playing in the yard when he approached.
Recognising him as an inspector by his black bag,
they fled over the crags when his jaunting car
halted.

" This seems to be a terrible state of affairs," said
Mr. Coonan to himself.

He went almost on tip-toe to the door, put his
head into the little hall-way and listened. To his
astonishment he heard Skerrett reading something
which he could not understand but which he guessed
to be Irish. Although an ardent Catholic and mildly
nationalist, Coonan severely disapproved of the
Irish language and of the republicanism with which
it was associated. In any case, its teaching was no
part of Skerrett's business in school ; so that Coonan
was horrified to find the man wasting the government's time.

" It's outrageous," he said to himself.

Then he coughed and strode quickly into

the school. Skerrett wheeled around and faced him.

" I'm Mr. Coonan, an inspector. I've come to examine you."

Skerrett settled his glasses more comfortably on the bridge of his nose and stared at Coonan.

" So you have come to inspect me," he said. " I've had no notice of this."

Coonan had never seen Skerrett before and he was rather taken aback by his dominant personality. In spite of his physical degeneration, Skerrett still had the appearance of a man to be feared. And he certainly looked at Coonan in no humble manner. Sensing that this visit was a prelude to his dismissal and that nothing he could do would influence the inspector in his favour, he went to no pains in order to make a good impression. With his head thrown back and his under lip thrust forward, he drew his right hand along his beard and examined the inspector from head to foot with great insolence.

" I was particularly ordered to give you no notice," said Coonan.

He could not prevent his voice being a little nervous. He was a tall, thin man, of poor health. He felt irritated by Skerrett's rude size and apparent strength.

" Huh ! " said Skerrett. " I suppose I can't complain. You have only to do what you're bid. Servants can't choose their conduct. Well, here I am and here is my school. I'm at your service."

The inspector went to the little table before the fireplace, put down his bag and looked about him.

There were only about twenty children present. The room looked empty. He noted the mangled condition of the benches. A few maps, hung on the walls, were in an equally bad state. A heap of broken slates lay in a corner. The floor was not very clean. The children were untidy and there was an expression of fear on all their faces.

" May I look at the roll ? " said the inspector.

Skerrett handed him the roll.

" What's your average supposed to be ? "

" Sixty," said Skerrett.

" How many are present to-day ? "

" There you are," said Skerrett, pointing to a little, oblong, black board, on which was written the number of pupils in each class and the total present. " There are twenty-three here to-day."

" Twenty-three," said the inspector. " One, two, three, four."

He began to count the number present in the school and found there were only twenty.

" Hum ! " he said. " How do you account for that ? There are twenty-three on the roll, but I can see only twenty here. Would you please count them and see if I'm wrong ? "

Skerrett marched haughtily down the room and counted the pupils. He could find only twenty. Astonished, he counted them again. Still he could find only twenty. He came to the table, opened the roll book and read out the names of those marked present in the morning. The three children whom the inspector had seen escaping over the crags failed to answer.

" Where are these boys ? " he shouted to the pupils. " Does any one know where they are ? "

" I know where they are," said the inspector curtly. " I saw them running away over the rocks as I was coming in."

" Then why didn't you say so ? " said Skerrett. " If you knew there were three missing why did you let me go on counting and reading out the roll ? "

" This is a funny way to run your school," said the inspector. " Is it usual for you not to know how many children you have present ? Can they leave the school when they please without asking your permission ? "

Skerrett looked him boldly in the face and said :

" They are encouraged to do as they please by those who are trying to drive me from my livelihood."

" And who are they may I ask ? " said the inspector.

" The manager of the school."

" You mean Father Moclair ? "

" I do."

" Well, I met him for the first time to-day coming up on the boat and he seemed to me a man that wouldn't injure a fly."

" Ha ! I knew you were well primed."

" I may tell you that's not the way to talk to an inspector," said Coonan. " I won't have it. I came here prepared to give you a fair and just examination, but you are doing your best to make that impossible."

" You came here determined to ruin me," said Skerrett. " Father Moclair gave you your orders."

" How dare you say that ? " cried Coonan. " How dare you speak evil against your parish priest at this moment when the whole parish is disgraced by the horrible outrage committed against him ? "

" Outrage ? " said Skerrett. " What outrage ? "

" Some villain tried to blow up his house with a bomb last night, while two innocent women were sleeping there without protection."

Skerrett gaped.

" A bomb ! " he cried. " By God ! Is that true ? "

" It is true," said Coonan. " He had more to trouble him than your school or gossip about you."

" My God ! " said Skerrett. " So his house has been bombed. I knew that something like this would happen. It's a terrible thing. You're right. It's a disgrace to the island. But let the disgrace be brought to the door of the person responsible."

" Eh ? I'm certain it is. They've already arrested a man called Griffin."

" Griffin ? Hum ! They have arrested him, have they ? Hum ! If he threw this bomb I'm sorry for him, although I have told him since he became a publican and gave up his honest trade that he was a scoundrel. He's a weak and greedy man, but that side of his character would never have come out, only for Moclair's bad example. And now this bomb is thrown. Money ! Money ! There are no bombs thrown where there's no money. An honest man is sometimes jailed and hanged, but he's never bombed. Tyrants are bombed. Greedy men that spread evil

passions among the people find these passions
thrown back at them like boomerangs."

" Are these the opinions you teach your scholars ? "
said Coonan.

" They are," said Skerrett proudly. " It's my duty
to teach what I believe is the truth. My duty is to help
them lead good, honest lives."

" By preaching disrespect for their parish priest ? "

" By teaching them to fear and despise whoever
and whatever is evil."

" Is that so ? " said Coonan, as he began to
examine the roll book. " Your average is supposed
to be sixty, but I see you have had no more than
thirty any day for the past two months."

" I have done all in my power to make them
attend school, but they are encouraged to stay
away."

" By whom ? "

" By the manager and his curate."

" Have you proof of this ? "

" How could I get proof ? There are no more than
two people in this parish who would not be afraid
to give evidence against him."

" These are dangerous charges to make without
proof."

" Look at those windows," said Skerrett. " I have
asked to have them repaired time and again, but no
notice is taken of me. It's deliberate, I say. A short
time ago, the children of Tobar Milis were sent to
Ardglas on purpose to lower my average."

" I have been told there was a serious reason for
that."

" The only reason for it was the wish to have me removed from my school."

Coonan made some notes and then ordered Skerrett to carry on with his teaching.

" Continue what you were doing when I came in," he said.

" Very well," said Skerrett.

He opened the book which he had been reading and marched down the room. It was a little book in the Irish language, dealing with the sagas that had grown up about Fionn MacCumhaill and his ancient warriors. He read aloud to the children. The inspector stopped him after a few minutes.

" Let me see that book," he said.

Skerrett came over and handed him the book. Coonan glanced at it.

" This is in Irish," he said, turning over the pages. " What is it about ? "

" Have you ever heard of Fionn MacCumhaill and his warriors, Oisin, Conan Maol, Goll Mac-Morna, Oscar and the rest of them ? "

" I've heard of them," said Coonan. " I've read some fairy stories about them. What have they to do with what you're supposed to teach in your school ? Is this how you waste your time, reading fairy stories in Irish ? "

" You have the mind of a slave, Mr. Coonan," cried Skerrett in a haughty and angry voice.

" How dare you say that to me ? " cried Coonan.

Skerrett laughed and stroked his beard. Then he drew back his shoulders with a jerk and continued :

" It's the truth. That's why I dare say it. My

business as a teacher in this school is to give my children a love for the heroic things in life, things they can dream about afterwards when they are working in their fields, or out at sea in their boats. What could be better than these tales of ancient heroes, their ancestors, who spoke their language and lived in this same country in freedom ? You want me to teach them things they'll never need when they turn their backs on this school. I'm damned if I will. Maybe these children will be free. Even if they never will, their children will be free. I'm sowing the seeds for the growing of a free race. That's what I'm doing. And these seeds'll grow in spite of you or Moclair, in spite of the whole gang of you. I'm a man, free and unsubdued. And when I die, if it be to-morrow, stoned to death by my enemies, I'll be remembered as a free man who never surrendered his faith or his independence. I'll stand out in the memory of the people as a man to be imitated, when skunks like you and Moclair are forgotten, or brought to mind only to be cursed. Write your report now, Mr. Coonan. Say you saw a man old before his years, half-blind, mad, saying queer things on the rocks of Nara, an outcast among the people. Do what you came to do and get me thrown out of this school. But you cannot defeat me."

He came up to the table, raised his clenched fist over his head and then brought it down with great force, so that the table shook.

" You cannot defeat me ! " he cried, almost in a shriek.

The inspector drew back a little, afraid that

Skerrett was going to strike him. Indeed, Skerrett looked so menacing in his exaltation that a braver man than Coonan would have been afraid of him. Like a dying fire that shoots forth flame with the passage of a wandering gust of wind, his anger fanned his waning strength, so that his body stiffened and grew full of throbbing energy. But it was only for a few moments. Even as his fist crashed on to the table, his body had begun to sag. His lip dropped. His whole face became a mirror of weariness. His head grew dizzy. He trembled at the knees. He lost the power to set his speech in order and could not remember what he wanted to say to this inspector, an outpouring of words that would do something to heal his wounded pride. Like a wounded bull in the arena, when the sword of death approaches, he watched the inspector with dull, questioning eyes, which no longer had sufficient force to flash defiance.

He thought that he was going to fall shamefully before the eyes of this man whom he despised. So he cried out :

" Go now. Leave my school. I'm still master here. Get out ! "

Coonan stared at him.

" Get out of my school, you ruffian," shouted Skerrett, picking up his cane from the table. " Get out before I lay this rod to your cowardly back."

" But . . . but——" began the inspector.

Skerrett raised the rod and cried again :

" Get out, I say."

He felt himself getting weaker and weaker. He felt that he must get out into the air or faint. There was a loud buzzing noise in his head. The inspector stuffed his notes into his bag hurriedly and turned to go. Suddenly he said in a very angry tone :

" I've never in my life been treated like this. It's an outrage. This'll be the end of you."

" Damn you and what you can do. You can do nothing to me, you rat. I defy you."

He followed Coonan out of the school and into the yard, waving his cane and shouting :

" Go now and tell Moclair what you have seen. Tell everybody how I kicked you out of my school. Tell them David Skerrett is still a free man and that he'll remain so, by God, while there's breath in him."

As the inspector hurriedly mounted to his seat on the jaunting car, Skerrett swung his cane over his head and shouted :

" Tell Moclair it will take more than a bomb to drive me from this island. Tell him I defy him, even if he brings the Pope of Rome to drive me from this place."

The jaunting car moved off quickly, with Skerrett waving his cane in defiance at it. When it passed out of sight, however, he dropped his cane and he had to lean against the gate post. He looked around him furtively. The two teachers in the girls' school were standing in the doorway watching him. He scowled at them and they went hurriedly indoors. Then he looked around the crags. There was brilliant sunlight and the air was still. The naked rocks glistened in the sun. All was still and grey, except for the brilliant gleams of the mica in granite boulders scattered here and there. Somehow, he thought these shining lights among the rocks were the eyes of devils grinning at him. Suddenly, he thought that the earth was a living being, making fun of his defeat. All was so silent and mysterious and unapproachable. He thought how puny and weak was man, wandering haphazard on this cruel earth, pressing its face with his feet, burrowing in its bosom and then passing to his death, when the vain quests of his life have dissolved in horrid annihilation. And it was made manifest to him as he watched this glistening crust of sun-baked rock, beneath its dome of sky, that there was no God to reward the just or to punish the wicked, nothing beyond this unconquerable earth but the phantasies born of man's fear and man's vanity. And he began to laugh softly to himself.

For the first time, his arrogant soul took wing into complete freedom and he decided that henceforth not even a belief in God would make him subservient to Moclair. He would kneel no more in confession to that demon. Rather sink into the bosom of this grinning, unsympathetic earth, to which all beings were the same, the bones of the wicked as the bones of the just, than mount into a fantastic paradise on the passport of Moclair.

Furtively, he looked at the forbidding rocks and his eyes were sombre with the dark wisdom that had suddenly come to him ; but his being was intoxicated by a strange force that was singing in the distance ; singing in the future, when his mind should be accustomed to being a law unto itself.

Then, like an old man, timid and uncertain of movement, he walked slowly back into his school and told the children to go home. Even before the last had hurried from the room, he sat down at the table, laid his head on his hands and closed his eyes. He still could see the rocks, grinning in the sun. And then he saw the stars at night, a multitude of grinning eyes, mocking foolish man. And then, he heard a loud cry which filled him with a strange terror, as he heard it in imagination make howling circles in the air. And he understood this cry meant that death threatened him.

He raised his head, shrugged himself and cried out :

" I refuse. I'm not beaten yet. Oho ! I now begin. Who threatens me ? David Skerrett threatened by a rat ? Am I afraid ? Not while there's breath in me. Come on all of you. I'm ready ! "

He staggered to his feet and put up his hands in defence ; and then the cry that had been ringing in his head suddenly vanished. His brain cleared and he found that perspiration was oozing from the pores of his forehead.

" I'm sick," he said. " I'm talking to myself. I must get away from here quickly. Quick ! Quick ! I'm going to fall. Then they'll find me here and disgrace me. I must escape from them."

Leaving the school door open, he went out on to the road and then over to his house, staggering along the roadside, clutching the fence to steady himself.

" Lizzie ! " he cried when he reached his gate. " Come out here. Give me a hand."

The servant ran down the garden to him. She put her arms about him and helped him into the house.

" I'm sick," he kept saying to her.

She put him to bed and then asked him whether she should send for the doctor.

" Don't send for the doctor," he cried excitedly. " Send for Michael Ferris. Send for Kearney too. Let me gather my friends about me."

Then he began to rave.

CHAPTER XXIV

SKERRETT lay in bed for five weeks with brain
fever, hovering between life and death. In the meantime, extraordinary things continued to happen on
the island.

On the Sunday following the outrage Father
Moclair preached a sermon from the altar at Tobar
Milis church. He said the whole of Catholic Ireland
was appalled at the crime committed by a native of
Holy Nara. This indeed was true, as contemporaries
will remember that the press gave considerable space
to the outrage and that several public men, both lay
and clerical, used the incident as a warning against
the revolutionary organisations which were then
beginning to be formed, for the purpose of setting up
an Irish republic. Of course, the outrage was in no
sense political ; but Father Moclair took advantage
of these utterances by public men, in order to
incriminate Skerrett, since the latter was well known
to be a republican.

" If we, the people of Nara," he said, " ever hope
to hold our heads up without shame, we must now
take drastic measures to punish those who dragged
our name into the gutter of contempt. We must root
out from our midst every trace of the evil influence
that has helped this crime to be committed. We must
seek out every individual even remotely connected

with this crime and we must stamp on that individual. We must have no mercy, for at this moment any feeling of sentiment is only weakness that will bring greater disasters on our heads. We must treat every one in any way connected with the perpetrators of this crime as social lepers. We must shun them like the plague. And if any man or woman even nods to them in the road, we must treat him or her in the same manner. Band yourselves together and watch day and night. The devil is in your midst, people of Nara. A wolf in sheep's clothing is in your midst. Of him, even more than of the misguided scoundrels who threw the bomb you must be aware. It was his teaching that planted the poison in the minds of the criminals. Until we shun this devil and treat him as a pariah, God will turn His divine face away from us. He will be deaf to our prayers and our land shall be barren. Our seas will refuse us fish. Disease will destroy our cattle. Brother will turn against brother and son against father. We'll be visited by all the horrors that are foretold with the coming of Anti-Christ."

By this sermon, the people were stirred up to such a state of religious fanaticism, that they would have torn limb from limb anybody whom the priest had said merited death. Once he had aroused this fanaticism, he preached moderation and tolerance, but his henchmen, O'Rourke, Finnigan, Culkin and others acted with unbelievable cruelty. The People's League, which had gone out of existence, was immediately reorganised and anybody who did not belong to it was boycotted and persecuted. Of

course, Griffin's relatives and friends were refused
admission and therefore boycotted. In this way
Moclair protected himself from being accused of
persecuting these people for personal reasons, since
they were ostensibly ostracised for political reasons.
Griffin and another young man called Hynes having
been sent to Galway for trial at the Assizes, the boycott of their relatives began before the accused men
had a chance in court of proving their innocence.
At first only three families came under the priest's
ban. But within a week this number had increased
to six and later the number reached thirteen, making
a total of seventy-one souls under social excommuni-
cation. The Kearneys were among the first to be
boycotted, since, apart from Barbara's relationship
to Griffin, they were friendly with Skerrett. For it
was against Skerrett that Moclair's hatred was
directed rather than against the others. He merely
drew in the others in order to make his persecution
of Skerrett in some way plausible.

Skerrett's servant had been in church when
Moclair delivered his sermon. On the way home
she was approached by her mother and some women
of her village, who told her that she must leave
Skerrett's employment at once. That evening she
packed her clothes into a bundle and fled from the
house, leaving the unfortunate man alone. When the
doctor came a little later he found Skerrett screaming
for water ; so he ran over to the Kearney's house
and asked one of them for the love of God to stay
with the schoolmaster until a nurse could be engaged.
The doctor, a man named Cummins, acted with

great humanity, although he was a relative of Moclair's and had received his position entirely owing to his cousin's influence, for he was quite useless as a doctor. Indeed, it is amazing that Skerrett survived under the circumstances. It was only his extraordinary vitality that saved him.

Barbara came to stay in the house until a nurse arrived from Galway. Moclair's henchmen protested against allowing the nurse to come, but the parish priest over-ruled them. Finnigan in particular was very insistent that Skerrett should be let die like a dog, without nurse or doctor. He appointed himself as guard over the house, to prevent anybody approaching it. He marched back and forth on the road like a policeman, accompanied by some young fellows who owed Skerrett a grudge for having flogged them when they were at school. They threatened and insulted the Kearneys as the latter entered or left the house. In Finnigan's absence, Culkin assumed the job of watching. Between them, they terrified Barbara Kearney to such an extent that she gave up visiting Skerrett after the nurse's arrival and persuaded her husband to do likewise. After that the only person that came was Ferris of Cappatagle. Owing to his influence among the people and his great repute, the League was afraid to boycott Ferris, so that he did as he pleased.

During the third week of his illness, Skerrett received notification that he was dismissed from his school. A fortnight later, just when he was preparing to leave his bed, another man came to take his place. At once Moclair ordered him to leave his residence, which now became the tenancy of the new teacher. The doctor went to Moclair and said :

" But he can't leave the house yet. He's in a very weak condition. If he moves now it might be fatal to him."

" You mind your own business," said Moclair. " It's not your business whether it's fatal to him or not. Out he gets at once."

" I'm ready to go," said Skerrett, when the news was brought to him. " Indeed I'm anxious to leave this house where I've suffered so much."

" You should go away somewhere for a holiday," said the doctor. " You have relations in Dublin, haven't you ? Couldn't you go and stay with them ? "

" I'll stay here," said Skerrett defiantly. " I'm going to Cappatagle. I'm going to my own house."

In spite of his weakness, although he was now unable to walk without the assistance of a heavy stick, he had lost none of his courage as the result of his sickness. He was, however, almost completely blind in the right eye and all his left side was threatened with paralysis. Yet he talked of nothing but of his confidence in being able to triumph over his enemies. There he was, crippled with sickness, almost blind, with only forty pounds in the world, after he had paid the doctor and his nurse, with only a single individual on the island that dared talk to him in public, and yet he felt sure that he would live to see himself again treated with honour and affection by the people.

He moved to Cappatagle in the first week of August. Ferris packed his furniture for him. A cart was needed to effect the removal and as Ferris had none himself, he went about the hamlet asking for the use of one. After some difficulty he persuaded a young man called Crogan to come with his horse and cart. Crogan insisted on covering the wheels of his cart and even his horse's hooves with sacking, lest some spy of Culkin's or of Finnigan's might hear the noise, coming to or going from Skerrett's house. At dead of night, they brought the furniture out of the house and put it on the cart. Then they stole away slowly. Skerrett sat on the cart and after it had gone some yards west from the gate, he suddenly gave way to his feelings. He shook his stick at the sky and cried out :

" I curse whoever has been responsible for all this. But whoever it is, I defy him to do his worst."

" Hush, brother," whispered the terrified Crogan. " Someone might hear you."

" Let him hear ! " cried Skerrett.

" That's all very well," muttered Crogan, " but I'd get boycotted if news of this got around."

" Ah ! Hell to your soul," said Ferris, " you have no more guts than a louse. Sure they can't boycott everybody. If they boycott any more they'll have no man left on their own side."

" True enough," said Crogan. " But all the same I don't want to get into trouble if I can help it."

As the cart passed each house, he whispered to the horse to keep quiet and he muttered prayers, begging the saints to prevent Finnigan or Culkin meeting his cart on the road. Now and again, Skerrett shook his stick at the sky, but he spoke no more, until the cart turned to the south along the narrow road that led to Cappatagle. Then he said :

" I'm now on the road to a new life."

" Bravo ! " cried Ferris. " By the blood of Christ ! I admire a man of your courage. Don't be afraid, brother. I and every man in my village'll stand by you. You're a man and I admire a man. You have your faults like the best of us ; but if you were a murderer twenty times over, you have the courage of a lion ; and so we'll stand by you. Long life to you."

He took Skerrett's hand and pressed it.

" Thanks, Michael," said Skerrett. " What you said has done me more good than all the doctors in the world could do for me."

Crogan halted his cart at the foot of the steep hill leading to Cappatagle.

" My horse couldn't go up that hill with a load," he said.

" Drive on," said Ferris, " and we'll pull the cart with us."

" It's no good," said Crogan. " My horse can't do it."

When Ferris urged him further he became angry.

" Is it through the village you want me to drive ? " he cried. " Is it how you want the people of the village to see me carrying furniture for a boycotted man ? "

" Well, then," cried Ferris, " I'll take it in spite of you. Leave go the horse's head."

He pushed Crogan away from the horse, took the reins and kicked the animal under the belly. The horse rushed up the hill in fright, with Crogan running alongside the cart, waving his arms and begging Ferris to halt. Although there was a moon, the night was dark as the sky was full of heavy vapour after the heat of the day. The road near the top of the hill was a cutting through limestone rocks, which rose above it to a height of about twenty feet on either side, making it quite dark. Ferris halted the cart at the top of this hill and called out :

" Come on, men of Cappatagle. Give a sick and homeless man help to put his furniture in shelter."

From the shadow of the rock came a voice :

" Yes. I'll give him a hand."

" In the name of God, we'll give a hand," said other voices.

A group of men appeared from the darkness and surrounded the cart. Then Ferris drove on.

" God bless you, brothers," Skerrett said in a broken voice. " May God reward you for your kindness."

Grealish, the old man who had escaped confirmation, said as he struck the padded wheel with his stick :

" 'Faith, it's in fine style you are coming to our village, brother, with carpets under your wheels."

The people tittered and then Ferris said :

" It was how Crogan was afraid the boycotters would hear him."

" Haven't I reason to be afraid ? " said Crogan anxiously.

" Ah ! Hell to your soul," said Grealish. " Sure a sick man can't be boycotted by any Christian. In any case, no man is going to be boycotted in this village, at the word of command of a poteen pedlar like Finnigan, or crouching Culkin, or fat-gut O'Rourke. Put that now in your pipe and smoke it. You can tell the people of Ballincarrig that Cappatagle is not going to boycott the noble friend of the poor, though poor enough he is himself now."

The other men voiced their agreement with the old man and Skerrett sitting in the cart felt tears gush to his eyes. It is only when a man is poor, sick or lonely that he can appreciate kindness to its full. He was now conquered by the simple charity of these people as he had never been by the most cruel blows of his fate. So that he was moved to tears. When the cart halted at the end of the narrow lane that led to the western end of the village and they took him down, he was trembling.

" Are you feeling weak, brother ? " said Ferris to him.

" It's not weakness," said Skerrett. " But I didn't expect this kindness. I'm a sick man, but I'm happy this night. Very happy indeed."

" Ah ! God give you peace, sir," said a woman who stood near.

" Amen," said another. " He'd bring tears from a stone in his condition."

It was a wild place where he had built his house, even compared to the wildness of the rest of the village. It was only about four hundred yards from the sea, whose solemn murmur was distinct although it was dead calm, wallowing by the rocky shore. A rough path of broken stones led through a crag that was naked of all vegetation up to the door. A fire had been lit by Ferris's wife in the kitchen and a lighted candle stood on the ledge of the chimney-place. Otherwise the house was quite empty when he entered. They brought in a chair from the cart and put him sitting by the fire.

" Ha ! " he cried, putting out his hands to the blaze of the peat sods. " I am now sitting at my own hearth. I'm a free man and no one can touch me, nor evict me from what is mine. With my own hands I built this house. My land is about me. At last I am secure. Let death come now when it pleases. When I die, I die by my own hearth. Good people, the happiness of this world comes from freedom like this."

They brought in the furniture and placed it in position. Women made a bed for him and prepared a meal, which he ate. Then put him to rest for the night. When he had retired, some of the men sat around the fire in the kitchen, smoking and discussing his position.

" Father Moclair won't let him stay long here," said one man.

" He can't touch him," said Ferris. " He's safe here."

" I'm not so sure of that," said the other. " The parish priest is like a ferret. What he gets his teeth in he holds."

It proved that this was so.

CHAPTER XXV

For a few weeks Skerrett lived at peace in his thatched cabin at Cappatagle. Under the leadership of Ferris, the people of the hamlet treated him with great kindness, so that he rapidly regained his strength and was able to go about freely. During this time, his manner remained subdued and almost timid, so that they felt that this once proud man was making an appeal to their pity and they were pleased.

" There you are," they said to one another, as they watched him go around the village, leaning heavily on a stick, patting the heads of little children, modest of speech, downcast, " even the misfortunes of this world have their use. For they put a strong rein to the evil of the human heart and let loose what's good and gentle."

Skerrett himself was not aware of any dissimulation in the practice of this humility. He was resolved to end his days submerged in the people of the village, identical with them in thought and outlook on life, as well as in speech, dress and habits, making no attempt to force his personality into the foreground ; but rather, like a wounded beast in the herd, choosing the deepest shadows for repose and the most humble position at the drinking well, lest prominence might attract attention to his wound and get him cast forth.

And he was very happy during those weeks, like a schoolboy from a city taking a holiday in the country. Everything looked new to him in the village life, even though he had thought himself familiar with every aspect of it. Now, however, he was seeing it from a different position. He was on a level with it, instead of admiring it from the height of a superior social position. So to speak, he had formerly masqueraded as a villager, whereas he was now one himself. The people no longer regarded him as a master and a benefactor, but as a hapless being who depended on them for protection. And as no sensation gives human beings greater spiritual pleasure than an active pity which does not entail too much hardship or expense, they were convinced that Skerrett was good, since being kind to him made themselves feel good. So they paid no attention to the attempts of the League to enforce the boycott on him, while he remained meek and accepted their services with humble gratitude.

If he had continued to behave himself in the same gentle way, they might have continued to give him asylum ; but I am not quite sure of that. Moclair's power was proof even against human pity. From the very beginning he would have caused Skerrett's expulsion from Cappatagle, had he not been too busy at that time with Griffin's trial. The trial began at Galway a few days after Skerrett's removal. It was a very scandalous affair, as the witnesses on both sides committed perjury without any compunction whatsoever. In fact, the only witness to tell what he believed to be the truth was the coastguard,

Jonathan Smallbotham. Under the circumstances, although Griffin was convicted and sentenced to three years penal servitude with hard labour, it still remains a matter of grave doubt whether he threw the bomb, or whether the whole thing was a plot on the part of Father Moclair, to make himself an object of public sympathy and to finally overcome all opposition to his plans. In any case, the outrage was eminently successful in achieving both of these objectives ; so much so, that when Mr. Davin acquired the farm at Ardcaol that autumn and immediately afterwards got married to Moclair's sister, not a voice was raised on the island to question the justice of the deal. Of course, the boycotted families made quite a solid group within the community, but they were afraid to raise their voices above a whisper. The only criticism of the priest's conduct came from the Protestant newspaper in Galway. Naturally, criticism from such " an enemy of the national cause " only strengthened Moclair's position in Nara.

When Griffin had been safely lodged in jail, Moclair returned to Ardglas. At his next appearance on the altar of Tobar Milis Church for the Sunday sermon, he drew the attention of the people to the fact that the devil was still at large on the island and busy with the seduction of the Cappatagle people.

" This causes me great sorrow," he said, " because, with a single unfortunate exception, the people of that village have been exemplary in their behaviour since I came to this island. Now, however, we may expect to hear dreadful news about them."

He was very mysterious about what the dreadful news might be, so that his speech strongly affected the Cappatagle people present ; especially the women, who in primitive communities are the carriers of superstition to a far greater extent than the men. Skerrett had not been to church, being still too weak to make the journey even if he wished to do so. Ferris brought him news of the fresh attack made on him by the priest. Skerrett was roused.

" I've been idle too long," he said. " From now I'll give him blow for blow."

" What madness have you in your mind now ? " said Ferris, who had grown more shrewd with the years. " The best thing you can do is to keep quiet and say nothing. Then maybe he'll forget about you."

" Forget about me ? " cried Skerrett. " I don't want to be forgotten. I'm not done with yet. I'm a young man yet."

He drew himself to his full height, threw out his chest and repeated : " I'm a young man yet, Michael."

The men of the village were in the habit of spending the evening around the hearth in Skerrett's kitchen, listening to his conversation. His kitchen had become a club-room since his arrival in the village. At first they had been timid of him, remembering the importance of his former position, but they soon got used to the reality of his reduced circumstances. Then indeed his kitchen became a school. Skerrett, comfortably settled in his easy chair before the hearth, stroked his beard and lectured them on his pet topics : how to set up an Irish Republic and how to make that Republic an ideal State, without injustice, suffering or waste. Not that his teaching had any effect on his listeners, for peasants are the least prone to conviction of all human beings on matters that affect their material lives. It is only on matters dealing with the supernatural that they are credulous. But they were amused by Skerrett and they pleased him by affecting to listen with open mouths to what he said. Afterwards, of course, they went away and made fun of him among themselves. In fact, he was becoming the village entertainer.

On Sunday afternoons after Mass, the people were in the habit of lying on the rocks by the roadside in the centre of the village, to spend the rest of the holiday in pleasant idleness and conversation. This Sunday the conversation was more serious than usual. They were discussing Father Moclair's sermon. Ferris and Grealish defended Skerrett and maintained that he was not possessed by the devil, but the others were of opinion that even though Skerrett might not be possessed by the devil it was dangerous to oppose Moclair.

" We don't want to bring the League down on top of us," they said.

" It might come to pass," they said, " that the people of our village'll be cursed from the altar."

While this discussion was in progress Skerrett appeared. Silence fell on the gathering at once.

Even the children that were playing on the road ran behind their parents and watched the approaching man timidly. Skerrett walked slowly, even though he held himself as straight as ever, and he leaned on a stick, which he carried in his left hand. His right leg was a trifle stiff, owing to the increasing lethargy of that side of his body. His belly had become misshapen. His beard had turned very grey and his face looked unhealthy. Angered by what Ferris had told him, the meek expression had gone from his eyes. They looked fierce behind his spectacles ; and yet they had lost confidence, for they had the furtive quickness of the man who is trying to hide some fear. When he reached the people he halted, drew back his shoulders and said arrogantly :

" God bless you."

They answered him in low voices. Hardly anybody looked at him. Then he spat on his stick.

" Ha ! " he cried. " So the big priest told you to-day I am the devil. Do you believe that ? "

" Musha, God bless you," said Grealish, " sure you know well we don't believe it."

The others remained silent. Skerrett looked from one to the other of them. He knew by their lowered eyes that they were afraid of what the priest had said. Instead of simulating fear himself and thus winning their sympathy, he lashed out at them.

" That's the kind of cowardly people you are, is it ? " he cried. " Afraid of that scoundrel. What can he do to you ? He can't turn you into goats."

" Don't blaspheme, sir," cried a man. " Sure how do we know what he could turn us into ? "

"We did what we could for you, brother," said another man. "Don't get us into trouble for it."

Skerrett got into a rage and waved his stick.

"You want to boycott me," he cried. "That's what you mean. Well ! Do it and be damned to you. I can do without you. I want no man to help me. I stand alone. I'll die alone. Damn the lot of you. You are a pack of cowardly dogs. I'd hate to call you brothers."

Ferris jumped to his feet and cried angrily :

"I'll not have you speak like that against the people of this village. We have treated you as best we could. Whatever we had we gave to you. We couldn't do more."

"Well, then finish what you have begun," said Skerrett. "Why do you turn against me now, when my enemy tells lies against me ? He has only to say that I'm the devil and you turn against me. I see it in your eyes. You are afraid of him. But I'm not afraid of God or devil. I know that the devil was invented by priests to terrify ignorant people like you. But I'm not an ignorant person. The devil has no power over me."

"If you keep your mouth shut," said Ferris, " and stay quietly in your house, it will be better for you. You'll do no good to yourself by shouting foolish things here. Go home quietly and things will be done for you in secret same as before."

"That's so," said the people. "Things will be done in secret for you."

"I want nothing done in secret for me," shouted Skerrett. "If you are afraid to do anything for me openly I don't want your secret help. To hell with the lot of you."

With that he turned away from them and strode towards his house. His angry outburst had made him feel very weak and his injured head was smarting with an acute pain that confused his thoughts. The day was very hot and this aggravated the disturbed state of his mind. He wanted to commit some violence in order to assert himself. So that in spite of his weakness he began to walk rapidly, swinging his stick, muttering threats against his enemies.

" I'll show them I'm not done with yet," he kept saying to himself.

When he had passed through the village and come to his house, he halted and looked at it. And suddenly it appeared sordid and humiliating to him. There it stood in the middle of a wild and naked crag, with its grey, limestone walls and its thatched roof, a tiny excrescence on the rock, like a limpet shell covering some paltry form of life. The labour it had cost him to build this cabin had been to no purpose ; for he was unable to begin a new life. He was merely hiding here on the charity of the villagers who were now about to boycott him, since Moclair's destroying hand had reached even this obscure corner.

Now he realised that his whole life had been an utter failure. All that he had touched had been accursed. One after the other, everything he held dear had been taken from him. He had been gradually stripped until he now stood alone in this tiny cabin on a lonely crag, by the edge of the ocean.

And then he thought of Moclair over in Ardglas, reigning like a king.

" By God ! " he cried aloud. " I'll go and get satisfaction from him. I'll not let him get any farther with this. He has struck me. The time has come to strike him."

This resolution so enthused him that he forgot he was an ill man. He strode into his house and began to strip off his clothes, scattering them about the floor.

" I'm finished with these rags," he cried aloud as he undressed. " I'm going to face him dressed like a gentleman. I've been a fool. I've been a damn fool, trying to win the people's respect by becoming like themselves. They only respect the man that walks on them and despises them. To him that has more shall be given. From him that has not, the very last thing he possesses shall be taken away. I curse the day I first came to this island. I wipe my feet on it."

Like a maniac, he pranced around the earthen floor in his shirt, stamping on the clothes he had cast from him. With this gesture, he stamped on his whole career ; or rather, on the wreck of the career he had tried to make. He had become a wild, brutal man as he had been when he first came to the island ; but with the difference that his brutality was now the child of despair.

Then he went to his bedroom and took from the trunk where they had lain since his coming to the village his " schoolmaster's clothes." When he opened the trunk, the first thing that met his eyes was the old black bonnet with feathers worn by his wife. He held it up, looked at it and then felt overcome by all the weight of his misery.

" In the asylum," he said. " She is in the asylum. He drove her there. He did. It was he was the cause of my son dying too. Didn't I see him on the day of the funeral, grinning at my sorrow, while he stuffed the offerings into his pocket ? Poor woman ! I made her unhappy, but who was really responsible for that ? He was. That devil was responsible for it. I'd never be on this cursed island only for him. By God ! If it's the last thing I'll do in this world, I'll kill him. I'll strike him down."

Then he dressed hurriedly and dashed out of the house, leaving the door open. He went through the village waving his stick and talking to himself. When he passed the meeting place, where the people were still lying, Ferris followed and tried to stop him.

" Where are you going ? " he said, laying hold of Skerrett's arm.

But Skerrett pushed the man aside.

" Don't you dare put a hand on me," he cried. " I'm going to get satisfaction."

Then he strode down the hill at a furious pace.

" He's gone out of his mind," said Ferris. " We should go after him."

" Let him go," said one of the men. " The police'll look after him. It's best to leave him alone."

The others agreed. They all wished to have nothing to do with Skerrett, the enemy of society.

CHAPTER XXVI

ONE HOUR and a half later, Skerrett arrived at Ardglas, exhausted but still determined to come to grips with his enemy. As he passed through the village a crowd of children and loiterers followed him, attracted by his distraught appearance. The children pelted him with stones and shouted insults. When he turned up the path leading to the parochial house, O'Rourke, then on his way to see Moclair, barred his passage and asked him where he was going.

" I want Moclair," shouted Skerrett. " Let me pass."

" About turn," said O'Rourke. " You're drunk. You can't see the parish priest in that state."

Skerrett raised his stick to strike O'Rourke, but the latter was too quick for him. A blow on the chin sent the unfortunate man heavily to the ground. The shock of the blow and of the fall unhinged his mind completely. When he got to his feet again, he began to stagger about, pawing the air with his hands and crying :

" Give me my sight. I can't see. Give me my sight, so I can tear him limb from limb. I'd kill the devil if I had my sight ! "

They had to tie him with a rope in order to bring him to the police barracks. They lodged him in a cell, where he spent the night roaring that he wanted to kill Moclair. The doctor certified him insane and on the following Tuesday he was taken down to the steamer, on the way to the county asylum. By that time he had grown calm and recovered his senses ; so that when on the way to the pier a crowd followed shouting insults at him, he smiled sadly and said to the policeman who was guarding him :

" This is a fitting end to a fool's life. I have spent myself for fifteen years to make life better for these people. That's my reward."

In the asylum he proved to be one of the most vicious and uncontrollable inmates, so that he was most of the time in a padded cell. He could not suffer any discipline and maintained that he was quite sane. In fact, great efforts were made by his friends in Dublin and elsewhere to effect his release. However, it was too late to do anything for him. The violence of his conduct during confinement played into the hands of his enemies, who claimed that he was a dangerous madman. In any case, his proud heart broke after six months and he died in the asylum hospital.

But he died undaunted as he had lived. The very last words he was heard to utter were :

" I defy them all. They can't make me bend the knee."

His wife survived him for three years, but she also died in the asylum.

CHAPTER XXVII

THIRTY years have now passed since Skerrett's death and already his name has become a glorious legend on that island, where his bones were not allowed to bleach and moulder into the substance of the rock, that was so like his spirit. His enemy Moclair, who left Nara two years after Skerrett to become bishop of the diocese, has also become a legend ; but his legend grows less with the years, while that of the schoolmaster grows greater. Indeed, both men are now only remembered for their virtues, while the evil in their natures is forgotten. And as Moclair's virtues were of the body, allied to the cunning which ministers to the temporal body's wants, so do they wither quickly into nothingness. Whereas the nobility of Skerrett's nature lay in his pursuit of godliness. He aimed at being a man who owns no master. And such men, though doomed to destruction by the timid herd, grow after death to the full proportion of their greatness.